Galileo

Galileo

Colin A. Ronan

G. P. Putnam's Sons, New York

Designed by Freda Harmer

House editor and picture research: Enid Gordon

Library of Congress Catalog Card Number: 74-76233
SBN: 399-11364-9

Printed in England

To Sir Bernard Miles who was Galileo in his production of Bertolt Brecht's play at the Mermaid Theatre in 1960

Acknowledgments

Acknowledgments are owed to the following for translations: Basic Books, S. A. Bedini and others in *Galileo, Man of Science*, edited by E. McMullin; Chicago University Press, G. de Santillana in *Dialogue on the Great World Systems* and in *The Crime of Galileo*; Dawson's of Pall Mall, E. Carlos in *The Sidereal Messenger*; Fawcet Premier, G. Bernardini and L. Fermi, *Galileo and the Scientific Revolution*; Macmillan (London), W. H. Shea in *Galileo's Intellectual Revolution*; Macmillan (New York), H. Crew and A. de Salvio in *Dialogues concerning Two New Sciences*; Pergamon Press, R. J. Seeger in *Galileo Galilei, his life and his works*; Pennsylvania University Press, S. Drake and C. D. O'Malley in *The Controversy on the Comets of 1618*.

Sources of Illustrations

Photographs and illustrations are supplied by, or reproduced by kind permission of the following: Alinari 10, 12, 30, 32*l*, 35*l*, 39, 40, 44, 47*a*, 49*b*, 60*r*, 66, 71, 80, 95*r*, 128*t*, 128*b*, 130, 133, 147, 161, 163, 166, 174, 177, 178, 192, 194*l*, 194*b*, 200, 224, 225, 226, 227, 239*b*, 240, 241*t*, 241*b*; J. Allan Cash 16; Biblioteca Laurenziana, Florence (photo Gabinetto Fotografico Nazionale) 15*r*; Biblioteca Nazionale, Florence 115; Bibliothèque Nationale (photo Françoise Foliot) 86, 88, 91*l*, 91*r*, 92*b*, 108, 167, 198; British Museum (photo John Freeman) 45, 54, 69; Christ Church College, Oxford (photo Oxford University Press) 32*b*; Paul Elek Ltd (photo Wim Swaan) 37, 63, 122, 136, 148–9; Ente Provinziale per il Turismo, Padua 90*b*, 93*t*, 93*b*; Gabinetto Fotografico, Florence 126; Gabinetto delle Stampe, Rome (photo Oscar Savio) 127, 129*a*; Gallerie dell' Accademia, Venice 46, 78; Galleria Nazionale d'Arte Antica, Rome (photo Mauro Pucciarelli) 210; Hermitage, Leningrad 13*l*; Hirmer Fotoarchiv, Munich 15*l*; Istituto di Studi Romani, Rome 154; Kunsthistorisches Museum, Vienna (photo André Held) 36*br*; Mansell Collection 85, 216, 218–9, 228; Mary Evans Picture Library 95*a*, 104, 123, 124*t*, 239*l*; Leonard von Matt 64; Museo di Brera, Milan (photo Josephine Powell) 36*bl*; Museo di Roma, Rome (photo Mauro Pucciarelli) 158–9, 211; Museo di Storia della Scienza, Florence (photo Electra Editrice) 34, 103, 120, 212, 242*l*, (photo Alinari) 95*r*, 96, (photo Scala) 101; Museo Poldi Pezzoli, Milan (photo Josephine Powell) 20; National Gallery, London 42, 62*l*, (by gracious permission of HM the Queen) 36*t*; National Maritime Museum, Greenwich 182; Pecci Blunt Collection (photo Josephine Powell) 156, 190, 204; Dr G.B. Pineider, Florence 58, 73, 77, 145, 222; Radio Times Hulton Picture Library 68, 129*b*; Ronan Picture Library 25, 27*l*, 83*l*, 83*r*, 90, 111, 113, 117, 124*b*, 142, 172, 228, 234, 237, 247, (and British Museum) 152, (and Royal Astronomical Society) 13*a*, 21, 27*r*, 33*t*, 33*b*, 48, 74, 98*b*, 143, 189, 235*t*, 235*b*, 248, 250, 251*a*, 251*b*, and tailpieces, (and E. P. Goldschmidt) 56, 98*t*, 106, 131, 168; Royal Collections, Windsor Castle (by gracious permission of HM the Queen) 41; Scala 51, 52, 101, 102, 119, 137, 138, 139, 140, 157, 160, 209, 232; Science Museum, London 242*r*; S. Croce, Florence (photo Josephine Powell) 244; Staatsgemäldesamm-lungen Bayerische Museum, Munich 62*r*; Uffizi, Florence (photo Josephine Powell) 18; Vatican Library 196, 221; Victoria and Albert Museum 110, 197*b*, 203, 217; Weidenfeld and Nicolson Archives 47*b*, 49*r*, 50, 60*l*, 197, 208.

Contents

Introduction

Galileo is science's most dramatic character, standing like a colossus astride the evolving world of the late Renaissance; he is the progenitor of the Age of Reason. Born of an impoverished patrician family, destined by his father for a medical career, his flair was for mathematics and physics, and for a new concept of the universe that spelled death to the old belief of Man as God's epitome of creation. Yet Galileo's conversion to these views was slow and, to begin with, uncertain. Educated in a Jesuit school, but taught at home to weigh facts and reject fancies, he grew up at once a devout Roman Catholic and a rebel philosopher.

A typical Renaissance man, Galileo's interests were wide and his tastes varied. He played the lute with great skill; he drew, painted and was an expert in the art of perspective – indeed, in his old age he confessed that if he had been given free rein he would have been an artist. Galileo also read avidly but critically, loving Virgil and the classics, adoring Ariosto but rejecting Tasso as tasteless. And for his own part he wrote well, in fine style, at once fluent and pithy, but his pen was barbed with a scathing wit. He, more than anyone in his day, could demolish opponents with a derisive ridicule that was amusing to read, but that made him bitter enemies.

It was Galileo's vitriolic wit that was partly the cause of his downfall. Showing itself first at Pisa when, as a young professor, he poked fun at the formal regulations on decorum for the academic staff, it coloured his attacks on the physical universe as Aristotle, and thus his contemporaries, saw it; it infused his arguments about sunspots with the Jesuit Scheiner, and reached its peak in a polemic masterpiece about comets that discomfited both Scheiner and another Jesuit, Orazio Grassi, so that in the end the whole Jesuit College in Rome was up in arms against him. This powerful enemy was joined by others, jealous of the favouritism Galileo received from the Tuscan Grand Dukes Cosimo and Ferdinand, and they plotted his destruction. Yet Galileo's trial and recantation were not only due to his biting wit.

Following Galileo's astonishing discoveries with the newly-invented telescope and his subsequent rise to fame, the Catholic Church was in the throes of the Counter Reformation and the Pope involved in a political embarrassment connected with a shift of power in the Thirty Years War. It was a time when tempers ran high and the majority of prelates felt they must assert their authority, a time when Galileo had become too well known and too much feared to be allowed to escape. This man, who advocated free thought in a country where individual opinion was anathema, who proselytized a new scientific outlook that did violence to the Scriptures, simply could not be tolerated. His popular writings that set individual observation above ancient authority, that welded mathematics and physics together in a totally new way which did violence to the old philosophy, were too dangerous and must be suppressed. With hindsight we can now see how right this new approach proved to be, but this lay beyond the comprehension of his dogmatic contemporaries. Yet by the harsh standards of the time, Galileo was leniently treated, and because of his obedience to his Church and his ability to recant, he lived to carry out fresh research and promote new ideas once more, even if the manuscript of his last book had to be smuggled out of Italy and published abroad.

Galileo may have had a predilection for the life of an artist, yet he was essentially a man of science. He lived and breathed a new and revolutionary scientific air, and it is not possible to separate the man from his science, to ignore his work and expect to see his character in the round. Nevertheless I have tried, in this book, to keep his science in perspective and yet set him against the backcloth of his age and, above all, to trace the inexorable sequence of events that forced Galileo into his inevitable clash with the Inquisition. To do this I have made use of recent historical research that has shown not only the full extent of his scientific brilliance but, equally significant, has taken a more penetrating look at the background to the trial, the sentence and Galileo's recantation.

In preparing the book I have been fortunate in having help from my wife Ann who read the manuscript and helped iron out many obscurities and infelicities of phrase, and supplied many of the black and white illustrations. I also owe a debt of gratitude to Mrs Enid Gordon of Messrs Weidenfeld and Nicolson for her editorial work and her imaginative assistance with the colour material. Lastly I should like to express my warmest thanks to Mr John Curtis for being not only a most charming but also a most understanding publisher.

COLIN A. RONAN
Barton, Cambridge, 1974

I
Ancient Wisdom

Galileo, the phenomenon, erupted into the intellectual world of sixteenth-century Italy. Musician and littérateur, mathematician and astronomer, his achievement was that he demolished all accepted knowledge of the physical universe and replaced it with new speculations; his tragedy that he ended his life a martyr for his challenge of authority. Yet it seems a strange irony of fate that his attack on established theories, which were themselves based on an idolatrous view of Greek science, stemmed from his own very real respect for the true science of ancient Greece, and the powerful minds of her scholars. The philosophers who had proposed the original theories formed the dynamic avant-garde of contemporary thought, propounding ideas that as often as not did violence to the cherished beliefs of a previous generation. These had been the men who, by imaginative insight and careful examination of the world around them, had formulated a universe at once aesthetically satisfying and logically faultless, a universe that absorbed all nature in its comprehensive embrace. And it is here that the irony really lies; the very completeness of the Greek scheme of things caused its degeneration from a vital, progressive view to a static system, impossible of improvement, that clamped a dead hand on any new ideas, and stifled any attempt to provide a new synthesis.

This intellectual tragedy arose not because of men's inability to recognize what had been done – this was too obvious to be missed – but because the whole corpus of Greek knowledge was lost to the western world for almost a thousand years and then, when it was rediscovered, the result was so overwhelming that the critical faculties that were brought into play were applied to the wrong material and for the wrong reasons. It was Galileo's genius that he could see through this and not only get back, as it were, to the pure Greek approach, but also that he built a new edifice on it, evolving methods that are as powerful and relevant today as they were in his own time. Yet to see his achievement in perspective, to appreciate why it was that his attack on authority was so serious and so fundamental, we must give the loss of Greek wisdom and its subsequent recovery at least a cursory glance.

The Greek civilization was a heterogeneous collection of city states that covered not only the Greek mainland, but also the whole area surrounding the Aegean. Some states were essentially monarchical, others were governed democratically or by an oligarchy, and some formed loose associations against common enemies such as Persia and Sparta. The growth of philosophy, which included mathematics and the study of what we now call science, was pursued avidly from at least as early as the sixth century BC, and even when the country came under Roman

Opposite Plato, holding the *Timaeus*, and Aristotle, holding the *Ethics*. Detail from Raphael's fresco, *The School of Athens*, in the apartments of Pope Julius II, in the Vatican.

Pythagoras, writing, with Averroes in a white turban, leaning over him. Detail from Raphael's *The School of Athens*.

domination in the second century BC, intellectually the Greeks conquered their conquerors, and their culture continued to spread in the Near East so effectively that a Greek-speaking Byzantine monarchy was in power long after the fall of the Roman Empire. In the early days Greek philosophy was centred round notable figures – the mathematician and religious mystic Pythagoras in the sixth century, Plato and Aristotle in the fourth – but the situation was changed by a shift of political power away from the city states. This happened between 359 and 323 BC with the rise and fall of the Macedonian empire, first under Philip II of Macedon and then his son Alexander the Great. Through their conquests Greece was unified and the tentacles of Greek influence extended as far as the Indian sub-continent, but with Alexander's untimely death in 323, his great empire disintegrated; India became herself again, and the remaining territories were divided among his three most powerful generals. All three were Macedonians, and all established dynasties, but each kept the Greek ideals of religious freedom and respect for learning. Indeed Ptolemy Soter, who commandeered Egypt, went further and at his newly-established capital at Alexandria – the large seaport Alexander had built a decade before – set up a Museum and Library that became the envy and admiration of the ancient world.

The Alexandrian foundation, built close to the royal palace, soon established a reputation and began to attract the finest scholars in the world. Euclid taught

Above, left The city of Alexandria on a Roman lamp of the first century AD. *Right* The astronomer Ptolemy. From G. Reisch, *Margarita Philosophica*, 1508.

there, Eratosthenes (who measured the size of the Earth) was one of the Librarians, and its standing was so great that Archimedes travelled all the way from Sicily to Alexandria to complete his studies. The climate was one of absolute freedom of thought, no restrictions were placed on enquiring minds and research took precedence over teaching. Just one result of this open atmosphere was a flourishing medical school where a host of anatomical discoveries were made, including the fact that the essential role of the heart is to pump blood, a discovery that the modern world attributes to a physician working in the seventeenth century AD. And it was in Alexandria, five hundred years after its foundation that Claudius Ptolemaeus, later to be known simply as Ptolemy, the greatest of all the Greek astronomers, flourished and produced his *Almagest*, an astronomical text that was to exert an immense influence on western thought, even as late as Galileo's time.

How extensive the Library was, how large the Museum, is now uncertain. Some accounts say the Library held a hundred thousand papyrus rolls, or two hundred thousand, or even half a million, although this last figure more likely refers to the number of works rather than the number of separate rolls. At all events it was an immense collection, swelled by an edict of Ptolemy's grandson, which decreed that every visitor to Alexandria must surrender his books to the Library for examination. If the Library already possessed them, they were returned; if not, they were retained and, for his enforced generosity, the donor was

13

provided with a cheap papyrus copy. Here, then, was the enshrined wisdom of more than two dozen generations of Greek scholars, to say nothing of those from Egypt itself and further afield; had it remained intact its influence on western civilization would surely have been incalculable. Yet it is idle to speculate because the Library did not remain inviolate, even though it suffered little damage when Julius Caesar laid siege to Alexandria in the first century B C. Three hundred years later it was to fare less well, when the ruthless but successful Queen Zenobia conquered Egypt, and it was utterly destroyed by mob violence in the fifth century and by Moslem zealots in the seventh.

These last two attacks were examples of that nauseating attitude which has dogged mankind from time immemorial – the fear and hatred of anything that lies outside the confines of a narrow preconceived mental outlook – an attitude that was anathema to Galileo, just as it is the bane of any enquiring mind. Epitomized by the seventh-century Moslem zeal of Caliph Omar, who destroyed the Library on the count that the books contained in it were either in accordance with the Koran and thus superfluous, or contrary to it and heretical, it was also the formal excuse used by the Patriarch Cyril in the fifth century. To this Alexandrian prelate the Library was a hot-bed of pagan learning and a danger to Christian piety, and the fact that its Librarian at the time was a friend of Cyril's bitter enemy, the Roman governor of Alexandria, only added fuel to the fires of hatred burning in his soul. The early Christian Church was, of course, apocalyptic in outlook; men still held themselves ready for Christ's second coming and fervently believed that the Day of Judgement was close at hand. Thus there was some excuse for an approach that saw personal salvation as the primary question, and looked on the study of philosophy and the natural world at best as an irrelevance, and at worst as a profligate waste of time that would be better spent in preparation for eternal life. Yet this outlook was not universal throughout Christendom; there were others like St Augustine who believed that the book of nature showed God's handiwork as much as did most of the events recorded in the Scriptures, and who therefore encouraged secular study. Yet with the destruction of the Alexandrian Library, the torch of Greek learning was finally snuffed out as far as western Christendom was concerned. Except for a few medical works, mainly by the Graeco-Roman surgeon Galen, the few books on astronomy and mathematics, and on the works of Plato and Aristotle that were in circulation were not originals, but merely second- or third-hand descriptions and commentaries. There was nothing left to stimulate original thought – no research centre such as Alexandria had been, no philosophical schools like Plato's Academy or Aristotle's Lyceum. Western Christendom entered an intellectual Dark Age which, except for an isolated literary revival under Charlemagne, was to last for more than seven hundred years.

Fortunately, the end of the Alexandrian Library did not mean the complete annihilation of Greek learning. As always with persecution and destruction, some-

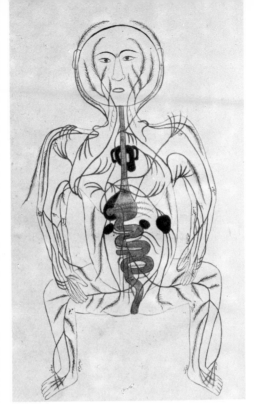

Above, left Hippocrates – from a Byzantine manuscript. *Right* Persian diagram of the blood system, derived from the anatomical studies of the Alexandrian school of medicine.

thing survives, and when Zenobia conquered Egypt, a few scholars saw the danger signals in time and fled, taking valuable manuscripts with them. They sought refuge in and around Byzantium, and the peaceful haven they found proved an attraction that others could not resist; gradually, and before the destruction by Cyril, crucial Greek works had thus found their way to the shores of the Bosporus. Yet Byzantium only remained a sanctuary for a time, for religious dissension tore the city apart early in the fifth century. Nestorius, the Bishop of Byzantium, claimed that Christ was divine not human, and this view was ruled to be heretical by an ecumenical council at Ephesus, with the result that the Emperor Theosodius had Nestorius and his supporters driven from the city and the surrounding neighbourhood. Since the Nestorians numbered a host of Greek scholars among their fraternity, when they left Byzantium – by that time called Constantinople – they took many original Greek manuscripts with them. The whole Nestorian Church migrated eastwards, some going as far as the south-west coast of India, others even to Ceylon. But the majority of the Greek scholars appears to have been a little less adventurous or less travel-prone, and they settled in Persia, clustering round Jundishapur. Here they remained in peace for the next two centuries, until the Moslem conquests began, and both Byzantium and Persia were overrun. Yet unlike many conquerors, the followers of the Prophet were for the most part, tolerant of other views – Christians and Jews were allowed to practice their own religions provided, of course, they acknowledged the civil and

15

military authority of Islam – and this was to prove an advantage from every point of view. For a time Jundishapur remained a centre of scientific learning but, later, there was a shift to Damascus. Yet even this proved only temporary, for when the descendants of Mohammed's uncle, the Abbasides, gained power and established their long-lived caliphate, they set up their capital in Baghdad, and the Greek manuscripts moved once more. They seem, or at least a great collection of them do, to have come under the control of a famous family of Nestorian medics and scholars – the Bukht-Yishu – who served the Abbasides for seven generations and, through their learning, persuaded the more enlightened caliphs to promote Greek culture. The Bukht-Yishu spoke Syriac and first of all were encouraged to translate the Greek texts they had into their own language, but later on Yuhanna Ibn Masawiah, who became medical adviser to the famous caliph Haroun-al-Raschid, whom Flecker has immortalized in his *Hassan*, made translations into Arabic. Gradually Arabic became the accepted language for scientific and medical works, and when Haroun-al-Raschid's son, the caliph Al-Mamun, created a translation centre in Baghdad, it was into Arabic that the Greek originals were transformed under the direction of yet another Nestorian, Honain Ibn Ishaq.

Baghdad's fame as a centre of learning spread far and wide, as did Moslem power, which at one time stretched so far north that it was only halted by Charles Martel at Tours. Yet if the Moslems conquered a large area, they needed trade, and travellers were able to move from Islam to western centres. Thus it was that the stories of Baghdad and its culture began to filter through, and although some Greek medical knowledge had, as it were, escaped across the Mediterranean to Salerno where there was a Greek-speaking colony and a medical school, the main body of Greek science still remained ensconced in Baghdad. Not until about the end of the eleventh century was there any change, when some scholars moved to Frederick II's newly-founded university at Naples; but it was only after Alphonso VI of Leon and El Cid between them turned the Moslems out of a great part of central Spain and relieved Toledo that a vast influx of Greek learning came to the West. Toledo was mainly Christian, although Arabic speaking, and it formed an ideal centre for the wholesale transmission of Arabic learning. Thus it was by way of Latin translations of Arabic commentaries and compilations that Greek culture began to move into the West. The texts were impure and sometimes distorted; they contained Moslem influence, they bore Islamic interpretations. Yet all this was unimportant at the time. What was significant, what was so vital, was the arrival of a whole new body of learning, an entire corpus of fresh views and novel facts into a mentally moribund civilization. This intellectual bombshell burst on western Christendom in the first half of the twelfth century; to the scholar steeped in traditional outlook it cast a blazing shaft of light into the fusty caverns of his mind. It was like looking on a new world for the first time. Things could never be quite the same again, although there were plenty who tried to keep them so, as Galileo was to find out.

Opposite Toledo was one of the greatest centres for the transmission to the West of Arabic learning and, through that, of Greek culture as a whole.

2
Background to the Renaissance

The multitude of works that poured from the scholars at Toledo covered a wide range of Greek learning, but while some of this was known in general terms, now at last detailed works were available. And in the sciences this was particularly true; books by Archimedes, by Hero of Alexandria, Aristotle, Ptolemy and Hippocrates, new material of Galen, as well as important works by Arabic authors like Avicenna, Rhazes and Alhazen, all came out of Toledo as the years passed. Not all that glittered was the pure gold of Greek scholarship; some books attributed to Greek authors such as Aristotle were spurious, and often the Arabic descriptions contained an Islamic bias, but by and large the treasure trove was everything the western scholars yearned for, and more. This cultural eldorado also imported a host of Arabic terms into the Latin of the west, terms like *azimuth* and *zenith*, words such as *algebra* and *cipher*, star names like *Aldebaran* and *Altair*, *Betelgeuse* and *Vega*. Nothing remained untouched; every aspect of learning was transformed by the new vision, the expanded outlook that this influx of a whole new culture brought about.

The Church could not have stemmed this tide of new knowledge even if it wanted to, but in fact it had no desire to do so. Most of the Latin translators were churchmen, simply because the majority of learning in western Christendom was concentrated among those clerics living either in monasteries or at the courts of prelates and princes, and if the old learning was to be made generally accessible, then it was an ecclesiastical responsibility. However as soon as the Arabic commentaries and Arabic editions came to be studied it was thought expedient to eradicate the Moslem bias, and even the original work of Greek philosophers required purging of pagan elements. Thus during the thirteenth century a concerted attempt was made to prepare texts and synthesize philosophical teaching so that the faithful should be edified and broadened, without being misled. Many scholars took part in this work, but towering above them all stands the figure of Thomas Aquinas. Son of a Neapolitan nobleman, Aquinas studied first at the university of Naples. He then took Dominican Orders and moved to Cologne to study Aristotelian philosophy under the West's leading scholar, Albertus Magnus. For a time Aquinas went to Paris, where he became embroiled in arguments about the soul and Aristotle's view of it – or rather the opinion of Aristotle as the Arabic commentaries of Averroes saw it. By now Aquinas had an unparalleled knowledge of Aristotle, strengthened by translations from the original Greek rather than the Arabic, which were being supplied to him by another Dominican scholar, William of Moerbeke, and he was able to show that pure Aristotle did

Opposite The medieval scholar in his study: St Augustine, by Botticelli.

St Thomas Aquinas, the instrument through which Aristotle's science and view of the universe became the only interpretations acceptable to the Roman Catholic Church.

not contain heretical elements. At least, he produced a synthesis that was entirely acceptable to the Church by eradicating aspects of Plato's philosophy which had been added to Aristotle over the centuries. This was an advance, but contained within it were the seeds of its own destruction. Being approved by the authorities, it became the sole interpretation to wear the cloak of orthodoxy, and in consequence it gradually grew to be tantamount to a dogma; Aquinas' view of Aristotle, his analysis of Aristotelian science, of Aristotelian physics, of the Aristotelian universe, was the only one for the Roman Catholic to adopt. The Church not only taught the faithful matters spiritual, but pronounced upon material questions as well.

It is easy now to criticize this attitude – especially in the light of what Galileo was to experience – but in the thirteenth century it seemed both natural and desirable. After all, the Church was the mediator between Man and God, and the universe was not some impersonal machine, but a vibrant living entity. Continually men thought of physical phenomena in animate terms, they used phrases loaded with vitalism. A lodestone attracted iron because the magnet was so loved by the iron: it was love that moved the Sun and stars. All this epitomized something more than a symbolic correspondence between Man and the universe, between the microcosm and the macrocosm. It was really that the hand of God

A geocentric picture of the universe, showing Aristotle's four elements, Earth, Water, Air and Fire, surrounded by the spheres of planets and fixed stars. From Raymond Lull, *Practica compendiosa artis Raymond Lull*, 1523.

was everywhere to be seen. His power was omnipresent. The heavens declared the glory of God, literally. The Church, then, had a definite duty of interpretation, and there was no room for deviation, and not much desire for it either. Men did not go about with independent ideas, formulating new theories, making novel interpretations of what they found around them. They looked to a common exegesis, a settled way of looking at things which married the profane and the divine, and in the Thomist interpretation they found it. Thomas Aquinas synthesized difficult problems like the Aristotelian ideas of matter and form with the Catholic doctrine of transubstantiation in the eucharist, and he married together Aristotelian potentiality with the outward bread and wine and the inward body and blood of Christ. He took the Aristotelian heavens and showed them to be God-ordained and man-centred. In brief, he made an extraordinarily complete dovetailing of Greek learning and Church doctrine; an amalgam of secular teaching and divine revelation that was an intellectual *tour de force*.

With this synthesis, and with the translations from Toledo, came a whole revivification of Greek physics. Concepts that had been ill-understood or completely unknown before were now the currency of the scholar. Aristotle's conception was of a universe in which the Sun, Moon and planets were fixed to spheres of pure transparent crystal, spheres that could not be observed but were

21

physically there nonetheless. The outermost, the *primum mobile*, was moved by God, and this kept all the rest in motion; beginning with the sphere of the stars and, inside this, seven other spheres, one each for the seven planets (the Sun and Moon being included in this category). In the centre of all lay the Earth, fixed and immovable, the centre-point and crowning glory of all creation.

The existence of the *primum mobile* was necessitated by Aristotle's belief that everything that moves requires a perpetual force to keep it going. This was a logical enough doctrine given that one can directly translate commonsense, everyday experience into a scientific theory. We see that a wagon moves only while an ox is pulling it, or that a chariot needs a horse to pull on the traces all the time to keep it in motion. It was this view that Galileo had to break down, even though it cost him a great deal of effort. And an equally difficult task for him was to deal with Aristotle's distinction between 'natural' and 'violent' motion. This distinction arose because Aristotle taught that there were four elements – Earth, Air, Fire and Water – and that all substances were combinations of these. Each element had its own natural place which it sought to reach, just as if it was an animate object with a will of its own. In this way all earthy substances tried to reach their natural home at the centre of the Earth, and so when dropped they fell to the ground. Water's place was the surface of the Earth, which was why it always spread out 'to seek its own level'. Air's natural place lay above the Water and, highest of all, was a sphere of Fire, which was why flames leapt upwards. Take a typical Aristotelian analogy – consider a piece of wood, and think what happens when it burns. You see the flames rising and hear the air hissing out. Water droplets form, and when the flames die away the earthy element is left lying on the ground in the form of grey ash. The kind of motion that the elements undertook when seeking their proper place in the scheme of things, he defined as 'natural motion'. He then classified any other kind of movement as 'violent motion' on the count that it did violence to natural behaviour; violent motion was the motion a body possessed when forced to move in some other way, when an ox pulls a cart, when a ball is thrown up into the air, when anything is impelled to change its place by a force impressed on it. And since a body would revert to its own natural behaviour once the force was removed, Aristotle was led to the conclusion that violent motion requires a continual application of force.

On their own the four elements could not account for the diversity observed in nature – the differences that could be derived from four variables were too few, the permutations were too restricted. Aristotle therefore coupled the four elements with a doctrine of four related qualities – hot, cold, wet and dry – and so extended the ground his theory could cover. For the most part, then, the whole argument seemed to explain things very well, and it is understandable that Galileo should meet such entrenched opposition. Indeed the whole of Aristotelian physics contained only one real weakness, and that was the way it accounted for the motion of a projectile like an arrow. Various involved solutions had been advanced to explain how it kept moving after it had left the bow, but all were somewhat unconvincing. However, taken in its entirety, the Aristotelian scheme was far too coherent and comprehensive to be cast aside on this count.

In addition to these outward physical explanations, Aristotle's views contained a deep and complex philosophical doctrine to explain the physical shape and essential nature of bodies, a doctrine that coloured the whole outlook so that it was impossible to give a purely mathematical description of nature such as Galileo was to seek. To the Aristotelian every body was not only made of matter (the four elements with the four qualities) but also contained 'form'. This was a potential quality, a kind of 'becoming' that imparted shape and therefore existence to matter. Both matter and form were inextricably linked since matter could not exist without form, and form required matter in order to exercise its influence. There were, of course, deeper philosophical questions with which the doctrines of elements, qualities, form and matter were involved, but enough has probably been said to provide at least a glimpse of the amazingly self-consistent scheme that Aristotle built up, a scheme that contained a host of implications that could, and did, provide plenty of scope to academics for discussion, and in which they were bound to have a vested interest. And since the scheme was so consistent, and since its parts were all interdependent, an attack on one part was a serious matter as it might lead to the collapse of the entire intellectual edifice, and require complete re-thinking of the whole way in which the physical world operated. So radical a change was bound to have opponents, and draw bitter attacks on any new interpretation.

The fact that the Aristotelian system of the world was so complete encouraged a stagnant attitude of mind. It was unnecessary to investigate nature, rather it was a case of looking round the natural world for confirmation that Aristotle was the supreme authority. Such an attitude, of course, fitted in admirably with the Christian dependence on authority, on its acceptance of a doctrine based on a specific interpretation of historical events, and it was doubtless that this was part of the attraction Aristotelianism exercised on the mind of pre-Renaissance as well as early Renaissance scholars.

Aristotle's natural world was a separate entity from Aristotle's universe. Celestial and terrestrial were divided by a deep-seated essential difference. The four elements had no place in the heavens, instead the celestial bodies were composed a fifth element with incorruptible qualities. Today this seems a strange if not senseless idea; the whole of modern astronomy and cosmology is based on the doctrine that the same elements exist throughout the entire universe, obeying the same laws as they do in a terrestrial environment. Without such a doctrine the modern scientific investigation of space and the objects in it, would be impossible, yet to the Aristotelian such a view would be anathema. And, to be fair, there was much sense in this at the time, for there appeared to be a basic difference between the heavens and the Earth; on the Earth everything was subject to change and decay, but the skies never changed. The same constellations were to be seen from one generation to the next, the Sun and Moon rose and set with ceaseless regularity, the planets perpetually weaved their paths among the stars. In short, the heavens provided an eternal pageant that repeated itself without essential change. And so strong were the arguments in favour of this view that such transitory phenomena as did appear in the sky were relegated to the terrestrial realm. Those odd terrifying celestial visitors called comets had to be put above the Earth, but at the same time kept below the crystal sphere of the Moon; the same was true of shooting stars or meteors, and of those much rarer objects, 'new' stars which suddenly blazed into prominence once every century or so. All were, in fact, classed with thunderstorms, whirlwinds and other aspects of weather lore; they were meteorological. And strange to say Galileo was to take a somewhat similar erroneous view, but his motivation was as far from Aristotle as it could be, as will become obvious later on.

There is one more aspect of Greek astronomical science that came through in its entirety when the transmission from Toledo got under way, and that was the planetary system of Ptolemy. To some extent this was a synthesis of previous ideas, but described in great mathematical detail, and so well described that it was not to be ousted until well into the Renaissance. Based on the fundamental Greek concept that the planets moved round the Earth at unvarying speeds in exactly circular paths, it used ingenious geometrical tricks to square this idealistic belief with the observed facts, which did not support unvarying circular motion. And Ptolemy achieved his aim with a degree of precision that was nothing short of remarkable, although some of his geometrical dexterity was later viewed with suspicion. There is no need here to go into his explanation, it is sufficient merely to note that two circles had to be used for each planet, a small circle (the epicycle) that spun round carrying the planet, and a large one (the deferent) that rotated, carrying the epicycle with it. The Earth was not at the centre of the larger circle, but offset from it, and it was here that some purists believed violence had been done to the principle of uniform circular motion.

The scientific treatises that were translated were welcomed with excitement, and assiduously studied. They opened up a new world, but a world that had to be assimilated, and this assimilation took time. Meanwhile their very presence gave men an urge to learn Greek, and to go back to the originals, and at the same time think and learn about the extraordinary civilization that had given birth to all this knowledge. They had known of the Greeks, but now that the fruits of antiquity were on their very desks they felt closer contact and a growing astonishment at the rich culture they were beginning to discover. Naturally the spread of the new knowledge was laborious: each manuscript had to be copied by a scribe, with the attendant danger of error, and those who could do this work were comparatively few in number. How long this might have lasted, how slow progress would have continued to be, is unknown because, at the beginning of the fifteenth century, an

The printing workshop of Jodocus Badius Ascensius in 1521. This is said to be the first printed illustration of a printing press.

invention arrived that was not only to change the face of scholarship but was to give the Renaissance its fantastic impetus. This was the printing press.

At first – that is around the 1420s – the printing press was used for making playing cards and duplicating great numbers of religious pictures, but by the middle of the century books had begun to be produced in the city of Mainz. How the invention arrived in western Europe is still not completely clear, but what is certain is that it originated some six centuries earlier in China and, like the invention of paper, reached the West from the Far East by way of trade and diplomatic missions. Its impact was tremendous, so tremendous that it is impossible to overestimate it. Figures can so often be misleading, but something of the importance of the printed book may be gauged from the fact that by the dawn of the sixteenth century something like eight million volumes were in circulation, more than all the scribes had produced in the previous thousand years. Of course quality is more important than quantity, but the significant point here is that knowledge and learning could now reach a public that had been starved of it before, a public that was small, select, university-educated, but of immense influence. Yet what was to make Galileo's texts so powerful and dangerous, was that most of his – unlike the others which were in Latin – were written in the vernacular and so were available to anyone who could read Italian. They were thus part of the growing movement that fostered the questioning mind, promoting an attitude in which men assessed things for themselves, and so helped plant the seeds of independent thought among those who had never had the power to question authority before.

At all events the printed book spread the newly-discovered culture widely, and so led to a general broadening of outlook. Men still referred to the authorities for their ideas, but now those authorities were not only the Church Fathers and a handful of Christian scholars, but Roman and Greek historians and the authors of masterpieces of classical literature. And as familiarity with the classics grew, men discussed among themselves the wonders of these past cultures, their respect for them increased and there developed a widespread desire to imitate the more attractive qualities of what seemed an almost golden age. This Renaissance humanism may have been a reaction against medieval monasticism and asceticism, but the interest was real enough. The sophisticated grandeur of the classical world informed their lives, their homes, their art and their architecture.

Those who had a penchant for science, for the study of the natural world, began also to look at related classical texts, and what they found surprised them. Nurtured on Arabic interpretations of Aristotelianism, they came face to face with the fact that Aristotle had not remained unchallenged. In one sense this was nothing new, for in the thirteenth and fourteenth centuries there were some medieval scholars who had found fault with the master and tried to improve his edifice by replacing the faulty bricks with fresh ones. What was novel about the rediscovery of the classical world was that it was not Aristotle-orientated, but it contained a collection of all shades of opinion, from those who, like Aristotle, thought the Earth was fixed, to those who believed it moved. There had been those who had talked of four elements, and those who had talked of less, and there were even some who had held that these views were oversimplifications – they thought that there were multifarious elements and had adopted an atomic theory to explain it all. In brief, the barriers were beginning to break down; the authority every scholar had cited turned out to be only one of many authorities.

The problem now was to choose which authority to follow, and which to cast out, and this meant taking a personal decision. No longer was it possible to rely on someone else's opinion and leave it at that: this would be intellectual cowardice. Now it was necessary to look critically at the evidence oneself and see what best fitted the facts. And this implied something even more radical – the possibility that no authority would do and one would be forced to formulate a completely new view. This was going against the grain with a vengeance; it was a complete reversal of the natural philosopher's role, a revolutionary approach that tore down the once unassailable genius of authority from its pedestal and substituted modern man in its place. Jack was not only as good as his master; he might well turn out to be better.

This new look at nature attracted bold and adventurous spirits. The new science had no place for the timid, it needed not only a new look but a new man. Yet it is

Left Nicholas Copernicus and, *below*, a diagram of his heliocentric system of the universe, from his *De Revolutionibus Orbium Coelestium*, 1543.

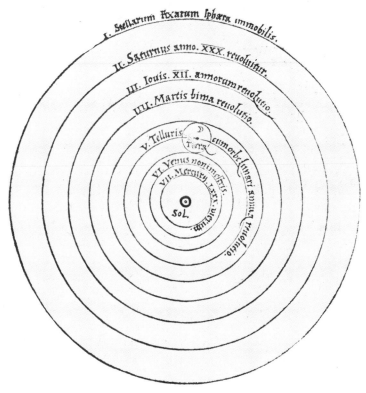

ironic that the first of the Renaissance scientists to propound a new view and act as midwife to the scientific revolution, still had a foot in the old medieval camp. Nicholas Copernicus, medical practitioner, administrator, ecclesiastic and expert in canon law, still hankered after authority, and for that very reason failed to follow his ideas to their logical conclusion. Even so his views, based on pre-Aristotelian and post-Aristotelian Greek theories, were to have an effect out of all proportion to their scientific use, an effect that Copernicus himself can hardly have foreseen, even in his most euphoric moments.

What Copernicus did was to dethrone the Earth from the centre of the universe, and relegate it to the status of a planet. Its place was taken by the Sun. As he himself remarked, when he began to read the Greek astronomers he discovered that a few had claimed that the Earth moved, and although the idea seemed absurd, the more he thought about it, the more it seemed to offer a plausible explanation of all observed motion. Aristotle, it is true, had inveighed against any idea of a moving Earth, but Copernicus was willing and able to refute his arguments by other equally valid ones. Aesthetically he found a Sun-centred universe superior to an Earth-centred one because he could make the geometry of planetary movement fit more closely to uniform circular motion than Ptolemy had done. His scheme did not involve the off-centre displacement that his Greek predecessor had been forced to use. Moreover the heliocentric theory was basically simpler than Ptolemy's geocentric one – it could get away with less epicycles to account for all the observations – although in some ways this simplicity was more apparent than real since computation of planetary positions was about as tedious and awkward on both theories.

The Copernican theory appealed to mathematicians, but was for a time rejected by those whose minds favoured purely physical explanations. This was not surprising as the theory did violence to the whole of Aristotelian physics – if the Earth went in orbit round the Sun, then if bodies fell to the centre of the universe they should fall towards the Sun not the Earth. And if they were to fall to the Earth – as, indeed, they were observed to do – then the whole scheme of natural and violent motion would require revision. What is more, if Copernicus were correct, a cyclic annual shift in star positions should be observed, and astronomers were agreed that there was no such change. We now know it is there, but it is too small for any instrument in Copernicus' day to have revealed, and it says something for Copernicus' intelligence that he appreciated that this might well be the case. The sphere of the stars, he said, was too far away for the change to be noticeable. Unfortunately this explanation, acceptable today, was looked on askance in his own time because it called for an immense gap between the outermost planet and the stars and what, it was argued, would be God's purpose in creating so huge a gap for no reason. Copernicus could hardly reply that it was an example of divine support for his theory and so matters had to rest, and rest for more than half a century before Galileo could adduce observational proof of a different kind.

The theory was only published in 1543, at the very end of Copernicus' life. With the title *On the Revolutions of the Celestial Orbs*, it was dedicated to Pope Paul III. The book had a preface extolling the theory's mathematical elegancies and warning the reader not to take the concept of a moving Earth too literally; but this was not written by Copernicus: its author was Andreas Osiander, a German Protestant divine who had piloted the work through the press, and no one seems to have worried over-much about it. To most readers Copernicus was proposing a heliocentric theory with an orbiting Earth. Yet few seemed to realize the implications of the theory, the results that were likely to accrue from dethroning the Earth and God's epitome of creation, Man, from the centre of the universe. Certainly not the Roman Catholic Church which, in the person of Paul III, accepted the dedication, and many of whose clerics and laity began seriously to consider whether it might, perhaps, be a true explanation of the heavens. Only two reformers, Luther and Melanchthon spoke out against it on religious grounds, Luther bluntly declaring, 'The fool will turn the whole science of Astronomy upside down. But as Holy Writ declares, it was the Sun and not the Earth which Joshua commanded to stand still', and to these critics it was the theory's inconsistency with a fundamentalist interpretation of Scripture that irked them.

It was not until some seventy years later that the Copernican theory was destined to occupy the centre of the stage, and to be the stumbling block that was to pitch Galileo headlong into the arms of the Inquisition.

3
Renaissance Italy

The date we take for the beginning of the Renaissance must necessarily be arbitrary, for there is no specific event which one can say is the unequivocal starting-point, and the moment any historian adopts will depend largely on his particular interest. The one thing that is agreed, though, is that whatever aspect of science and the arts we turn to, the Renaissance seems to have flowered in Italy about a century earlier than anywhere else. Although by some reckonings the availability of the printed book in about 1450 may be rather late, this is certainly the date from which the movement began to gather momentum, especially in the scientific field, for to begin with Renaissance science lagged a little behind the revival in literature and the fine arts.

Why did the Renaissance begin in Italy? What caused it to grow in a land that was no more than a loose conglomeration of city states with no cultural unity? What was so fertile about the intellectual soil that the new attitude, a fresh appreciation of humanistic values, should blossom there first? There is no simple answer, for it seems partly to have been due to the genius of the people, partly to the state of economic and intellectual development, partly to a sense of political independence, and partly to other factors less easy to define; what is more it did not begin all over the country simultaneously. It started first of all in Tuscany, a state with a tradition of learning, a tradition that permeated both court and cloister, with the result that Tuscan towns in general, and Florence in particular, were especially sensitive to any intellectual change. Here it was that the Italian Renaissance took root.

To begin with, the growth of Renaissance humanism was slow even in Florence; it took time before it was of sufficient stature to compete with the long-established medievalism. Superficially, perhaps, many things were slow to change; if we think of Botticelli's Venus standing on her shell on the waves, she is, to the inexpert eye, really rather like an underdressed version of one of his madonnas. So many of the pioneers and patrons displayed the familiar dichotomy of the human mind and were unable to purge their thoughts of received attitudes, and we find Lorenzo the Magnificent pressing his scholars for translations of the most recently discovered original classical texts while, at the same time asking a friend to comb the bookshops for so typical a product of medieval scholarship as a commentary on Aristotle's *Ethics*. Yet gradually, almost imperceptibly, the new humanistic attitude began to pervade every aspect of cultural life, broadening it, extending its boundaries far beyond the confines of religious symbolism which was so dear to the medieval mind. Above all, its effect was to secularize and to see

Opposite Sixtus IV appointing the humanist Platina as Librarian of the Vatican in 1478. A typical Renaissance pope, Sixtus was an active politician and a great patron of the arts. Fresco from the school of Melozzo da Forli.

In the early part of the fifteenth century paintings such as Mantegna's *St James on his Way to Torture (left)* were typical, and only one painting in twenty dealt with a non-religious subject. A century later the proportion had increased fivefold and by the end of the sixteenth century amazingly realistic pictures such as Annibale Carracci's *The Butcher's Shop (below)* were on the increase.

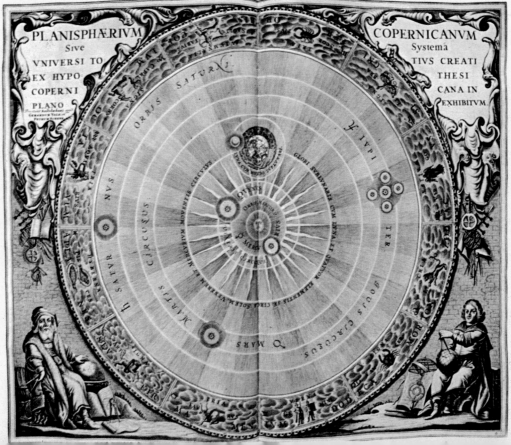

Previous page, top The Ptolemaic system of the universe, showing the Earth surrounded by Water, Air and Fire. *Bottom* The Copernican system of the universe. Both from Andreas Cellarius, *Harmonia Macroscosmica*, 1708.

Opposite A huge armillary sphere built for Ferdinand I de' Medici by the mathematician Antonio Santucci delle Pomarance between 1588 and 1593.

Right Objets d'art such as this ewer of oriental sardonyx and silver which belonged to the collection of Lorenzo the Magnificent, were much sought after by wealthy collectors in fifteenth-century Italy.

beauty in the real world, not in a world limited to sacred imagery. Whereas only one painting in twenty dealt with a non-religious subject in 1420, by the next century the proportion had increased fivefold. Everywhere realism began to replace formalized representation; the wax images in churches became increasingly lifelike. There was a fashion for making masks from the face of a living person rather than the usual deathmask, and men's attention was centred on life here and now instead of death and the hereafter – there was a positive mental attitude. Many who could afford it began to build collections of *objets d'art* in a way never attempted before. There had always been collections of manuscripts and official gifts by governors and princes, but now it became the vogue to go out of one's way and even employ agents to procure choice items. The range of interest was as wide as the collector's purse could make it; the magistrate Federigo Contarini, whom Galileo knew and who died in the first decade of the seventeenth century after a long and successful life, amassed a vast library, a fine display of bronzes, another of vases, a gallery of paintings, a collection of mathematical and astronomical instruments and, as if this were not enough, he accumulated minerals and fossils as well. Yet Contarini's collections were not unusual for the discovery of the wealth of Greek culture fired a new craze of collecting anything old. Where the antiquities were beautiful, or where they were collected and arranged to show a general pattern of antique culture this was fine, but more often than not people merely gathered anything, good, bad and indifferent, just because it was from the past. A mad scramble for old rubbish, as Galileo was to call it.

On a more constructive plane, the humanist view led to a re-examination of Greek philosophy and Greek literature, and it was not long before the set medieval views about Plato and Aristotle were challenged, the inconsistencies recognized,

Opposite Three great patrons of Renaissance Italy: *Top* Federigo da Montefeltro, Duke of Urbino, attending a lecture at his court by a humanist scholar, probably Paul of Middleburg. By Justus of Ghent. *Bottom, left* Ludovico Sforza, Duke of Milan. Lombard school. *Right* Isabella d'Este, wife of Francesco Gonzaga, Marquis of Mantua. By Titian.

Above Coloured stucco bust of Niccolò Macchiavelli. Florentine school.

and the pen used as a weapon to demolish opponents mercilessly. Satire – a genre in which Galileo was to excel – became rife, and even the humanist attitude itself came in for attack when it reached the silly stage of extolling the 'perfection' of ancient literature, and accepting quite uncritically everything ancient historians had written. One of the most severe critics here was Girolamo Mei whose great love of Greek music was to bring him into contact with Galileo's family.

Renaissance Italy was alive with new ideas, independent views, and reassessments of accepted opinions and, as might be expected in an age when everything was questioned, some of the new concepts were political. For purely practical reasons there was the beginning of a breakdown between classes – nobility was still important, but the merchants, growing richer as trade expanded, had an increasingly influential say in public affairs, while the artisan was exerting his own pressures on a labour-hungry society that was becoming increasingly technical, if not technological, with the new works of Renaissance engineers like Francesco di Giorgio and Agostino Ramelli. At the same time, in the diplomatic field, Niccolò Machiavelli had produced his famous treatise on statecraft which drew aside the curtain of hypocrisy that surrounded power politics, and bluntly stated the way a ruler should act to gain his ends. Politics, he said, was autonomous, beyond the power of good or bad morals; it had its own laws and it was useless even to attempt to rebel against them. His book, *The Prince*, setting this out so clearly, was never intended for public gaze: it was written solely for Lorenzo de' Medici, but once it had been published it brought a new dimension into the political scene. The very idea that politics should lie above the ordinary laws of morality, should have an independent existence outside and beyond the Church, was disturbing. This in itself was not new. and probably it had always been the practice to set the end above the means, but this was the first time it had been expressed explicitly in public. Now the secret was out and that there were two standards of conduct, one for the ruler and another for the ruled, was made evident. Why then should double standards be the privilege of the few?

The growth of independence, of freedom to think as one wished, to form one's own judgements – this was the essence that spread as the Renaissance progressed. Yet it must not be overstressed. The intellectuals did not reject the Church, did not replace Christianity by some materialist doctrine, and Galileo for one, was ever a true churchman, who did not deviate in his fundamental beliefs. The scholars did not decide everything they had been taught was wrong, that the medieval concept of purpose in the universe was invalid, they merely began to open their minds to the possibility that there were new ways of looking at things. Because Copernicus proposed a new universe, because Aristotle's physics began to look a little threadbare in places, they did not leap at the one and reject the other. The process of re-assessment was slow and piecemeal. Its importance was that it happened at all. The very act of daring to query the authority of the past was what was significant and novel, not how far the questioning went.

The mechanical clock in the Sforza castle at Milan was installed in 1478.

There was another aspect of the Italian Renaissance, of the growth of intellectual independence and intellectual explanation, that was symptomatic of a new movement with social consequences: there was a widening dichotomy between popular art and art for the elite. This did not only arise because the well-to-do had leisure and money to specialize and to refine their taste, but to a great extent because of the increasing cheapness of printing. By the early sixteenth century, technical improvements in printing had brought the price of books down, so that a wider demand could be satisfied. Broadsheets poured from the presses, particularly in Venice, and chap-books crammed with popular tales were sold everywhere among those who could read or even just enjoy the pictures. And there were other technical innovations that arrived and began to alter life in what was essentially a fluid society.

The mechanical clock appeared in the West some time in the fourteenth century, and by the second half of the fifteenth was becoming more common. In 1450 a public clock was installed in the town hall in Bologna, in 1478 at the Duke's castle in Milan, and the clock in the Piazza S. Marco in Venice was put in place just before the close of the century, in 1499. Portable clocks were also manufactured for the well-off, and the astrologer Giacomo da Piacenza is said to have

Leonardo da Vinci, *Self Portrait.*

slept with an alarm clock at his bedside. The clock ushered in a new outlook on time. The irregular hours previously used, hours that depended on the length of sunlight each day, and so on the season, were replaced by hours of equal duration. Short intervals of time were now measured; seconds and minutes came into every-day speech, brief moments were now stated in numbers, not in the vague terms of the time taken to say *Ave Maria.* Time became precious; people began to speak of saving time, of spending it carefully – time was money.

Yet another novelty was the production of inexpensive flat mirrors in Venice in the fifteenth century. By the sixteenth century production was increased and dispersed; and even in Florence the mirror makers were numerous enough to have a separate niche of their own in the annual carnival, singing a song extolling the virtue of the mirror for showing a man his defects which, unlike the defects in others, he did not find so easy to pick out. The mirror therefore epitomized yet another fresh aspect of the Renaissance, Man's awareness of himself as a person with individual leanings and an individual outlook. And it also probably had something to do with the artist's realization and rediscovery of the art of perspective, for although distorting mirrors had been a customary feature of medieval fairs, the flat non-distorting mirror was a source of visual reality.

The Renaissance man was a new man, typified in his best aspects by Leonardo da Vinci. Although the son of a well-to-do father, he was illegitimate, and since his mother was of lowlier stock, he did not receive a formal university education but an apprenticeship. A Florentine, he went to the studio of Andrea Verrocchio and there not only did he learn the crafts of painting and drawing, and casting bronzes,

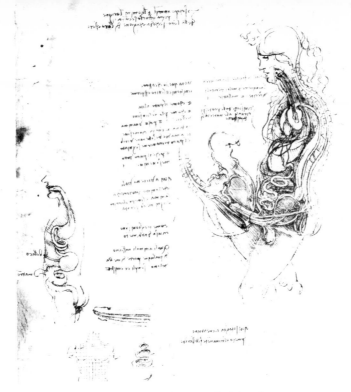

Leonardo da Vinci, anatomical drawing.

but he talked and was talked to. He was stimulated to think and think for himself. For a time he was employed by Ludovico Sforza, Duke of Milan, and when the French conquered the city, Leonardo, after a short exile, returned, getting on well with the French and studying geometry and anatomy under Luca Pacioli and Marcantonio della Torre. After the French were turned out of Milan so was Leonardo, classed probably as a collaborator. He moved to Rome and, finally, to France. In a sense he was an international man, at home with like minds, with those who used their hands as well as their brains, rather than with men whose one claim to brotherhood was nationality. His interests were as broad as his travels – he painted superbly, drew magnificently, and spent hours sketching out details of machinery and all kinds of devices. How much, or how little, Leonardo himself invented is a moot point – much that he drew was not new and many of the novel ideas attributed only to him were being actively discussed at the time he was at work. What is significant now is his omnivorous appetite for practical learning, for unfettered enquiry. At a time when it was still anathema to dissect the human body, he managed (as presumably others did) to acquire some for anatomical study, and although he had no assistant to help him, he would stop the gory business and turn to the delicate process of drawing, then go back to dissection, draw again, and so on. When one considers that there was no running water, no refrigerators (and Milan was warm), his achievements were remarkable. Yet Leonardo published nothing; he compiled copious notebooks but, unlike Galileo, made nothing available to the world.

4
Florence, Venice and Rome

The Renaissance Italy of Galileo was not only a collection of separate states but a heterogeneous collection of methods of government as well, a conglomeration of principalities and republics; in one state the people held the power, in another a hereditary ruler. Yet no two principalities were quite alike: a prince might rule despotically, or he might rule through an oligarchy like a Privy Council or the College of Cardinals in Rome. Rome was a principality with a select few governing under the papal crown. Florence and Venice were the most politically enlightened, if one takes political involvement of the public as an example of enlightened rule. In Venice public participation, which began at the age of twenty-five, was denied to shopkeepers and craftsmen, but in Florence no one was excluded and political maturity was judged to begin at fourteen.

The various methods of rule gave rise to a realization that there was more than one way to govern a state. Minds were not closed, and even though there might be – and were – power struggles, no one believed in a finality, in a changeless system, however much they might hope for it. In Florence, at the close of the fifteenth century, people went so far as to hold a conference on the advantages of different kinds of government – democracy or oligarchy, or a compromise between them both. And this was not the only debate of its kind that the Renaissance atmosphere engendered; there were discussions, and not only in Florence, about the relative merits of family and personal ability, of descent versus achievement. Was there, perhaps, an inherent class division based on action rather than ancestry? Should men be classified into those who pray, those who fight and those who work? And could one achieve position by study as well as virtue? Could one climb the social ladder by learning, as the humanists claimed? Whatever the answers it was clear that many options were open, and that social flux and change was in the air. When Galileo was born this was the atmosphere in which he was nurtured, this was the attitude he found around him. This, too, was at least one factor that made him want to appeal to the masses and write in the vernacular. Herein lay his strength – and his danger; Galileo was a force the authorities could not afford to neglect.

In Galileo's time Florence was nominally a republic, governed by the people, but in practice the power lay in the hands of the Duke. This had not always been so; in the middle of the fifteenth century a ruling council of 200 was established under Cosimo de' Medici the Elder, merchant, banker, art collector and general benefactor of the city. Then the Council was reduced to something like a third of its size, and then about a decade later the Medici were driven out and a Great

Opposite Portrait of Leonardo Loredan, Doge of Venice, by Giovanni Bellini. Of all the Italian city states of the Renaissance, Venice was the most stable as well as the most independent.

A view of sixteenth-century Florence, with a religious procession. School of Vasari.

Council established instead. Within twenty years the Medici were back, then ousted a second time, but by 1532, some thirty years before Galileo was born, they had returned and Florence had settled down with a Great Council and a Senate to rule under the Medici Grand Duke. At last it was reasonably stable, and Dante's comment of over two centuries earlier that Florence was like a sick woman twisting and turning in bed, was no longer valid.

The Florentine Council and Senate were elected, but there was a chancery staffed by permanent civil servants. Rome too had its permanent staff, and Venice; then, as now, no elected administration could run a state, even a comparatively small one, without a corpus of civil servants to provide some kind of continuity. Rome indeed had a host of specially trained clerics to staff the headquarters of a vast ecclesiastical machine, as well as the usual civil servant administrators.

Venice was the most stable and the most independent of all the Italian republics; it also possessed the most balanced arrangement of government that can best be described as a pyramid of power. At the top was the Doge who, like the Pope,

The Doge of Venice with members of the Great Council. Sketch attributed to Antonio Varegiano.

once elected remained in office for life. Under him came a Council of Ten and a Council of 'Sages', six men who, in rotation, prepared business for the Council as a whole. There was also a Senate which was the legislative body. This contained more than a hundred members, half chosen by the outgoing Senate and half by the Great Council, while a caucus of 1,300 elected persons which also elected magistrates, judges, ambassadors and other senior office holders formed the base of the pyramid. The power of the Doge was limited and he could only defy the Council of Ten at his peril, and when Doge Francesco Foscari did so in 1457, the Council forced him to resign. In the Venice of this period democracy and freedom were cherished in the religious as well as the political field, and the power of Rome was restricted. It was this shield against the Inquisition which Galileo was invited to take advantage of at a crucial time although, for his own reasons, he would not do so.

Industrially Venice was far more powerful than either Florence or Rome, although she herself was no match for Milan which was the industrial centre of

Glassmaking *(above)* was one of the most important Venetian industries and objects such as the glass ewer *(below, right)* in the shape of a ship, with blue and gilt rigging, and the glass bowl *(below, left)* enamelled with the Medici arms of a Pope (either Leo x or Clement VII) were much sought after in the other Italian states and abroad.

Opposite A view of St Mark's Square, Venice, with the Corpus Christi procession, painted by Gentile Bellini in 1496.

sixteenth-century Italy. Above all Venice was noted for its glassmaking, ship-building and publishing. Of these three glassmaking was probably the most important, there having been glassworks in Venice since Roman times. In 1290, just before the Renaissance, the industry had expanded rapidly and, because of the fire hazard involved, the government had decided that it should be moved across the lagoon to the island of Murano. Phials, mirrors, spectacle lenses, drinking glasses and chandeliers were the mainstays which became known all over Europe; the glassworkers themselves were highly paid compared with other artisans, but this was scarcely compensation for the fact that they were virtually captives and were subject to very heavy penalties if they absconded from the island. Shipbuilding was another large employer of labour and as early as 1420 at least 6,000 skilled craftsmen were to be found in the shipyards. That it was so large was due, of course, to Venice's position as a great maritime power.

Printing and publishing, the life-blood of the Renaissance, reached a peak in Venice after Erhard Ratdolt moved there in 1475, and Aldo Manuzio arrived from the Papal States in 1490. Among many other publications, Ratdolt was responsible for the first printed edition of Euclid in 1482, and Manuzio, who introduced italic type, established the famous Aldine Press, noted for the beauty and exceptionally high quality of its productions. It was in Venice, too, that the first printed edition of that *vade mecum* of astronomy, Ptolemy's *Almagest*, came out in 1515. Unhappily though Venice did not retain its superiority for, in 1596, after

48

Opposite Printing and publishing reached a peak in Venice after 1475 when Erhard Ratdolt moved there from Germany. First page of the first printed edition of Euclid's *Opus Elementorum*, published by Ratdolt in Venice in 1482.

Right One of the chief sources of Florentine wealth was their textile industry. This picture of a dye-works was painted *c.* 1570 for Cosimo I de' Medici by Mirabello Cavolori. Another of the great Florentine industries was jewellery, such as the siren, dragon, butterfly and cockerel *(below)*, made of gold, baroque pearls and precious stones.

Overleaf, left The upper echelons of the Roman Catholic Church in Renaissance Italy contained a very high proportion of noblemen, such as the Medici pope Leo X, painted here by Raphael, with Cardinals Giulio de' Medici and Luigi de' Rossi. *Right* A view of Florence by Vasari, from a fresco in the Palazzo Vecchio.

Pope Clement VIII instituted the *Index of Prohibited Books*, the heavy hand of censorship came down on the presses, and the book publishers left the republic and moved to the less restricted atmosphere of the Netherlands.

Another source of Venetian wealth was the large textile industry which expanded so rapidly that during the first half of the sixteenth century it multiplied some five times. Even so, it was no real competitor for Florence whose production of woollens and silks formed the chief industry of the Tuscan state. The Florentines also had large dye-works, they manufactured jewellery and, with a Medici as their Grand Duke, had a member of a famous banking house at their head. The Medici were fabulously rich, and wisely their fortunes were not based solely on banking; they had a guiding hand in many industrial enterprises and their managerial abilities were so noted that they were employed by the Pope to run the alum industry that was the mainstay of the wealth of the Papal States. Alum was important, indeed vital, in the dyeing trade where it was used as a mordant, and it was also widely used in tanning. The Papal monopoly was centred at Tolfa, the one place in Italy where the alum-bearing rock was to be found, and the secrets of the extraction process were closely guarded, as too was the monopoly itself; on more than one occasion the Papacy used the threat of excommunication to deter those who dared to consider importing alum from abroad because of high prices charged for the indigenous product.

It is obvious from the trading activities of the Medici if for no other reasons, that in Renaissance Italy no social stigma was attached to trade: there were noble houses that were looked up to, but there was no eternal barrier fixed preventing some new family from reaching noble heights. Money, not aristocratic blood, was the determining factor. By and large, then, the upper strata of society were ill-defined, and there was constant intercourse between nobles, merchants and professional men, as Galileo's adult life showed so clearly. However, among the peasants and servants there was, as in most societies, a far more stringent class structure with a great deal of in-built social differentiation. Even so, in Renaissance Italy there was one powerful organization that in a very real sense cut across all social barriers, bridging the gap between the nobles, the professionals and the working class, and this was the Church. Perhaps, when one considers the enormous numbers of clergy – when Galileo was a young boy, one in twelve of the total population of Rome was either a cleric or a nun – this is not surprising. Yet it was not the only reason: the broad social spectrum within the Church was also partly due to an element of secularization that made it quite common to find friars practising everyday trades, and nothing unusual to come across a worker priest. Another contributory cause was that the upper echelons of the Church hierarchy contained a high proportion of nobility, so that at the Council of Trent in the late 1540s, three quarters of the bishops attending it came from noble families, and there were princes who became popes and cardinals. This is not to be wondered at since the more senior ecclesiastical offices went to those who could

Opposite The enlargement and fortification by the Medici of the harbour at Leghorn was commemorated in a *pietre dure* table, designed by Ligozzi and cut by Cristofano Gaffurri between 1600 and 1604.

Pope Leo x's bull excommunicating Martin Luther was publicly denounced by Luther in December 1520.

afford them, and some positions cost their holders a small fortune to run.

Generally speaking, then, Galileo found himself in an open society, ready in many quarters to consider new ideas, not hidebound by a strict class structure but, one which encouraged cross-fertilization between princes and merchants, between the professions and the nobility. Yet in spite of its breadth and culture, it was not a free society. The Church held a strong grip on education and, as far as it could, on secular thought. Throughout the ages it had commanded a monopoly of learning, since so many academics were priests or members of religious orders, but it was only in the decades following 1520 that the Church started to exert a stranglehold on almost all intellectual speculation. This hardening of attitudes was Rome's response to the schism which became inevitable in December 1520 when, in defiance, Martin Luther publicly immolated Leo x's papal bull excommunicating him, and so set the Reformation in motion. Luther was part of a widespread rebellion against the canker in the Church – the commercialism, the corruption and the host of other faults that are so often the besetting sins of a large institutionalized authority – and like other reformers, his call was for a return to the Scriptures and to the straightforwardness and purity of the early Christian church, a call that found sympathetic ears even in Italy itself where, between 1530 and 1545, Protestantism made some headway in the northern states and in Naples.

Rome could not sit quiet, and so the Inquisition was strengthened and goaded into a new spate of activity, while within the Church itself there was a movement towards a moral revival amongst the clergy and a return to the true Catholic spirit as expressed by the Fathers of the Church. Symptomatic of this 'counter reformation' was Ignatius Loyola's founding of the Society of Jesus in 1534. This religious order was dedicated to teaching the young, preaching and instructing adults, dispatching missionaries and, above all, stamping out heresy whenever and wherever it should be found. The Society, not formally embraced into the Church until 1540, soon gained a wide following, and was especially attractive to the more intellectually inclined clergy, and before long it became one of the most powerful elements in the Church. Galileo was educated at a Jesuit school, and one of his greatest tactical errors was that he later aroused the Society's bitter antagonism.

In addition to the righteous indignation and messianic proclamations of the Protestant Reformers, towards the end of the sixteenth century the Church of Rome found itself beleaguered by another movement that turned out to be a hotbed of revolutionary zeal, and this was the cult of religious Hermetism. It was a doctrine based on an immense historical mistake, but was none the less powerful for that. We now know its origin lay in the second century AD when there were many in western Christendom who believed, as many Renaissance humanists were later to do, that the fount of all serious occult knowledge had lain in ancient Egypt, a view that crystallized into the legend that the progenitor of this knowledge was the mystical figure Hermes Trismegistus, Hermes the Thrice Great. Accompanying the legend was a whole corpus of writings that drew parallels between Christ, the gospels, and the Old Testament, and covered them with a thick layer of Egyptian mysticism. When these documents filtered through to the West with other material from Greece and the ancient world, their date was unknown, and from internal evidence it was erroneously concluded that Hermes Trismegistus was contemporaneous with Moses. If this were so, and no one who read the works doubted it, then here was a collection of mystical writings of the utmost significance, a collection that apparently had its origin in ancient Egypt yet contained knowledge of the most detailed kind about the ministry and sufferings of Jesus Christ, and gave the full import of the Christian message. A fabulous storehouse of wisdom, a fantastic example of holy precognition, it could not fail to have the most profound effect on any mystically orientated believer.

To begin with, four of the Hermetic treatises were translated by Marsilio Ficino of Florence, a protégé of Cosimo de' Medici into whose possession the manuscripts had found their way. This was in 1463, but in subsequent years they were supplemented by Pico della Mirandola, a pupil of Ficino's, who extended the doctrines by adding Cabalism, a strange mixture of occult lore and numerology. Cabalism and the Hermetic ideas complemented each other and the result-

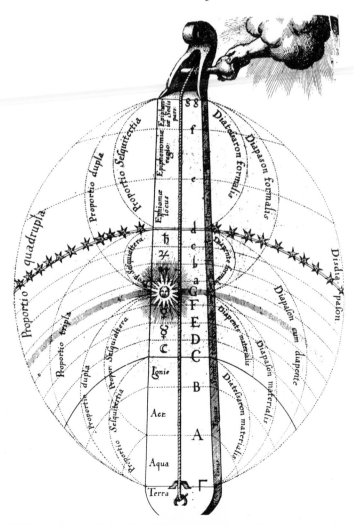

ing conglomeration of occultism, magic and religion exerted a great influence on many fifteenth- and sixteenth-century intellectuals. It was especially effective among those who still had one foot in the world of medieval mysticism in spite of the awakening of the Renaissance, men like the notorious Lenzuoli Borgia who became Pope Alexander VI, Lorenzo de' Medici, Botticelli, Francesco Giorgio and, later, the Jesuit Martin Del Rio who did his best to reconcile these doctrines with the traditional Roman Catholic outlook.

Their importance on Renaissance thought has only been recognized by historians comparatively recently, and the fact that it was to exert some influence on Galileo's life at a crucial time is still not widely appreciated. Not that Galileo was himself a Hermetist, not that we have any evidence that he ever gave a moment's consideration to Hermetic magic, but because a chance set of circumstances brought Copernicanism and Hermetic doctrines of Church reform together, with the result that the heliocentric theory became tarred with the brush of apostasy, and among some ecclesiastics earned the reputation of a doctrine dangerous to the faith.

Opposite The Hermetic concept of the divine harmony of the universe, symbolized by the 'divine mono-chord' – a hotchpotch of mathematics, mysticism and cosmology. From Robert Fludd, *History of the Universe*, 1617–19.

5
Galileo's Early Years

Galileo Galilei was born in Pisa on Shrove Tuesday, 15 February 1564, the very same year that saw the birth of Shakespeare. Known universally now by his first name, he came from an old noble Florentine family that had seen better times, and whose surname had originally been Bonajuti. A Tommaso Bonajuti who, some seven generations earlier, had been elected to the College of Twelve which formed part of the government of Tuscany, and it was he who assumed the name of Galilei, a name that his successors kept.

Galileo's father was Vincenzo Galilei, a musician who was forty-two when he married Giulia Ammanati in Pisa in 1562, and Galileo was the eldest of a family of seven. We know very little about his brothers and sisters; there were two brothers, Michelangelo and Benedetto, and four sisters. Two of the sisters, Virginia and Livia married and settled in Florence, but what happened to the other two girls is a mystery; we do not even know their names. Galileo himself never referred to them and there are, apparently, no records describing them, so it would seem probable that, like many children in the sixteenth century, they died in infancy; this was certainly what happened to Benedetto. At all events, none of them played any significant part in Galileo's life except to be a financial burden to him after his father's death. We know as little about Galileo's earliest years as we know about the lives of his siblings, and all that is recorded is that the family remained in Pisa for the first six years or so of his life, and then, when his father went to Florence, they lodged with friends in Pisa until 1574, when Galileo was ten, and they all moved to Florence permanently.

At Pisa Galileo had a private tutor, and while in modern society such a privilege is confined to the wealthy, in Galileo's time a poor cleric could command no more than a working man, and although the Galilei's funds might be limited and even insignificant beside those of the wealthy nobles and merchants, they would still be comfortably placed compared with a labourer's family, and could afford to educate their son at home. Galileo's tutor was one Jacopo Borghini, and although we do not know just what he taught him, it is safe to assume that they laboured over the usual subjects; some grammar, a little literature, some basic arithmetic and a small amount of geometry, perhaps.

On looking at matters generally, it seems that Galileo, like so many sons, imbibed much from his father, although of course we do not know how close they were, and whether they got on well together or not. Yet they had many interests in common, and it is certain that it was from his father that Galileo derived his great love of music and his intense interest in mathematics. Glancing back with

The house near the Porta Fiorentina at Pisa, where Galileo was born on 15 February 1564.

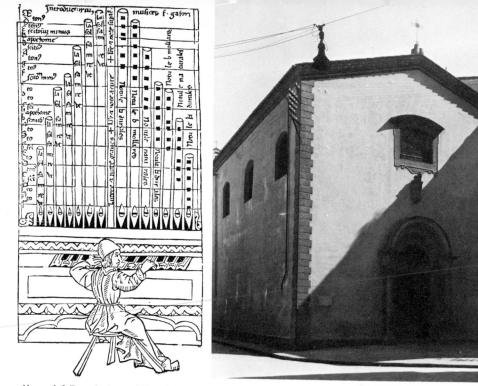

Above, left Frontispiece of Franchino Gafurio's *Theory of Music*, 1492, compiled for Lodovico Sforza and which Vincenzo Galilei may have studied. *Right* The church of San Simone, in Florence, built by the Galilei family.

the benefit of hindsight, knowing what Galileo was to make of his life, what he was to accomplish and where he was to fail, one can see similarities with his father all along the line. In Galileo's case the characteristics were bolder, the achievements greater, the arguments more vituperative, and the results far more dramatic, but they followed a pattern that, if not the same, at least was similar in many ways.

Vincenzo Galilei was a Florentine. Born sometime about 1520, his early education is unclear, but when he was about twenty he began to study music seriously, and besides getting a sound theoretical grounding, learned the lute and gained a considerable reputation as a performer. However he became increasingly interested in musical theory, and in due course decided to go to Venice and study there with Geoseffo Zarlino, a man of much the same age who was known for his erudition and had been appointed to the coveted post of Maestro di Cappella at St Mark's. Zarlino had recently published a large tome *The Institutes of Harmony* and was considered the great authority on musical theory and on all matters of intonation and tuning. Galilei seems to have stayed in Venice for no more than two years – and possibly for less – before he returned to Florence, married Giulia Ammanati and then settled down in Pisa.

During the 1570s, when his family was lodging with friends in Pisa, Vincenzo began a correspondence with the Renaissance scholar and Hellenist, Girolamo Mei, who lived in Rome and was intensely interested in Greek music. Zarlino had said much about the subject himself in his *Institutes*, discussing music and mathematics and, in particular, Pythagoras' and Ptolemy's ideas of numbers and 'harmony, and Vincenzo's enthusiasm was fired. He did not keep his new-found passion to himself, any more than his eldest son was to do later on over his purely scientific interests. Vincenzo was a member of a select and famous group of Florentine musicians known as the Camerata, that Count Bardi di Verne had formed primarily to discuss and play new music. The new music they were concerned with was monody, a style in which the melody is given to a single voice only, with or without an accompaniment, and both Count Bardi and Vincenzo composed in this way, Vincenzo writing for voice and for voice and lute. With the assistance of the Camerata, and helpful comments from Mei, he carried out experiments on tuning and, in particular, on the whole scheme promoted by Zarlino which was concerned with Pythagoras' idea that consonance depended on the notes given by vibrating strings whose lengths could be expressed by the numbers two, three and four. Zarlino had followed Ptolemy and added a new 'sonorous' number, number six. This was, of course, all purely theoretical, and what Vincenzo and his friends did was to experiment; they constructed a single stringed instrument, the monochord, just as Pythagoras had done, and they tried out the relationships given by the sonorous numbers. Their results were discouraging, and Vincenzo came to the conclusion that whatever theory might say, this did not square with musical practice. What is more, he felt that no purely numerical system could do so, and as Mei had stressed in correspondence with him, nothing could replace the musician's ear, however mathematically ingenious it might be.

Vincenzo's experimental approach is interesting, for this was just the way Galileo was later to attack the problems and arguments that faced him. It makes one pose the question whether the young Galileo saw, perhaps even helped in, trials of this kind. At the time Vincenzo was busy with all this – in the late 1570s – the family was all together again and in Florence, and Galileo was in his early 'teens. The boy was a fine lute player – later he was to excel even his father in charm of style and delicacy of touch – and was also a more than competent organist, so with an obviously musical bent, he would have been worth asking on so subjective a matter. And it is certainly not stretching a point to suppose that Galileo's experimental attitude to questions in physics was stimulated by his father's approach to vibrating strings which, after all, are an integral part of the physics of sound.

Another aspect of the similarity between father and son showed up when Vincenzo, convinced that his experiments had proved his point, wrote to Zarlino to tell him that he was wrong, and that musical intervals must be determined by the musical ear not by some mathematical formula. An acrimonious and polemical correspondence grew up between them, and when Vincenzo decided to publish his views, Zarlino did everything to prevent the book being issued. Vincenzo had intended his *Dialogue on Ancient and Modern Music* to come out in Venice but this Zarlino managed to prevent, although he could not stop it being published beyond

Above, left Ariosto, the author of *Orlando Furioso*, and Galileo's favourite poet. Portrait by Titan. *Right Boy Playing the Lute*, by Caravaggio. Galileo learnt to play the lute at an early age and his music remained a great joy to him throughout his life.

Opposite Florence Cathedral, Santa Maria del Fiore, seen from Giotto's *campanile*.

the borders of the Venetian state. In 1581 it appeared in Florence, but Zarlino did not give in; he stopped the Venetian booksellers handling it and then set about writing and publishing a *Musical Supplement* to his *Institutes*. The *Supplement* came out in 1588, seven years after Vincenzo's book, but the damage was done, and although he answered his critics, and in particular Vincenzo, the importance of musical experience, of musical sensitivity, could not be denied.

The atmosphere of Galileo's home was musical and artistic and its influence stayed with him. He kept up his lute playing throughout his life and when, towards the end he became blind, it was a source of great comfort to him. Yet important though music was it was not the only art in which he took an interest. Galileo was very fond of poetry and a lifelong devotee of Ariosto, but above all, even above his music, it seems, he loved to draw and to paint. Towards the end of his life he said that if he had been completely free to choose a career, he would have become a painter, and even if this was an exaggeration, or an over-romantic piece of reminiscence, there is no doubt that he showed great talent, and considerable knowledge too. His friend, the artist Lodovico Cardi, five years his senior, and perhaps better known as Cigoli, the 'Florentine Correggio', was later to say that it was Galileo who taught him all he knew about perspective, a confession indeed from one who was later to write a book on the subject.

The young Galileo was not narrow in his outlook. Not only did he have artistic leanings, he also loved mechanics and spent a great deal of time making mechanical devices, just as Newton was to do eighty years later. This may sound no more than many children do today with construction kits, making mechanical toys purely as an amusement, as a passing phase in their development, but we live in a mechanical environment; Galileo did not. His mechanical bent was a foretaste of an interest that was to last throughout his life, one that he was to return to time and again in between more purely theoretical bouts of activity, and it was a factor that led to his great respect for the ancient Greek mathematician and mechanician Archimedes.

When the Galilei family all moved to Florence in 1574, Galileo was sent to school. He went to the famous eleventh-century monastery of Santa Maria at Vallombrosa on the east side of Florence; a school run by the Jesuits. Here he received the usual sound Renaissance foundation, he learned Latin – in which he probably had a good grounding already – Greek, mathematics that would also include physics, astronomy, and various subjects that we should now classify as the humanities. He would also receive very sound religious training, and indeed this so moved him that when he reached the age of fourteen he entered the Society as a novice. His father was horrified and wasted no time in withdrawing him from the school, using the excuse that Galileo needed special medical attention for his eyesight. His father tried to get him a scholarship to the university at Pisa, where the age of entry was then much earlier than now, but he failed and, in the end, the boy returned to Vallombrosa obviously with strict instructions that on no account was he to consider becoming a novice. How well Galileo did at school is not clear, but there is every reason to assume that he was an apt pupil, if his subsequent career is anything to go by. His father, it seems, had hopes that he might go into commerce and trade as a cloth-dealer, a sensible enough suggestion considering the strength of the Florentine textile trade. But Galileo's interests, and presumably his progress at Vallombrosa, made it obvious that this plan would not work. Galileo would never be happy in the business world, and it is to Vincenzo's credit that he realized this. His son was cut out for some different pursuit. However Vincenzo was not a rich man and he did not want Galileo to be troubled by financial worries, so after thinking things over, he decided the best thing was to combine his son's academic talents with a reasonably lucrative profession. He should go to Pisa and read medicine. Doctors were well paid, and professors of medicine received higher salaries than most of their colleagues – at Padua, for instance, the professor of medicine was paid at more than three times the rate of the holder of the mathematics chair. And what is more, had not Galileo's great-great-grandfather held the medical chair at Florence? So he was entered as a medical student, and in September 1581, at the age of seventeen, he left Florence and went to Pisa, lodging there with a cousin and her family.

Opposite The eleventh-century monastery of Santa Maria di Vallombrosa where Galileo was sent to school.

65

6
University Student and Scholar

In the late sixteenth century Italy was exceptionally rich in centres of learning. Compared with other countries, universities proliferated, and when Galileo began life as a student in 1581 there were thirteen of them, while England and Scotland still had only three between them for it was another year before Edinburgh was to be added to the list. This, then, was the importance attached to learning, although we must remember that the Renaissance university was very different from its twentieth-century counterpart. There was a far greater reliance on authoritarian teaching, and research took a very minor place in the general activities. Perhaps one factor that played an important part in this state of affairs was a much younger general age of entry, for boys in their early teens would scarcely have the intellectual maturity to assess as well as to absorb, and their professors were forced to assume the role of school-teachers. The undergraduate began by studying a general course, taking in the seven 'liberal arts' of grammar, logic and rhetoric, arithmetic, geometry, music and astronomy. This was the formal scheme, the official curriculum, but, in practice, it varied from one university to another, and there was an unwritten arrangement in most that the student learned poetry and history as well as the official subjects. All teaching was in Latin, the international language of academic communities, and the hallmark of a learned and cultured gentleman. And not only was the teaching in Latin, but the students were expected to speak Latin out of the lecture hall as well as in it, and snoopers or 'wolves' (*lupi*) were employed to see that this rule was obeyed; if it were broken the student was fined. After one had passed the general arts course then, and only then, was it possible to proceed to a higher course of study and obtain a degree in theology, in law, or in medicine. For an older entrant like Galileo, who had had the benefit of a private tutor and a sound education at home, it was possible to begin straightway on a degree course.

Since the Renaissance had first flowered in Italy, one might have expected that by the time Galileo was old enough to become a student the Italian universities would have been centres of advanced thought, but this was not the case. Most did not encourage a new outlook, and regarded a creative mind with some disfavour; the dead hand of authority was everywhere – or nearly everywhere – in evidence. The trouble seems to have been partly the entrenched belief in Aristotelian philosophy and science, the attitude that took it as read that the Greeks had observed everything and considered everything; one might, conceivably, recapture the golden age but one could never surpass it. And just as the Greeks had excelled in science and philosophy, so too were other authors, even Renaissance authors,

Opposite The façade of Pisa Cathedral where, in 1582, Galileo probably made his discovery of the pendulum's isochronism.

A view of Pisa: the quay of Santa Maria della Spina over the Arno.

elevated to an exaggerated position; at best one might emulate them but that was as far as it was possible to go. All this had a numbing effect on the intellectual vigour of university circles. Men studied and commented on this or that classic work, but were unmoved by it. True critical scholarship was impossible because criticism, if it were not to be purely destructive, had to lead to a positive result and this could mean, and probably would mean, setting out on an independent path.

What of Galileo himself at Pisa? How did he fare, coming from a home background that was full of new ideas, that was no respecter of pronouncements even from authorities of impeccable reputation? Independent test, individual experiment, this is what he had been taught to regard as the touchstone of learning, not what was enshrined in books that described in unimaginative prose ideas that had ceased to be novel almost two thousand years before. How did he react? Did he accept the situation, decide to humour the authorities and get his degree? Or was he too much of an individualist to accept the dogma without protest? As soon became evident, even the youthful Galileo was not one to drink in without murmur the words of wisdom meted out by his teachers. He would not take as evidence something enshrined in a book, or told him as a fact, unless it could be shown incontrovertibly to be so or, better still, be confirmed by experiment. It was not long, then, before he began to question and, when the answers became

The teaching of medicine at the university of Pisa was based on the writings of Galen.

unsatisfactory, to argue with his lecturers. At every turn he would query the Aristotelian natural philosophy, what Aristotle propounded on the movement of bodies, on the nature of heat and cold, on the four elements; every physical fact, every scientific argument he would examine to the annoyance, and often the discomfort, of his tutors. It is little wonder, then, that he was not popular with the staff, and earned himself the nickname of 'The Wrangler'.

When it came to medicine itself, Galileo found the whole situation more tedious than he had ever imagined. In the first place, he had no particular love for the subject and it was not his wish to be a doctor or to practice medicine; his real interests lay elsewhere, and the way medicine, an eminently practical subject, was taught, seemed to him completely arid. His criticism was not ill-deserved, either. The whole of academic medicine was based on authority, on the discoveries made in earlier times, and in particular on the work of the highly successful Graeco-Roman, Galen. Galen was a keen experimentalist who wrote well and enshrined his experience in a number of medical works but, ironically, because the reverence accorded to him in medieval and Renaissance times was so great, independent experiment and investigation in medicine was thought unnecessary. The teaching of medicine was based on Galen's writing, and traditionally his anatomical work was read by the professor and a cadaver was dissected by a menial who worked under the eye of a professional assistant (the 'demonstrator'). Although the habit had to some extent, been broken down at Padua by Vesalius who, earlier in the century had personally carried out dissections and found some of Galen's descriptions to be in error, the basic medical instruction Galileo received was still founded on Galen, and thus on the four elements and the four qualities of Greek philosophy, and the four bodily 'humours' that had been introduced into early medicine by Hippocrates or his immediate followers. Galen was still the authority, the fount of wisdom, the man whose truly encyclopaedic medical knowledge must be followed to the letter. It was to this that Galileo so strongly objected. He was irked by the dogmatism that he realized was the very antithesis of what Galen would have wished.

However, it would be wrong to imply that the entire medical staff at Pisa were dyed-in-the-wool Galenists, for although the professor of medicine, Andrea Cesalpino, was conservatively minded, he was a sound practical physician. Cesalpino believed it better to return to the original teachings and methods of Hippocrates, than keep slavishly to Galen's interpretations of the Hippocratic corpus, partly because they fitted in better with Aristotelian doctrine, and partly because he found them more effective and more in keeping with his experience. Moreover, one of Cesalpino's duties was to act as Keeper of the university's Botanic Garden, and it was here that he discovered that some of the ancient authorities were not completely correct, and he found himself forced to caution his students over blind acceptance of all the information given in the old herbals. Whether, in fact, Galileo ever received lectures from Cesalpino, whether he ever knew of the professor's wariness over authority, is uncertain, but it seems probable. If so, then something of this attitude would have been bound to rub off, especially since it would confirm his own convictions.

It was while at Pisa that Galileo is supposed to have made his first independent discovery. The story goes that during a sermon in the cathedral sometime late in 1582, he noticed a huge chandelier gently swinging to and fro after it had been lit; and being bored by the sermon, he began to time its swings against his pulse. To his surprise, he found that the swings all occupied the same time, whether they were the longer swings he had observed to begin with or the short ones as the chandelier slowed down. The great chandelier was, in fact, acting like a pendulum, and Galileo's observations showed him that any pendulum must therefore be isochronous, performing all swings in equal times.

Whether the story is true or apocryphal is not so very important, but anyone visiting Pisa cathedral should not be deceived if they are told that the chandelier hanging there now is the very one Galileo used to make his observation, for it was not installed until 1587. The only point in doubt is the date at which Galileo made the discovery for, as far as we know, the first time he mentioned the isochronism of a pendulum was in 1602. His experience is supposed to have led him to invent and build a device called the pulsilogium, a simple contrivance for measuring a

Opposite The so-called 'Chandelier of Galileo' in Pisa Cathedral, was in fact installed five years after Galileo's discovery of the isochronism of the pendulum.

patient's pulse rate, and consisting of a small metal weight on the end of a string, the top of which was fixed to one end of a small horizontal scale. By moving one's fingers along the string and holding it at a point along the scale one could alter the free length of the string, and thus of the pendulum. Since the time a pendulum takes to swing depends on its length, and not on the weight of the pendulum bob, the time of swing could be adjusted to coincide with the pulse, and the result read off the scale. It was ingenious and, in the days before most physicians possessed pocket watches, it gave a desirable precision to the measurement of pulse beats. A number of elaborate versions of the device were designed, some probably by Galileo himself, but the man who really made use of it was Santorio Santorio of Padua, who was extremely interested in trying to bring exact measurement into medical research, and is generally credited with being the first person to attempt to study metabolism precisely. Santorio published descriptions of pulsilogia in 1620 and in 1625, and for a time it seems to have had some vogue, although it went out of fashion after his death in 1636. Did Galileo invent the device, or did he merely apply it? We do not know as he never laid claim to having done so but it seems quite likely he did. Certainly the idea of the pulse as a measure of time was not new, for Zarlino had suggested its use for timing intervals in music, and Galileo may well have been aware of this through his father, but the important fact of the observation was the isochronism, the fact that time constancy was independent of size of swing. This was significant and was to be used by Galileo towards the end of his life in a device that could well have developed into the pendulum clock.

The pulsilogium and the observation of the chandelier show one aspect of Galileo that was later to become all important – he relished measurement, and had an intense interest in problems of physics. Indeed, he had little fondness for medicine, and in 1585 he left Pisa and, like so many students at the time, without a degree.

What was Galileo to do? He was now twenty-one and must soon consider earning a living but, unfortunately from the financial point of view, his main interest was mathematics. This was the subject that really intrigued him; this, with its sixteenth-century ramifications of physics, was what Galileo wanted to study. He had felt frustrated because the chair of mathematics at Pisa had been vacant while he was there, and so he had had no access to formal mathematical teaching within the university. However, he managed to persuade his father to let him have some private tuition, and he took lessons from Ostilio Ricci, whom he met in the summer of 1583. Ricci was a friend of his father's, a member of the Florence Academy of Design and had, it seems, once been a pupil of the famous Italian mathematician Niccolò Tartaglia who, amongst his many activities, had edited the works of Archimedes. Galileo was soon to become a devotee of his astonishing Greek scientist, it was doubtless by way of Ricci's teaching that he first fell under Archimedes' spell. 'Those who read his works,' Galileo was soon to write,

The mathematician Ostilio Ricci, a friend of Vincenzo Galilei, gave Galileo private tuition in mathematics and was particularly responsible for fostering Galileo's interest in Archimedes.

'realise only too clearly how inferior are all other minds compared with Archimedes', and what small hope is left of ever discovering things similar to the ones he discovered.'[1] An overdose of reverence, a smattering of the prevalent attitude of inordinate respect for past achievements perhaps, but Galileo was obviously brimming over with youthful enthusiasm for someone who had been a legend even in his own time, and if there was only small hope of making new discoveries in the subjects Archimedes had studied, at least he did not rule it out entirely, even then.

As soon as he came down from Pisa, Galileo lost no time in immersing himself in mathematics; he read Euclid and went on with Archimedes and soon began to give private lessons himself, even travelling the thirty miles or so to Siena to do some teaching there. In 1586, a year after he had left Pisa, Galileo busied himself with hydrostatics, and constructed an improved form of the hydrostatic balance. What set him off along this track, was the intriguing story of King Heiron's golden crown, a story that is worth re-telling. Heiron II of Syracuse was a friend and kinsman of Archimedes, and when he suspected that a golden crown he had commissioned was adulterated with silver, he appealed to the mathematician to help solve the problem. Archimedes is said to have come on the answer while in his bath tub as soon as he became aware of the buoyancy of his own body, and

Archimedes in his bath. From Gaultherus Rivius, *Architechtur . . . Mathematischen . . . Kunst*, 1547.

jumped out shouting '*Eureka*' (I have found it). His solution was one that he could apply as a basic principle to various problems of fluids and floatation and led to the hydrostatic balance. Here a body is first weighed in air, and then weighed while immersed in water. The second time it weighs less because it is buoyed up by the weight of the amount of water it has displaced. In the case of Heiron's crown, if made of gold the difference between the weighings would be greater than if it were made of silver, since gold is denser than silver. Thus Archimedes was able to work out the proportions of the two precious metals without destroying the crown. Galileo analysed the whole procedure, redesigned the balance, and circulated a manuscript among his friends describing his work. Known as *The Little Balance* it remained unpublished until after his death, but this was of no moment; what was important was that it brought him to the notice of scientific circles in Florence, and began to establish his reputation as a mathematician.

He produced another manuscript, this time dealing with the centre of gravity or balancing point of solid bodies. Again it was circulated among friends and it, too, remained unpublished until, in 1638, it came out as an appendix to his book *Discourses . . . on Two New Sciences*, a classic work on moving bodies and the strength of materials that he wrote towards the end of his life. His enthusiasm for mathematics seems to have been unbounded, but so was his frustration. He wanted to teach mathematics, and to carry out further research – in brief to obtain a university post. Yet in spite of his manuscripts and his lecturing in Siena, there was no response. No one seemed to take the slightest notice. No offer came from Pisa, none from Siena. With the typical impatience of a young man Galileo expected results too quickly, and he thought everyone should react immediately. Perhaps there were ways of stimulating action, at least in some quarter or another? What of a journey to Rome? There were plenty there to whom he could arrange introductions, and above all there was Christopher Clavius, Jesuit mathematician and astronomer at the Collegio Romano whom Galileo wanted to meet and who, he thought, might conceivably be able to help.

Galileo went to Rome in 1587, travelling with the heir to the rich Ricasoli family. Once there he met Clavius, with whom he seems to have got on very well, for throughout the older man's life they remained on the most cordial terms even though Clavius was never able to bring himself to accept Galileo's theories. What came out of the interview with Clavius we do not know, but one thing seems certain, there was nothing about an appointment to teach mathematics at Siena or anywhere else. In one sense Galileo seems to have been utterly dispirited, and had talks with Ricasoli about the possibility of going out to the Near East to seek his fortune, but all this came to nothing. His whole journey seems to have been abortive for he was not even to make a rich friend who could be a patron throughout his life, for Ricasoli suffered from some kind of mental illness and his family had to take legal action to annul a will that he had drawn up and to recover the grossly extravagant gifts which he had impulsively distributed far and wide. Galileo became involved in this, but only in so far as he had to make a deposition about various things he witnessed.

At last, in 1588, came the first signs of recognition; Galileo was invited to give a short series of addresses to the Academy of Florence on the topography of hell as given in Dante's *Divine Comedy*. Today this sounds the most unlikely subject, having little if any relevance to mathematics, astronomy, or science in general, and seems to be a particularly useless exercise into the bargain except, perhaps, for a literary scholar. Yet in the 1580s it was both relevant and an honour. True, it did expect some considerable knowledge of Dante's poem, but this was to be expected of any cultured Italian; after all the *Divine Comedy* was one of the greatest literary flowers of Italian Renaissance and no education would be complete without a study of it. And the prevalent idea was still that the Earth was in the centre of the universe, in spite of anything Copernicus might have suggested to the contrary; heaven lay above the Earth and hell below, at least in theory. But the subject had another side: the description Dante gave of the infernal regions raised certain ambiguities, particularly as far as its geographical position and territorial extent were concerned, and scholars were divided in their opinion. Analyses had been made, and there were two schools of thought; on the one hand there were those who followed the Florentine geographer Antonio Manetti who, a century before, had made the first detailed investigation; on the other there was the Venetian Alessandro Vellutello who had strongly attacked Manetti and substantially modified Manetti's conclusions. Who was right? Clearly the Florentine Academy hoped it was Manetti, and expected Galileo to use both his literary knowledge and mathematical skill in support of Manetti's interpretation. It was a wonderful opportunity. The very invitation was a recognition of his scholarship and his ability to think clearly, a tribute indeed from Florence's leading cognoscenti: if he could acquit himself well, then all kinds of doors should open.

Galileo wisely avoided all rhetoric, even though this was the customary accompaniment to an academic discourse, and just concentrated on the text, the two interpretations, and a penetrating mathematical analysis of the topography. Using the theory of conic sections which he knew well from his studies of Archimedes, and having the tact – a quality he did not often show – to apologize to the learned company for offending their sensitive ears with the bald technical terms of mathematics, he demonstrated that Manetti had indeed been correct and Vellutello wrong. Florence was vindicated, Venice repudiated, Galileo's success was enormous and his reputation assured. His love of literature, ancient and modern – he adored Ovid, Virgil and Seneca, although Ariosto held pride of place – and his predilection for mathematics had both been used to the full. In the face of such an obvious triumph his father was defeated, and there was no further criticism of his wish to pursue a mathematical career.

The success of his lectures to the Academy gave Galileo the self-confidence he needed. He wanted to be a mathematician? Then he would become one, and go on applying for a mathematical post until he was successful. To suit action to words he began by trying for the chair of mathematics at Padua, but his application was not accepted. This does not seem to have depressed him, but now he determined to make use of his friends, some of whom could be powerful allies. In particular the Marquis Guidobaldo del Monte of Pesaro, who had been one of the first to recognize Galileo's genius and had been at pains to introduce him to all the right people in the appropriate literary and scientific circles, was asked to support a fresh application, this time to the university of Bologna. Guidobaldo seems to have been only too happy to help, but even with his support, Galileo was turned down, and the appointment went to Giovanni Magini. Magini, a conservative young man, probably received the chair because he was better qualified than Galileo, having a far greater knowledge of astronomy, a subject with which Galileo had no more than a nodding acquaintance at this time, but which a professor of mathematics was supposed to teach.

Guidobaldo was probably as sorry as his protégé that they had drawn a blank at Bologna, but all was not lost. Padua and Bologna might be doors that were closed, at least temporarily, but the university of Pisa, after all these years, was still without any occupant for its mathematical chair. Here, surely, was an opening that Galileo could take, especially with the support of someone like Guidobaldo

It was through the influence of his friend, Marquis Guidobaldo del Monte, that, in 1589, Galileo obtained the Chair of Mathematics at Pisa.

who had close connections with the city. And so it turned out, Guidobaldo used his influence and prevailed on his brother, who was a Cardinal, to lend his support, and in 1589, the very year that Vincenzo Galilei's *Dialogue on Music* came out, Galileo was installed as Professor of Mathematics at Pisa. The appointment was only for three years in the first instance, a usual procedure, and the salary a mere pittance of some 60 florins a year – about one thirtieth of what the professor of medicine earned – but at least he now had academic standing. With what, if any, misgivings the Appointment Board at Pisa decided to have the Wrangler back in their midst, we do not know – perhaps, with the del Montes exerting pressure, they had no choice, or no desire for choice – but it was not to be long before they were to find that the new professor was every bit as radical as his student days promised he might be.

7
Professor at Pisa

Galileo was twenty-five when he became professor at Pisa, not so young as it might seem, since in the sixteenth century life expectancy was shorter than it is today, and both men and women appear to have matured earlier. How did he feel, returning as professor to the university at which he had studied but from which he had never graduated? Probably a sense of well-being and satisfaction – it was after all, a boost to his self-esteem to know that his onetime academic seniors had decided to accept him into their circle, even if they had needed the del Montes to persuade them – but these feelings were probably tempered a little when he began to think about the Aristotelians. They would be only too happy to hold disputations provided these were confined within a rigid framework, narrow in its vision and antagonistic to any concept that disobeyed the basic tenets of Aristotelian physics. No, he would clearly have trouble there. And another annoyance was the stiff formality of the university itself; this was something that irked Galileo and was to tempt him to exercise his wit at the Establishment's expense.

Another new member of staff in 1589 was Jacopo Mazzoni who was appointed to the chair of philosophy. Mazzoni was a confirmed Aristotelian, and indeed he could hardly have obtained his post if he were not, but he was already friendly with Galileo, and in spite of their difference in outlook they remained on easy terms. A second piece of good fortune was that when Cesalpino resigned the chair of medicine to go and serve Pope Clement VIII, his successor was Girolamo Mercuriale, another of Galileo's friends. With these two allies close to hand, he obviously did not feel completely isolated in the war he knew he was going to wage against Aristotle's physics for, as early as 1589, Galileo had firmly arrived at the conclusion that, when it came to discussing the precise way in which bodies fall to the ground, one thing was certain: Aristotle was wrong. He might have to stand alone when it came to his scientific arguments, Mazzoni could not support him there, but at least he was assured of human sympathy and understanding when things became difficult, as surely they were bound to do.

The analysis of how bodies fall is important, important to the physicist, important to the engineer, and also important to the astronomer if he is going to move away from the Greek universe into the new cosmos of Copernicus. Galileo did not at this time accept the Copernican theory, although he had certainly heard about it, and his interest in falling bodies was primarily from a physicist's point of view. This did not make it any the less urgent a question, and he set about devising trials and tests of his ideas that would prove him right, and provide him with hard evidence that he could use in his arguments against current theory.

Opposite Pisa: the cathedral and the Leaning Tower from which Galileo supposedly made his experiments on the fall of weights.

Why do bodies fall to the ground? Because, said Aristotle, they were seeking their natural place which was the centre of the Earth which, itself, lay at the centre of the universe. At this stage Galileo might have his doubts about the validity of the argument, an argument that had little meaning if the Earth were not the centre of all things, but he was not disposed to discuss the point. What he was willing, indeed keen, to do was to attack the underlying Aristotelian theory that bodies had a natural appetite to reach their natural place, an appetite that depended on the earthiness of the body. Put into modern language, what Aristotle claimed was that a body's propensity to fall depended on its weight. The heavier it was, the stronger its appetite to reach the centre of the Earth. In other words, the heavier a body the faster it would fall. This, Galileo said, was wrong; totally and utterly mistaken, for bodies do not fall at a rate depending on their weight, and as he wrote in 1590: 'We certainly see by trial that if two spheres of equal size, one of which is double the other in weight, are dropped from a tower, the heavier one does not reach the ground twice as fast.'[1]

There is a story, and a very well-known one, that Galileo proved his point and demolished the Aristotelian view, by a public demonstration made from the Leaning Tower of Pisa. According to the testimony of his last pupil and first biographer, Vincenzo Viviani, the entire university had been specially assembled for the occasion and Galileo, dropping two quite different weights, showed that they both hit the ground at the same instant, not one after the other as they should have done if Aristotle were right. And, Viviani goes on, he hammered his point home by repeated experiments. Viviani's account, however, stands alone, and

A romanticized painting by Giuseppe Bezzuoli of Galileo conducting an experiment on the fall of weights.

there is no corroborative evidence, and no university record, to lend support to the story; we would have expected to find some reference, however garbled, in the archives, if the whole university had been called together especially to witness this great demolition of Aristotelian wisdom. Equally it is extremely unlikely that Viviani fabricated the whole incident, for there would be little point in his doing so. On the other hand he may well have exaggerated things in the mistaken belief that he was adding to his master's stature by doing so; still a third possibility is that a more or less private demonstration grew out of all proportion in an old man's recollections, for it does seem likely that Galileo did make at least a few trials from the Leaning Tower. In his writings he keeps referring to dropping bodies from towers, and in more than one case specifically claims to have done repeated tests of this kind. The Leaning Tower, begun in 1174, tilted over during construction due to soil subsidence, and although the angle of inclination was nowhere near as great as it is now, it would have provided Galileo with an ideal testing site all the same. However, it is important to realize that what Galileo did was to disprove the Aristotelian claim, not devise a precise experimental test of whether or not all bodies do in fact fall at the same rate. The greater effect of air resistance on a lighter body compared with a very heavy one would vitiate any result, as, too, would the very real problems of releasing both weights at the same instant, and determining whether they did land at the identical moment. Galileo was aware of this as anyone, he knew that it was impossible for him to measure such discrete parcels of time, and so he only set out to show that one weight ten times heavier than another did not fall to the ground ten times faster, which is what the Aristotelian doctrine demanded. This was a gross enough difference to be demonstrated clearly by dropping weights from a tower.

Galileo was not the first to suggest that all falling bodies dropped at the same speed for in 1533 the Venetian Giovanni Benedetti, another of Tartaglia's pupils, had proposed just this, and in 1586 a test was made and the results published by the Flemish engineer Simon Stevin. Galileo may not have known of this work, since he claimed that the idea came to him during a hailstorm when he noticed that large and small hailstones hit the ground together, but the question here is not one of priority: it is one of intent. Galileo's aim was to make an independent critical examination of every tenet of Aristotle's physics, and where he found it in error, which it mostly was, boldly to say so. And equally important to his contemporaries was the technique he adopted to do this, a technique that can most simply be described as conducting thought experiments. Essentially this was a method of visualizing the ideal conditions under which an experiment could be performed (in the case of falling bodies this would be to neglect air resistances, timing errors in release of the weights, and so on), and then working out the consequences mathematically. It was what Archimedes had often done, and would appeal to a mathematical mind, to one whose outlook on the physical universe was quantitative, who wanted to express everything in numbers, or explain things by way of geometrical constructions. At heart Galileo was one with Euclid, Ptolemy and Archimedes, not with Aristotle who, as we now know, was scientifically at his best on biological subjects, and who looked at everything from a qualitative point of view.

At the time of the supposed Leaning Tower demonstration, Galileo was occupied in writing a book on motion. Untitled, it was not prepared for his students, and he most likely had a more erudite readership in mind but, in the event, he never actually published it. All the same, writing it was obviously a useful exercise, for it would have helped to get his ideas straight in his own mind, and his basic criticism down on paper. The little treatise, known as *On Motion*, is important to the historian because it shows how Galileo's mind was working at this time, and it demonstrates the development of his ideas on kinematics, a subject which he was later to include in a full-scale book. Why Galileo did not attempt to publish his little tract is not absolutely certain, but it was probably because in 1590 he was still having difficulties about how to reconcile theory with experience when it came to falling weights on the one hand, and the way bodies roll down inclined planes on the other. There seemed to be discrepancies between the two, inconsistencies that showed up in the mathematical reasoning, but that theoretically should not have been there. With hindsight we can now see, as Galileo himself later saw, that the inconsistencies were not real; they arose only because, at the time, he thought the speed of a falling body increased to a certain value and then remained the same. In fact, it does not do this at all. A body goes on gathering speed as it falls; there is continual acceleration. This was a rule of behaviour which Galileo had to discover on his own account, and although it was not long before he was able to specify it, in 1590 this gap in his explanations was a very real stumbling block which would be pounced on by his Aristotelian opponents. But by the time he had solved his problem, he was too preoccupied with other interests to bother to see *On Motion* through the press.

What *On Motion* shows so clearly is Galileo's ability to branch out along a new line, and in a new way, in his study of the natural world. In one very real sense Galileo's greatest contribution to science was the mathematical approach he took to physical problems and his geometrical and numerical analyses of the way the world works, what can only be called his mathematization of nature. It was an innovation, but it proved so useful, and opened the door to such clear and precise thinking, that it has been followed ever since. In one way then, *On Motion* was a very advanced work, but in another it was somewhat conservative, as Galileo at this time still held to the customary view that the Earth lay in the centre of the universe. He had not accepted the Copernican view, and for the very good reason that there was no proof of its validity. Yet this is not to say that Galileo accepted the Aristotelian universe in its entirety, or that he took the whole concept of a fixed Earth in the generally accepted sense. In fact, in the book he shows himself quite ready to consider the Earth rotating on its axis; not orbiting round the Sun,

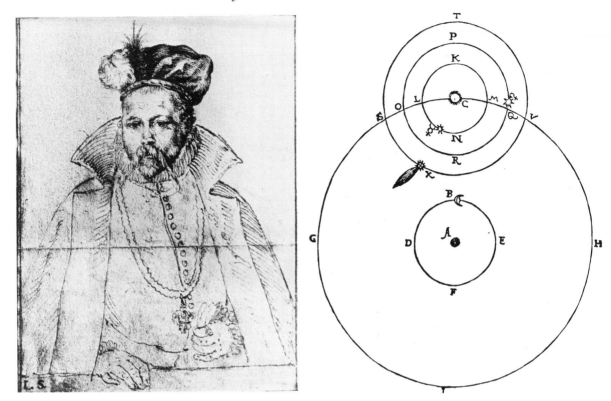

Tycho Brahe *(left),* the Danish astronomer who attempted a compromise between the Aristotelian and Copernican views of the universe and *(right)* his planetary system showing at X the comet of 1577, beyond the sphere of the Moon where, according to Aristotle, no change could take place.

but spinning round once every twenty-four hours, a view that was at variance with the Aristotelian outlook and against which a host of arguments had been marshalled. Copernicus had attacked these and, roughly speaking, we can put Galileo's opinion at this time on a par with the theory that the Danish astronomer Tycho Brahe favoured. Tycho was a staunch protestant, and as such was motivated by a fundamentalist approach to the biblical teaching of a fixed Earth, an approach that led him to attempt a compromise between the Aristotelian and Copernican universes. In the end he kept the Earth in the centre of things, with the Sun and Moon orbiting round it, but he allowed the planets to orbit the Sun not the Earth. Tycho's scheme had been described in a book he had published in 1588, and although it is unlikely Galileo had read it, it was probably discussed openly enough in Pisan academic circles for him to have a working knowledge of it.

There is one more aspect of Galileo's unpublished tract that must be mentioned, and this is its author's pugnacious attitude. In his criticism of Aristotle he is merciless, time and again attacking the twin concepts of violent and natural motion which, to his mind, split the subject so hopelessly that it became impossible to consider motion as a single phenomenon. In six of the chapters Galileo begins '... in which it is concluded against Aristotle ...',[2] while elsewhere he says that '... in practically everything he wrote about local [i.e. terrestrial] motion, he wrote the opposite of truth ...'[3] The real master to turn to, Galileo said, was the 'divine Archimedes'. His criticism was perfectly justified and, in attacking Aristotle's two classes of motion, Galileo hit at the very nub of the problem. Once the separation of movement into two distinct classes was removed, a new synthesis was possible, but not before. Galileo's genius was his recognition of this fundamental fact.

On Motion was circulated privately, and must have made a considerable impression on those able to appreciate its mathematics. But did it add to the natural antagonism of the Aristotelian faction of the university? And did its contentious language and the fact that it was obviously a protest, a radical document against the foundations of all physics teaching, worry the university authorities? We do not know for certain, but it would surely be strange if it did not. Here was the young mathematics professor pointing out bluntly that his predecessors were all wrong, and in removing one dichotomy, only replacing it with another. Aristotle's two motions were in error, and Aristotle's physics should therefore be expunged. The mathematicians would not have Aristotle at any price, yet the philosophers could not leave Aristotle; he was their divine guide. Was philosophy to be divorced from mathematics, were these two interrelated disciplines now to part company?

Galileo had certainly not made his own academic path any smoother, nor had he made it easy for senior members of the University to accept his ideas without swallowing their pride, for soon after arriving to take up his chair, he had written a satire on the ordinance that every university professor must wear his academic gown at all times, and not only within the confines of the university itself, but in the outside world as well. It was a gift for ridicule and Galileo had grasped the opportunity with both hands. He described the plight of a young university professor with a meagre stipend of 60 *scudi* a year (his own salary), less deductions for unexcused absences from his lectures (in his own case these amounted to almost ten per. cent) who had to display the robe at all times for the sake of academic dignity. What of the intimate adventures of a young man – are these to be conducted in a robe or the ordinance broken? In the rough and tumble of the market, is he to wear the robe over his own shabby garments while he haggles for his frugal supplies? Does this add to the university's prestige? The young professor longs for ancient times when men went naked and were judged by their achievements – a parody harking back to the humanist dream of a Golden Age.

The poem was no student prank but rather a superb piece of satire. Written not in Latin, but in authentic popular dialect in the style of Francesco Berni, the brilliant Florentine satirist of the previous generation, it was a subtle mixture of elegiac sadness and blunt speech. As a bonus for the reader Galileo indulged in the

A view of the Camposanto at Pisa, built in the thirteenth century.

Florentine sport of attacking the clergy, the long cassock providing him with every kind of irreverent innuendo. His remarks were not always new, but he was following in a noble tradition, for Lorenzo de' Medici had once referred to those robes 'under which they get ready to kick even before one sees their leg', and the cumulative effect was masterly.

Galileo's tact was never much in evidence – and his outspoken criticisms were scarcely likely to endear him to the Establishment. The satire on the gown was only one of his more blatant indiscretions; and although he may have been almost over extravagant in his praise of those whose work he approved, such as his adored Ariosto, he was a stern and often abusive critic when it came to those whom he considered had earned his disapproval. He said that Tasso, whom he abhorred, 'besmeared too much paper'[4] and in the end only 'made pap for cats'.[5] This may all have been Renaissance rumbustiousness, but it was not the tone expected from a young professor who still had his way to make academically, and it seems that Galileo acquired a bad reputation on more than one count. Not only was it thought that his behaviour undermined what the university valued so highly, the dignity of his position, but he was also known as a man of loose morals, although this may have owed more to the imagination of his enemies than to any basis in fact. By 1592, the last year of his appointment, the Aristotelians had suffered so much at his hands that, by way of revenge, they managed to pack out his lectures and hiss at his every word. When his term of employment expired, Galileo did not apply for it to be renewed; indeed, there seemed little point as it was doubtful whether he would be considered suitable. More important still, he did not relish spending any longer in an uncongenial atmosphere, and thought it better to try to find a more sympathetic post elsewhere.

He decided to leave Pisa and return to Florence even though such a step was a difficult one from the domestic point of view. In the middle of 1591 Vincenzo had died, and this meant that all the family responsibilities fell on Galileo's shoulders as he was the eldest son; not least of these was the problem of providing a dowry for his sister Virginia, who had recently married Benedetto Landucci, son of the Tuscan ambassador to Rome. As well as Virginia there was his mother, another sister Livia, and a younger brother, all to be provided for, and it seems that his father's estate was trifling. Inadequate though the 60 *scudi* he received from Pisa may have been, it was better than the absolutely nothing he was earning as an out-of-work professor. It was imperative, then, for him to find some source of income, but in an era when patronage was all important, where was he to turn for help? He was in a situation that was to crop up repeatedly throughout his life, where his independence of mind and the forthright way he

ILLVSTRISSIMVS IOANNES MEDICES
MAGNI COSMI FILIVS, IOANNIS NEPOS
Franco Forma

Giovanni de' Medici, governor of Leghorn, was one of the earliest victims of Galileo's uncompromising attitude to what he considered scientific misconceptions.

expressed himself made him his own worst enemy, and this was as true on his home ground of Florence as it was in Pisa. Along with his other gifts was one for antagonizing people, due mainly to his inability to suffer fools. Among those he upset was Giovanni de' Medici. As governor of Leghorn and a member of one of the most powerful of European families, even if the man had been a moron it would have been politic to humour him, but this seems to have been beyond Galileo's powers. When the governor, who fancied himself as an architect and an engineer, consulted Galileo over the dredging of Leghorn harbour, and showed him his own scheme for doing the work by using large flat-bottomed cranes, Galileo could not forbear telling him that the whole scheme, based on the widespread belief that a flat surface would give additional buoyancy, was founded on an Aristotelian misconception, the fallacy of which had been recognized centuries back by the divine Archimedes.

In spite of himself Galileo did still have some friends, and Guidobaldo del Monte who had worked so hard to gain him the chair was as staunch a supporter as ever, and does not seem to have been discouraged by his protégé's failure to gain acceptance amongst the academic community at Pisa. He had recommended a young man whom he liked, and for whose intellect he had the greatest respect; if Pisa had not proved congenial then some more suitable opening must be found for him. He enlisted the help of other friends and, in particular, that of the erudite Genoese, Gianvincenzo Pinelli, whose home in Padua was a clearing house for ideas from both city and university. With his university connections Guidobaldo was sure that Pinelli would be able to exercise some influence to get Galileo appointed to the chair of mathematics at Padua, which was still vacant after more than seven years. With these two men of influence behind him, Galileo was in a strong position, and it was not long before he took up his second appointment.

GENVENSIS. ✠ IOANNES VICENTIVS PINELLVS PATRICIVS

ΚΑΙ ΚΕΡΑΙΟΙΣ ΑΠΕΡΙΣΤΕΡΑΙ ΠΝΕΣΘΕ ΦΡΟΝΙΜΟΙ ΩΣ ΟΙ ΟΦΕΙΣ

8
Venice and Padua

At the end of the summer of 1592, Galileo set out accompanied by a solitary trunk containing all his worldly possessions. But he had no need to feel despondent, for ahead lay Padua, a city noted for its freedom and independence of thought, a place pregnant with possibilities for making new converts to the anti-Aristotelian cause. And not only was there a new battlefield, but he was being paid three times as much to wage war on it as the miserly Pisans had given him. And what added even more zest to his situation was that he had been given the chair instead of that arch-Aristotelian Magini, whose four-year appointment at Bologna was soon to expire. Magini was furious that his application should be turned down and bore Galileo a grudge ever after, proving a considerable nuisance in later years.

Galileo found Padua suited him well. The atmosphere of independence was no myth, and after the Aristotelian narrowness of Pisa he at last felt free to breathe the cool fresh air of speculation. The university was large – at times it had a student population of 8,000 – and if the State made it a regulation that Padua was the only university Venetians were allowed to attend, it nevertheless welcomed foreign students and foreign academics, men like the anatomist Vesalius, Copernicus and William Harvey, who was to prove the circulation of the blood.

In Padua Galileo was made welcome by the Pinelli circle, and given the free run of Pinelli's astonishing library of some 80,000 volumes, many in manuscript, which must have seemed an El Dorado to an almost penniless professor. As well as access to his host's thousands of books, he also had the less tangible, but much greater, pleasure of finding sympathetic minds with whom he could form life-long friendships. It was at Pinelli's house that he met Paolo Sarpi, some dozen years his senior, whose immensely broad range of interests included science and mathematics, although his main subjects were theology and history. It was Sarpi who seems to have been the driving force behind Venice's resistance to papal power, and whose critical *History of the Council of Trent* made him famous throughout Europe.

Among other friends that Galileo made was Cesare Cremonini, a professor of philosophy, renowned in his own day for the brilliance of his defence of the Aristotelian viewpoint, and in spite of their opposing views the two men were able to agree to differ, and like each other immensely. He also became intimate with two of his most brilliant pupils, Benedetto Castelli and Giovanfrancesco Sagredo. Castelli, a cleric who later became the Pope's adviser on hydraulic

Opposite Galileo's years in Padua were enriched by his friendship with Gianvincenzo Pinelli, a Genoese patrician and the leading patron of artists and intellectuals in Padua.

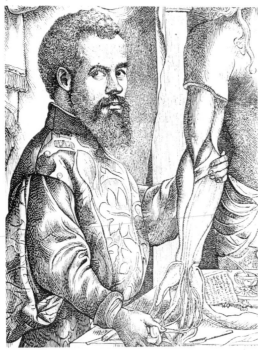

Left Andreas Vesalius, the brilliant Belgian anatomist who worked and lectured at the famous medical school at Padua, some fifty years before Galileo became a university professor there. *Below* The Theatre of Anatomy at Padua university, where Vesalius lectured.

engineering was to figure frequently in Galileo's life, especially when he became embroiled with the Church. Sagredo, who took up a diplomatic career, was a nobleman and a *bon viveur*, and was to be immortalized in Galileo's controversial *Dialogue*, where he is represented as the epitome of the enquiring mind of the Venetian intelligentsia.

Happily the attitude of the Paduan university authorities was far less rigid than was the case at Pisa, and they had a more lenient attitude to both staff and students. Although term began on 1 November, Galileo was readily given time to find suitable accommodation and settle his personal affairs before presenting his inaugural lecture. By now he had decided that he needed space to set up a work-shop for making scientific and mathematical instruments; these he intended to sell to supplement his income which was still inadequate to support so many family commitments. He therefore required something larger than a simple room or couple of rooms, and he settled for a whole house in which he could not

Two close friends of Galileo's at Padua: *Below, left* Cesare Cremonini, professor of philosophy at the university. *Right* The Venetian Paolo Sarpi, a Servite friar, whom he met at Pinelli's house.

only have his workshop and his own quarters, but where also there was enough accommodation for him to let out rooms to students and their servants. It was a sensible enough arrangement, and when his brother Michelangelo came to join him there was still plenty of space. Michelangelo seems to have been rather a burden, making few, if any, financial contributions to the family income, and when the remaining sister, Livia, married (probably about 1592) it was again Galileo who had to find the dowry. We do not know what sum was expected, but in 1593 he had still not yet paid it and was threatened with an arrest for debt.

By the time December had arrived Galileo was ready with his inaugural address, which he delivered with infinite care, winning 'the greatest admiration'[1] not only for his erudition but also for his eloquence. Now that he had formally taken his place, what was it he had to teach and what constituted a university mathematics course at this time? Pride of place was given to Euclid's *Elements of Geometry*, coupled with Ptolemy's system of planetary motion which used Euclidean geometry and was mathematically elegant and a good exercise in applying geometry to solve the theoretical problem of planetary motion. The

Below A contemporary engraving of the façade of Padua university. *Opposite, top* The central court, or Cortile del Bò at the university and *(bottom)* Galileo's lecturing pulpit in the School of Mathematics.

mathematics of the sphere (positional astronomy) was included, as it was important when it came to computing the aspects of the heavens at different times and was useful in dealing with astrology and various geographical problems. Finally there was a book called *Questions of Mechanics* which was then believed to be by Aristotle. Galileo's reaction to this collection of medieval dogmatics unfairly fathered on Aristotle can easily be imagined, and although there was nothing official he could do about it, he had his own method of counteracting its influence. Altogether it was a very conservative course, keeping mathematical facility mainly to the realm of geometry, and was somewhat restricted in scope, but this was an advantage for Galileo because when his students wanted instruction over a broader range, he was able to satisfy them by giving private tuition and so supplement his official stipend.

To help his students, and to provide an antidote to Aristotle, Galileo issued a series of short treatises. Untitled and unsigned, they were modified from time to time as his own research progressed; one still exists in three 'editions', one each for 1593, 1594 and 1600. Known as *Mechanics*, it is interesting because it shows Galileo continuing his own independent approach to mechanical problems and, when his research led him in that direction, neglecting well-accepted ideas. For instance he discusses the behaviour of objects rolling down inclined planes, so necessary for a proper understanding of accelerated motion and falling bodies, and goes into the subject in greater detail than he had ever done before. He stresses the fact not fully realized or expressed so clearly by anyone else, that a body on a horizontal plane only needs the smallest force to move it. This was of the most profound importance. He had already given a proof of it in his tract *On Motion*, but here it leads him on to what later became known as the concept of inertia, the property of bodies to remain still unless some force acts on them, and then to continue in motion until they are stopped. This, put into formal language more than half a century later, became what we now know as Newton's first law of motion, but in 1593 it was not only a novel idea, it was a concept that hit at the very vitals of Aristotle's physics. To Aristotle no body could be in a state of rest because it was forever seeking its natural place, and no body would keep on moving until something stopped it, because it required a force to push it along all the time. Yet in spite of what *Questions of Mechanics* said, and in the face of official teaching, Galileo knew otherwise, and saw that his students knew too. And it says much for the broad outlook of Padua that no objections were raised.

Not content with demolishing the mechanical aspects of the current physical doctrines, Galileo set out to examine the phenomenon of heat, and although we know he did the work while at Padua, we are not sure exactly when. What he did was to investigate a way of measuring temperature, and constructed what we should today call an air thermometer. This consisted of a glass bulb with a long thin neck: the bulb was warmed – in the hands, for instance – and then the device was inverted in water. The warm air in the bulb contracted, with the result that

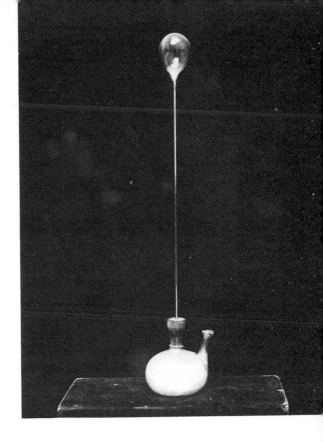

Above, left The so-called 'Tower of Galileo' at Padua, where many of his observations were said to have been made. From a nineteenth-century engraving. *Right* Galileo's air thermometer which he devised while at Padua.

some water was drawn into the narrow neck. The amount of water sucked in depended on the contraction of the air, which would be greater the higher the original temperature to which it had been heated. Now, of course, we use the expansion of mercury, not air, in a glass bulb, and do not have to plunge the thermometer into water to get a reading; but at the end of the sixteenth century such measuring devices were in their infancy. It does not seem proper to attribute the invention of the air thermometer to Galileo, for its principle was known in Greek times and had recently been mentioned again in a book called *Natural Magic* by Giambattista della Porta, but Galileo does deserve credit for being the first to use a device of this kind as an indicator of change in temperature. In one sense it lacked the precision of a true thermometer, and perhaps it should really be called a thermoscope, but Galileo's pupil Sagredo did use it later to measure temperatures and, more importantly, it was developed by Santorio in the Paduan Medical School as a means of determining body temperature.

In spite of his lecturing, private teaching and research, Galileo still had time and energy enough to pursue his intention of developing a workshop for producing scientific instruments, and as if this were not enough, designing the odd piece of larger equipment. But his instrument making was the most profitable. In these early years his greatest commercial success was his so-called geometrical and

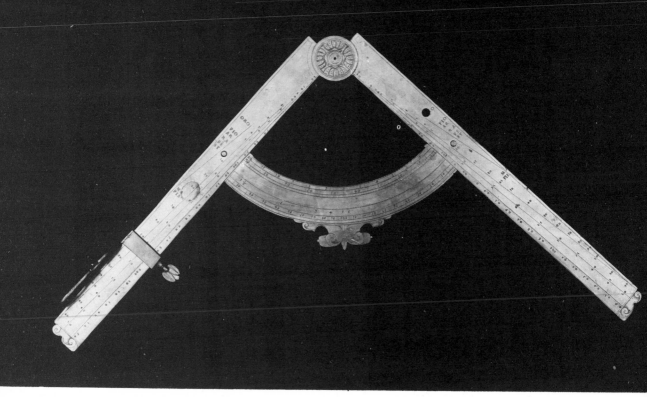

Galileo's geometric and military compass, which he designed and built in 1597.

military compass that could be used both for measuring and for making calculations. There is, and was, much argument about who originally invented the compass, but most of, if not all, the difficulty appears to be due to the fact that the same name was used for a variety of instruments. Thus, Federigo Commandino, mathematical tutor to the Duke of Urbino, designed a 'proportional compass' that was essentially a pair of compasses that allowed the user to divide a straight line into any number of divisions he wanted. This useful little tool became widely known, as Commandino employed an expert instrument maker, Simone Baroccio, to produce it for him, and Baroccio manufactured copies. Guidobaldo del Monte examined one of those when he was visiting Commandino, but after he had left he felt sure that he could do the job better and at lower cost, so he then set about re-designing the compass and commissioned Baroccio to make one for him. These devices gradually spread to other European countries, receiving minor modifications and improvements on their way. By the time Galileo came across the proportional compass, it was already well-known and available in a number of different designs, and although we have no direct evidence about how his attention was first drawn to it, as Guidobaldo del Monte was one of his patrons it is safe to assume it was through him that Galileo's interest was aroused.

In improving the proportional compass Galileo really re-designed the whole device, effectively combining two instruments in one; no longer was it necessary to buy a proportional compass and a quadrant for measuring angles, for the

96

Galilean design did both tasks equally well. Basically, it was a pair of compasses, the arms of which were engraved with numerous scales, and which could be used to give a graphical solution to such problems as multiplication and division of a given length, working out the squares and cubes of numbers, and the more difficult task of finding square roots. This was indeed an improvement over any previous proportional compass, yet it was not all the instrument could do, for it even allowed one to work out the densities of different metals and stones. In fact there were so many scales that the instrument proved extraordinarily versatile, being used in gunnery, surveying, navigation and in constructing sundials. And it was not only versatile, it was also so accurate that a line could be divided up with a precision of one part in a thousand, and it was not replaced by any other equivalent device until the slide-rule was introduced 300 years later.

Still we have not exhausted the instrument's potentialities, for so far we have only considered one of its functions: its use as a portable calculator. But there was another side to it: each compass was provided with a curved metal arc that could be screwed between the arms, and when this was done the arms were open by exactly a right-angle, and the instrument became a quadrant. With a plumb-line fixed to the pivot it could now be used for measuring escarpments and the heights of walls and towers, and there was also a detachable foot so that it could be steadied on a flat surface in order to obtain more accurate readings. Used on its side, the quadrant was invaluable for castramentation. There is no doubt that this indispensable geometrical and military compass was Galileo's own design.

Early in 1598 Galileo sent an instrument, complete with an illustrated description, to Giovanfrancesco Sagredo, and also showed one to Paolo Sarpi. The result was that demand for the instrument began to spread, and by July of the next year it was so great that Galileo found that he needed assistance; he engaged the instrument maker, Marcantonio Mazolleni to help him in his workshop. Mazolleni stayed with him for the next ten years and the accounts show quite clearly that one of his first jobs was to construct a number of compasses. According to Galileo, Mazolleni made in all more than a hundred of the standard model, plus a few in gold or silver for specially rich and notable patrons like the Grand Duke of Tuscany and the Landgrave of Hesse. In the end Galileo claimed that more than three hundred compasses were built and distributed. This may be an exaggeration, although it is true that orders came from all over Europe, yet as neither Galileo or Mazolleni signed the instruments, we cannot check the validity of Galileo's claim or the pedigree of the few examples which have survived.

Now that his workshop could supply so useful an instrument, Galileo's financial difficulties were to some extent eased, but it was only to be expected that at some stage someone should claim priority of invention in the hope of at least dividing the spoils. There was a slight skirmish along these lines either in 1602 or 1603, when the well-known Flemish instrument maker Johann Zugmesser came to Padua. He brought a proportional compass with him and claimed to be the

Two uses of the quadrant: Galileo's invention did away with the need for separate instruments for different tasks.

inventor, but the whole matter was sorted out when it became clear that Galileo's instrument was very different. Real trouble did not begin until 1607 when there were two claimants: a young man named Baldassare Capra and his father Aurelio, who were Milanese and who had settled in Padua about the time of Galileo's arrival there. They claimed that, with Simon Mayr, who had been on the staff at Padua and was one of Baldassare's teachers, they had invented the self-same instrument as Galileo's and Baldassare cited a little Latin treatise he had written on the use of the instrument as additional evidence for their claim. The incident seems to have been prompted mainly by spite, for Galileo had crossed swords with Baldassare and Mayr a few years earlier when he was accused of not giving them credit for an astronomical discovery. It appears now that Baldassare and his father borrowed one of Galileo's instruments from a quite independent owner and kept it for a couple of months while they became familiar with its use. In addition, Baldassare made a habit of visiting Mazolleni in the workshop and familiarizing himself with the way the compass was made. What with the Capras and the trouble with Zugmesser, Galileo had had enough and he sensibly decided he would prosecute. He went to Venice and presented a statement to the appropriate magistrate for Padua, and Baldassare was summoned to appear in court. Whether Baldassare and his father expected this reaction is not clear, but Mayr, the brains of the group, was in Germany and there was little alternative but for Baldassare to give evidence; after all, on his own admission, he was the author of a Latin treatise on the instrument. At all events Baldassare Capra made a very poor showing and it gradually became evident that he did not know what he was talking about: Galileo later said he believed that it was Mayr and not Baldassare who had written the treatise, and this would explain Baldassare's ignorance. When at last the trial came to an end and sentence was pronounced, Galileo was victorious, the offending book was suppressed and Baldassare received a severe censure. The Capras returned to Milan not long afterwards while, for his part, Galileo published a heated *Defence*. In some quarters he was criticized for this, as many of his acquaintances felt that to be castigated in court was sufficient punishment for the Capras and that the matter should have been allowed to rest there.

While the Capra-Mayr affair was in progress, Galileo was occupied with a fresh interest: this time it was magnetism. He had read William Gilbert's *On The Magnet* which was published in London in 1600 and had been intrigued. Gilbert did not discover magnetism; the power of the lodestone to attract iron was known to the Greeks; the magnetic compass had been in use by western mariners since the twelfth century and by the Chinese far earlier than this, and della Porta and others had written about it. What Gilbert did was to collate all the evidence, construct magnets of various kinds out of lodestone, design and build magnetic indicating instruments for his experiments and, in brief, take a thoroughly scientific view of the whole subject. Certainly he was never able to account for magnetism itself, which was not achieved until this century, but he did reach the then startling conclusion that the Earth itself is a magnet.

Because he was too preoccupied with other matters, Galileo did not do any magnetic experiments until 1607, but before this he expressed his opinion of Gilbert: 'I have the highest praise, admiration and envy for this author, who framed such a stupendous concept concerning an object which innumerable men of splendid intellect had handled without paying any attention to it. . . .'[2] It is evident that he had made a mental note to do something himself as soon as he had time. When he did start examining magnetism, it was during a vacation, when he was back in Florence, and though on holiday acting as private tutor to the young Cosimo de' Medici, who was then seventeen and soon to succeed to the dukedom. Cosimo said he wanted a lodestone himself. To find one suitable for so exalted a person took time, and it had to be large and of good quality. Galileo asked among his friends. Sagredo, it so happened, had a fine example but he wanted 400 gold *scudi* for it, a sum that Cosimo's emissaries said was far too expensive. After some bargaining, a lower price was finally agreed upon, and both sides seem to have been happy with the bargain. Galileo's own experiments were conducted with smaller and less expensive examples, and were concerned almost entirely with 'arming' the stone, that is finding the magnetic poles of a stone and then sheathing it in iron (the armour). The purpose of this was to concentrate the magnetism at the poles so that the stone would then pick up heavier weights. Soon after 1608, Galileo was deflected from his interest in magnetism by other more pressing and scientifically more exciting research, and he did not return to the subject until some eighteen years later, when once again he concentrated on better ways of arming. His experiments were successful; he improved on Gilbert's method, and to such a degree that Benedetto Castelli could report he had seen a lodestone of no more than six ounces support an iron weight of 150 ounces. Yet here Galileo's excursions into magnetism seem to have stopped; once he had done all he could in concentrating the magnetism to greatest effect, he went no further. He never entered into the theory of magnetism, never discussed the nature of the magnetic force. Magnetism was no more than an intriguing and pleasant bypath along which he wandered for a time.

Unlike his two sisters, Galileo never married although, while at Padua he took a mistress, Marina Gamba. We do not know why he did not enter a more formal union but it may well have been that he was too poor to be acceptable to the family of a woman with the same social background as his own, and so felt himself forced into a temporary relationship. Nevertheless he seems to have had a happy relationship with her for well over ten years. During this time they had three children – two girls and a boy. The two girls, named after Galileo's sisters, Livia and Virginia, were brought up in Florence by his mother, not a very happy arrangement as the grandmother was a peevish and difficult woman. To calm

Opposite Two of Galileo's telescopes and the front lens from another.

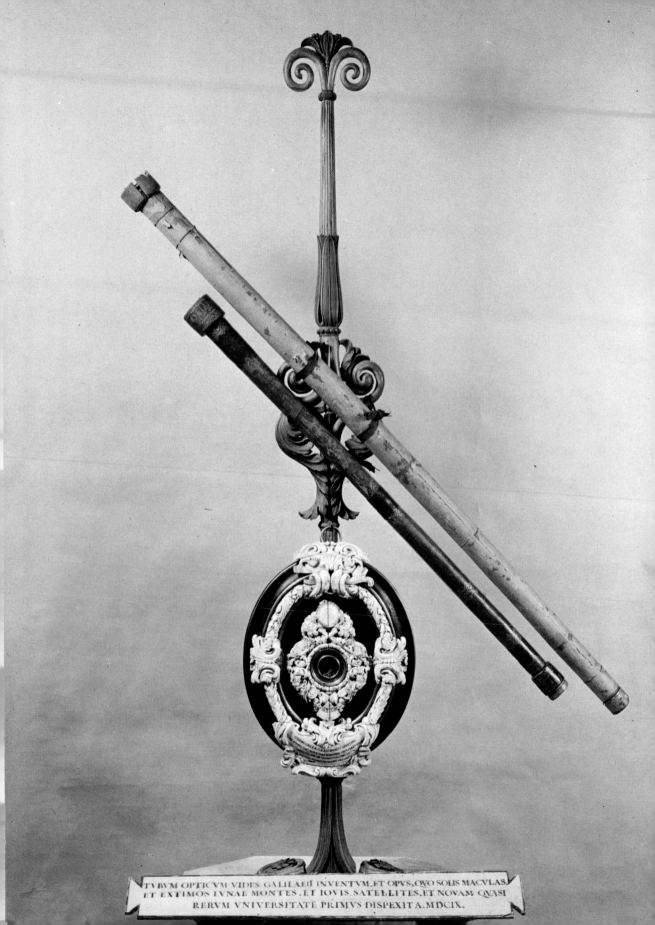

TVBVM OPTICVM VIDES GALILAEII INVENTVM, ET OPVS, QVO SOLIS MACVLAS,
ET EXTIMOS IVNAE MONTES, ET IOVIS SATELLITES, ET NOVAM QVASI
RERVM VNIVERSITATE PRIMVS DISPEXIT A. MDCIX.

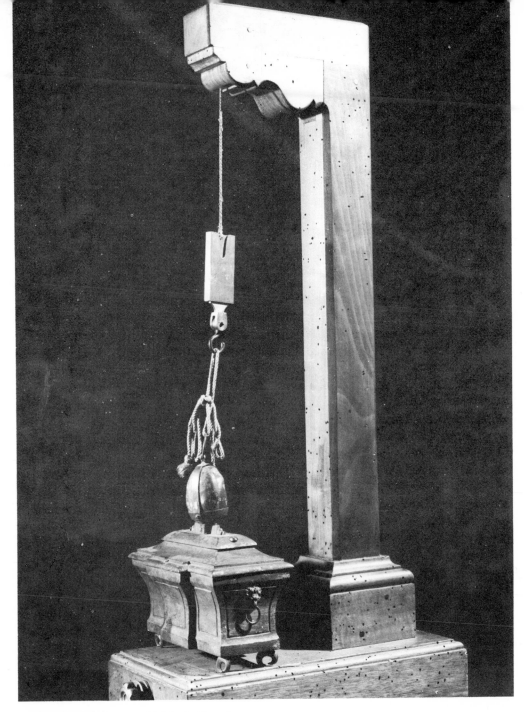

Above Galileo's lodestone which he built *c.* 1607.

Opposite A Medici jewel, by Bernardino Gaffurri, 1599, representing the Piazza della Signoria in Florence, with the statue of Cosimo I de' Medici in the foreground. Mosaic of semi-precious stones and gold.

what was obviously an unhappy situation, Galileo managed in due course to get both his daughters into a convent near Arcetri, close to Florence, even though they were not really old enough. The two girls were temperamentally very different; Livia, the younger, who took the name Arcangela upon entering the convent, was rather like her grandmother, but not so Virginia. She was a sensitive and gentle soul and, under the name Maria Celeste, carried on a long and tender correspondence with her father, a correspondence that he treasured and which brought him great comfort in his loneliest moments. Unhappily, neither outlived their father.

Galileo's son, Vincenzo, is a somewhat shadowy figure who only comes into the picture in his father's later years. As an infant he had been looked after by Marina but when he was old enough he travelled to Florence to live with his grandmother. It is sometimes said that he and his father did not get on, but there is no evidence of this, and possibly he is often confused with a cousin, also called Vincenzo. The relationship between Marina Gamba and Galileo was very much one of convenience and when, in due course, Galileo left Padua, there was no ill feeling; in fact Marina married and settled down not long afterwards.

Opposite A woodcut of Venice in Galileo's time.

9
The Telescope

Galileo was restless. In spite of the freedom he found in Padua, the friends he had made there, the mentally stimulating life he led, and even the profits from the instrument-making business, he still wanted to return to Florence. His friends all tried to persuade him against the move, but he seems to have been like a moth drawn to a candle flame. Florence appeared to offer such brilliant opportunities, for Cosimo de' Medici was now Grand Duke of Tuscany and not only was he a pupil, but he held Galileo in great respect and affection. What chance, then, did he have of securing a position such as Court Mathematician or General Scientific Adviser to the Grand Duke? A position like this, with its luxury, its easy living and the host of pickings that went with being near the centre of power, would suit him admirably; it was so much more desirable than having to spend one's time teaching students and having to conform to some imposed curriculum, however broadly based. Yet how could it be created, and why, if it were, should it go to him? The truth of the matter was that at this stage of his career Galileo, whatever his local reputation might be, was an international nonentity. He had insufficient eminence to raise him above the jealousies and backbiting of court life, and his standing was not enough to reflect sufficient credit on his patron. It was an intractable problem until, quite suddenly, in 1609, there was an event that changed the whole situation: the telescope arrived in Italy.

The mystery of the origin of the telescope has still not been fully solved and nobody knows who invented it. It first created a stir in the Netherlands in 1608 when three men applied for a patent virtually simultaneously, although it is highly unlikely that any of these was justified in claiming to be the inventor. Whatever the rights and wrongs of priority, news of the amazing new instrument reached Galileo via Paolo Sarpi. Because of his diplomatic and theological interests Sarpi had a vast network of correspondents all over Europe, and from one of these he received a vague mention of an instrument for seeing at a distance which had been offered to the States General in the Netherlands as a possible military aid in their continuing struggle against Philip II of Spain. Galileo showed immediate interest, and since Sarpi could tell him nothing more, a letter was sent to Jacques Badovere, a former student who was then in Paris, to see if he could find out further details.

The invention had spread like wildfire and Badovere reported by April 1609 that telescopes were on sale in Paris. These early instruments were of atrocious quality: the spherical aberration was pronounced, which meant that most of the distant scene was blurred, and because of chromatic aberration every

Opposite Galileo presenting his telescope to the Muses and pointing out a heliocentric system. From *Opere di Galileo Galilei*, 1655–6.

object seemed to be surrounded by coloured fringes. Really, they amounted to no more than optical toys, and sold purely and simply because they were novelties, and expensive novelties at that. Badovere's news was passed on to Galileo when he was in Venice in July, but more exciting still he now learned that there was an actual instrument in Padua. He dashed back and managed to get a description that, although not complete, did give him the basic information. He learned that the instrument consisted of a metal tube with a lens at each end. This was enough: as a physicist he had sufficient knowledge of perspective and the behaviour of light to enable him to work out what lenses he would need to fit into a tube to magnify a distant scene. On his very first night back in Padua he went into his workshop and made a model that functioned after a fashion. It was not a good telescope but at least it demonstrated the principle, and he then began to build others.

At about the same time the Doge was offered one of the telescopes, apparently for a small fortune, and the Senate could not decide whether to accept it or not. Sarpi was asked his opinion and given the telescope to examine, with the warning that it had been handed to the Doge's representatives on the strict condition that it would not be taken to pieces. Sarpi did not think much of it himself, but he wanted a second opinion and asked Galileo to have a look at it. As soon as he

Doge Leonardo Donato for whom Galileo made his famous improved telescope in 1609.

saw it, Galileo realized not only what a poor instrument it was, but that even his experimental models outstripped it, and he told Sarpi that, in his opinion, the Senate should on no account buy it. Indeed, he said that if only he could have a little time he, Galileo, would produce something far better and so Sarpi agreed to delay making his report for a while. This, Galileo saw as his great opportunity: if he could make a telescope that was a substantial improvement over any imported one, then the Doge would be pleased and his own reputation enhanced. He already knew of a number of simple but effective steps he could take to better the sample, foremost of which was to have carefully made lenses of the best Venetian glass instead of the usual inaccurately ground spectacle lenses then being used. He set to work, presumably with Mazolleni's help, to grind and polish two matched lenses. The technique itself, widely used for spectacle making, was no secret, but how many lenses Galileo made and rejected before he had a satisfactory pair can only be guessed. It was probably considerable, because we know that in his later telescopes he found he had to throw out a high proportion for the simple reason that the optical requirements for even a moderately satisfactory telescope lens are infinitely greater than those for a pair of spectacles. Yet better lenses were not the complete answer and Galileo still had the problems of spherical and chromatic aberration to overcome if he was not to get unacceptably fuzzy images and coloured fringes. He found there was little he could do over the coloured fringes, as they seemed to be an inherent fault of telescopes, but they could be made less obtrusive if he could only get a clear picture. Spherical aberration, he appreciated, was caused by the inability of a lens to bring together light passing through its centre with light from its edge; and he found that the simplest answer was to make the front lens larger than he wanted, and then place a mask over the outer part and let light pass only through the central region.

By late August he was able to build a neat and effective telescope that magnified nine times; or, as Galileo put it, an object nine miles away was brought so close that it seemed to be only one mile off. And his telescope had another advantage: it gave an upright image, a fact that we may take for granted but which was then, it seems, an innovation, as the Dutch telescopes gave an inverted image. As soon as he saw it, Sarpi was delighted; he told the Doge and Senate about the instrument and arrangements were made for it to be tested. On 21 August Senator Antonio di Girolamo Priuli accompanied other colleagues up the campanile of St Mark's and saw

the marvellous and effective singularity of the spy-glass of ... Galileo, which consisted of a tinned iron tube covered on the outside with a variety of crimson cotton material ... with two glasses, one ... concave, and the other not, on either end, with which, when raised to one eye and the other eye closed, any one of us were able to see distinctly as far as ... the campanile and cupola with the façade of the church of Saint Giustina [in] Padua. It was also possible to distinguish those who entered and departed from the church of Saint Giacomo [in] Murano, and one could see persons entering and dismounting from the gondolas at the ferry at the Collona at the beginning of the Canal of the Glass-workers, with many other details in the lagoon and the city which were truly admirable ... multiplying the vision with it more than nine times.[1]

Since the distance from Venice to Padua was some twenty-four miles, it is not surprising that the Senate was extremely impressed with the telescope which Galileo formally presented to the Doge, who responded by electing him to his chair at Padua for life and granting him a salary of 1,000 florins a year, an unprecedented sum for a professor of mathematics.

With a comfortable salary and a life appointment, many men would have been content to sit back and rest on their laurels, to take life more easily. This was not Galileo's way, however. When a project interested him he usually became thoroughly absorbed, and was impelled to follow it through until he reached his goal: in the case of the telescope his aim was greater magnification. This meant refining his techniques and so he turned his entire workshop facilities over to telescope-making, partly so he could try out detailed improvements at every stage of manufacture, and partly to meet a sudden spate of orders for telescopes like

Below A contemporary view of St Mark's Square, Venice, with on the left, the Campanile from which on 21 August 1609 Galileo's telescope was first tested by the Venetian Senators.

Opposite Galileo demonstrating his telescope to the Doge and the Venetian Senators. From R. Franklin, *Nature Displayed*, 1747.

the one now in the Doge's possession. For even at this early stage no one could match Galileo for quality; the professional spectacle-makers had not by then appreciated the unusually fine workmanship needed to make telescope lenses, nor the fine tolerances within which they had to be fitted in the tube to work satisfactorily. Yet in spite of their inferiority their products sold well enough since none of Galileo's were available on the open market: his entire production was absorbed in satisfying the needs of princes and prelates. The Doge ordered a dozen, Cosimo de' Medici wanted one as soon as possible, and other orders followed without remission, so that the workshop was soon turning out a constant stream of instruments. Precisely how many were made is uncertain since only about one in ten were considered of suitable optical quality to be sent away, but we do know the number was high and came to something well over a hundred. As far as his own experiments were concerned it was not long after he had supplied the Doge with his first telescope that Galileo managed to construct others with 'more nicety',[2] one of which magnified thirty times. It was with this instrument that he seriously began to examine the heavens and make a series of discoveries that were to make him famous.

Turning his attention to the skies was something of a new departure for Galileo. His interest in astronomy had been minimal until five years earlier, in 1604, when he had become involved in two astronomical questions. The first was why, if the Earth moved in space, one still only saw a hemisphere of sky. According to Galileo's Pisan friend, Jacopo Mazzoni, this should not be so; moving away from the centre of the celestial sphere must surely bring one closer to one side, and so render more than half the sphere visible. And Mazzoni went further; using some contentions of Aristotle, he even claimed that if one moved only far enough from the centre of the universe by climbing to the summit of a very high mountain, it would be possible to see more than half the sky at once. When Galileo read this he was sure there was a flaw in the argument, but to prove his case he made a mathematical analysis of the whole question and found that without any shadow of doubt the Aristotle-Mazzoni argument was wrong. This marked a turning point in his outlook, for while he had previously toyed with the idea that Copernicus might be right, he now found it was possible in one case at least, to formulate a mathematical proof that the concept of a stationary Earth was wrong, and mathematics could not lie. From now on he felt that Copernicus must be right, and he even wrote to Kepler to say so; but Kepler was already one of the converted, and Galileo knew that he must find more positive evidence before he dared come out into the open himself as a pro-Copernican. This is why he found it prudent to sit on the fence during the second astronomical event of 1604, when a new star, a nova, appeared suddenly in the October skies, and everyone began seeking his opinion of it. The Aristotelians were arguing that it was a meteorological phenomenon not a celestial one, but they were bound

Johannes Kepler, the brilliant German astronomer with whom Galileo corresponded for many years, published his momentous book, *Astronomia Nova*, the same year that Galileo developed his telescope.

to do this because Aristotle had been emphatic in pronouncing the heavens as changeless. What did Galileo think? Did he agree with Tycho Brahe who, some thirty years earlier, had claimed that the nova of 1572 lay beyond the sphere of the Moon, and was a celestial phenomenon in spite of what Aristotle might say? In the end Galileo could not avoid the question; public interest and academic pressure were too great, and when at last it was announced that he would deliver three public lectures on the subject, the whole intellectual community flocked to hear him, so there was no single hall in Padua that could accommodate the crowds. Personally Galileo did not favour Tycho's theories though he did set some store by his observations, but precisely what he said we do not know. From indirect evidence it seems that he confined himself to a detailed discussion of all the scientific possibilities and left the question open. He was too unsure of himself to do otherwise; to mount a full-scale anti-Aristotelian campaign in public he needed to have a good physical explanation of what the nova was and observational evidence to back it up; yet he had neither. His audience might be disappointed, since they were not treated to the display of verbal fireworks they had doubtless hoped for, but Galileo felt he had no alternative but to play safe, however galling it might be. However once the telescope had arrived, once he had managed to perfect his technique so that he could reach a magnification of anything between nine and thirty times, he at least had means of seeking the observational proof he needed. The nova had faded, but he felt sure that the heavens could provide plenty of other evidence.

What Galileo saw when he used the telescope astronomically astounded him. At every turn, whichever way he looked, cracks appeared in the fabric of the Aristotelian cosmos. Every observation showed him something new, every observation provided direct visual evidence against the classic arguments for a stationary Earth. Here, with a simple metal tube and two lenses, he had made a rod for beating the Aristotelians, demolishing their universe and exorcizing the demon of Greek invincibility in science.

His observations were so important, so epoch making, that he decided to publish them at once, since it would probably be just a matter of time before someone else turned the telescope on the heavens and claimed priority for discoveries that were really his. So Galileo wasted no time and as early as March 1610 he was able to publish a slim volume called *The Starry Messenger*, 'unfolding great and marvellous sights'[3] – a comment that may sound too much of a eulogy but was no more than sober fact. Writing in a clear and simple style, Galileo announced his astonishing results. 'It is,' he said, 'a most beautiful and delightful sight to behold the body of the Moon ... about thirty times larger ...; and ... one may know with the certainty that is due to the use of our senses, that the Moon certainly does not possess a smooth and polished surface ...'[4] – which is what the Aristotelians claimed. Rather, Galileo says, its surface is 'rough and uneven, and, just like the surface of the Earth itself, is everywhere full of vast protruberances, deep chasms, and sinuosities'.[5] There are in fact 'lofty mountains and deep valleys'[6] and not content with a purely qualitative description, he goes on to describe measurements he has made of the shadows cast by the mountains which, with information on the relative positions of the Sun and Moon, he could use for computing the height of the mountains themselves: he found them, as astronomers have done since, higher than terrestrial mountains. To Aristotle the Moon and every other celestial object was a perfect body, not subject to change and decay; yet here was evidence that showed that one at least was just like the Earth, another material body, another earthy globe. These lunar observations alone would have created a storm of argument, a round of vehement claim and counter-claim, but they were not all the telescope showed. The *Starry Messenger* had many other 'marvellous sights' to unfold.

Applied to the starry background of the sky, the telescope showed a host of stars not visible to the eye alone, a vast concourse unknown and unimagined by the Greeks, too dim for them to have classified on their magnitude or brightness scale. Now 'beyond the stars of the sixth magnitude you will behold through the

Galileo's own drawings of the phases of the Moon. From the manuscript of *The Starry Messenger*.

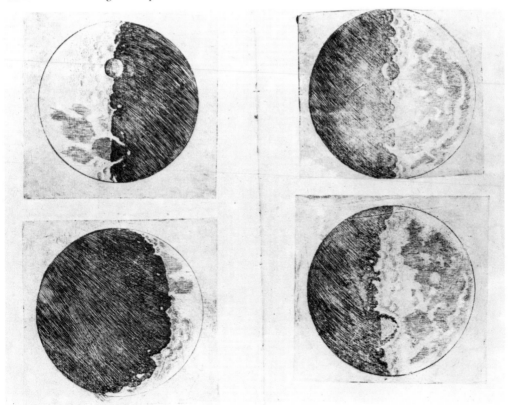

spy-glass a host of other stars, which escape the unassisted sight, so numerous as to be almost beyond belief, for you may see more than six other differences of magnitude'.[7] And the better to convince his readers, Galileo becomes more specific, directing the telescope to the sword and belt of Orion, and to the beautiful cluster, the Pleiades. 'I have selected the three stars in Orion's Belt and the six in his Sword, which have been long well-known groups, and I have added eighty other stars . . . in their vicinity. . . .'[8] Again, over the Pleiades, Galileo takes the six or seven visible to the unaided eye and then says: 'Near these there lie more than forty others invisible to the naked eye. . . .'[9]

Next he turned his attention to the Milky Way, that hazy irregular band of starlight that seems to stretch unbroken right across the sky: the Greeks had been undecided about its cause, but now Galileo could settle the matter once and for all. 'By the aid of the spy-glass,' he tells us, 'any one may behold this in a manner which so distinctly appeals to the senses that all the disputes that have tormented philosophers through so many ages are exploded at once by the irrefragable evidence of our eyes, and we are freed from wordy disputes upon this subject, for the Galaxy is nothing else but a mass of innumerable stars planted together in clusters.'[10]

These stellar observations were important for two reasons. In the first place, the discovery that the Milky Way is composed of myriads of stars, demonstrated the power of accurate observation with a suitable instrument. This was to be a hall-mark of later science – the development and use of special equipment for obtaining answers to specific questions – and it established observation as a primary source of evidence. No longer was it to be a matter of who could get the better in a disputation, the touchstone was to be the evidence of the senses. Secondly, the fact that the telescope showed stars invisible to the naked eye made it evident that however intelligent they might have been, there were things the Greeks did not and could not know, yet things that would certainly have caused them to modify their theories if they had been aware of them. And this was not a matter for disputation, it was a matter of self-evident fact. Go and look for yourselves, Galileo said, and you will see the proof with your own eyes.

In the closing section of *The Starry Messenger* Galileo described his observations of Jupiter, perhaps the most important of his astronomical discoveries. First he saw it possessed a disk, small but unmistakable; second, and far more significant, it was accompanied by four satellites. A series of observations made in January, February and at the beginning of March 1610, showed him that four bright stars that he had noticed close to Jupiter were actually in orbit around it; he had watched them change their positions until at last it had become clear that this was the only rational explanation of their behaviour. To astronomers this might seem no more than an interesting new fact; another body in space had been observed with a satellite system; there existed a copy of the Earth-Moon arrangement but on more elaborate lines. Yet the really vital thing about the observations

116

was their anti-Aristotelian and pro-Copernican context, for they were the most powerful of all Galileo's observational counterblasts to the accepted physical and astronomical ideas of his day. It had been argued, and with great cogency, that if Copernicus were right and the Earth did move in space, then the Moon would be left behind. There was no doctrine of universal gravitation, so there seemed no physical reason why the Moon should follow the Earth. There was of course the doctrine of natural place, but if the Earth were removed from its natural place there was no reason why this should force the Moon to forsake its natural orbit round the centre of the universe. Yet all Aristotelians agreed that Jupiter moved in space, and now it was observed to be doing so complete with a family of orbiting satellites, and what was true for Jupiter and his moons should be true for the Earth and her Moon. Aristotelian physics was not only wrong, it was seen to be wrong: as Galileo wrote, 'now we have not one planet only revolving about another, while both traverse a vast orbit about the Sun, but our sense of sight presents to us four satellites circling about Jupiter, like the Moon

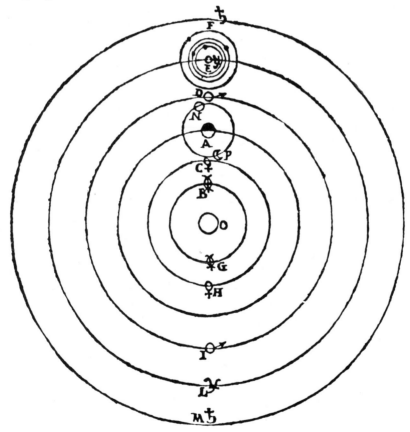

Galileo's drawing of the Copernican system of the universe, showing his own discovery of the four satellites of Jupiter. From his *Dialogue*, 1632.

about the Earth, while the whole system travels over a mighty orbit about the Sun in the space of twelve years'.[11] – a clear explanation of what his observations meant and an unequivocal statement of his Copernican outlook. There were no doubts about that now; Galileo was publicly committed to the ranks of the new cosmologists.

The Starry Messenger was a best-seller, and a second edition was published at Frankfurt within a matter of months. In Prague the Tuscan ambassador, Giulano de' Medici gave Kepler a copy with a request from Galileo for comments. When this was followed soon after by a similar request from his patron, the Emperor Rudolph II, Kepler quickly set about putting pen to paper, and in a few months produced a pamphlet called *A Discussion with the Starry Messenger*. In this he extolled Galileo's work, even though at the time he had no telescope and had not even looked through one. Soon after, however, Kepler did have the opportunity to observe through one of Galileo's telescopes and thereupon published a second pamphlet; indeed he became so intrigued with the instrument that he temporarily broke off his own research to write a book on lenses and even to design an alternative telescopic arrangement that had some astronomical advantages over the Galilean type.

Kepler's and Galileo's publications stimulated a spate of telescope building and observing over the next few decades, but more immediate was the jeopardy into which Aristotelian philosophy was thrown due to the observations recorded in the *Starry Messenger*. For the first time since Aristotle's original work in the fourth century BC, there was visual evidence to prove him wrong. Galileo was now clear where he stood and said so; and it was not long before a philosophical storm broke about his head, although, when it did, he had already left Padua and settled in Florence, a move that was to have the most profound implications on his later career.

Opposite Grand Duke Cosimo II de' Medici, with his wife, Maria Maddalena of Hapsburg, and their son, the future Ferdinand II. Cosimo, who came to power in 1609, had been a pupil of Galileo's since the summer of 1605.

10

Return to Florence

Galileo's negotiations to return to Florence were conducted secretly, but to oil the diplomatic wheels, he openly dedicated *The Starry Messenger* to Cosimo de' Medici, and named Jupiter's satellites the 'Medicean Stars'. With *The Starry Messenger* Galileo became famous overnight. The whole of Europe talked about his discoveries, and at last he was able to negotiate with the court officials from a position of strength. To give himself sufficient leisure to do the research he had in mind, he wanted to be relieved of the task of lecturing if he was given a university post, and implied that he would not accept a salary that forced him to take in many private pupils. And there was an additional problem: a university post meant Pisa, and Galileo did not wish to live in Pisa; he wanted to settle in Florence. All this he made clear to his friend Belisario Vinta, the Tuscan Secretary of State and, in spite of the conditions, by May 1610 Vinta was in a position to write to Galileo to say that the Grand Duke would be pleased to nominate him First Mathematician of the University of Pisa, pay him a thousand florins a year, relieve him of any need to deliver lectures, and set aside the ordinance which made it obligatory to reside in Pisa. This seemed generous enough but Galileo said that he wanted more, not financially, but by way of position, for by May it had become clear in his own mind that he would probably have the whole philosophical faculty from Pisa attacking his observations in a last-ditch attempt to vindicate Aristotle. He needed official recognition as a philosopher; he had to be in a position that was unassailable by the university set; and he got his way: in addition to his appointment to Pisa, he was also formally styled 'Philosopher and Mathematician to the Grand-Duke'.

In June 1610, less than a year after the Senate had increased his salary so generously, Galileo resigned from Padua. For his part he claimed that the Senate had not kept all the promises they had made when the enthusiasm for his telescope was at its height, but whether his grievances were real or not, the fact remains that his departure was precipitous. Admittedly, he tried to arrange for a replacement, hoping to persuade Kepler to take his place, but Kepler declined although, as events turned out, it would have been to his advantage to have gone there. Indeed in the long run Galileo would have done better to have remained in Padua under the protection of the Venetian state. When Sagredo returned from diplomatic duties in the East, and learned of Galileo's move to Florence, he was aghast at the thought of what might happen. 'Where', he wrote to Galileo 'will you find the same liberty as here in Venetian territory. ... Also, your being in a place where the authority of the friends of Berlinzone [a nickname for the

Opposite An astrolabe which belonged to Galileo. It was built about 1584 in Padua and mounted into an octagonal table.

Above Galileo showing Cosimo II his discovery of the satellites of Jupiter which he had diplomatically named the 'Medicean Stars.'

Jesuits], from what I am told, stands high gives me grave cause for worry.'[1] Sagredo had good reason to be concerned about the Jesuits, for the Senate had found it necessary to expel them from Venice only a few years before for political intrigue, yet Galileo was not worried on their count; as far as he was concerned they were intelligent men, humanists and lovers of science, and he believed he could look to them for support. It was the unimaginative university men that concerned him, the diehards who wore Aristotelian blinkers: these were the ones who would stand in the way of his proselytizing the Copernican gospel; these were the people he must destroy, and he could only do so from a position of unassailable authority such as the Grand Duke had now been persuaded to give him. Of course there were dangers; Galileo was exchanging a formal contract of employment, legally enforceable, for the promise of a prince which could be revoked at any time. Yet he had faith in the Grand Duke, a faith which he was never given reason to doubt although, as he was later to find to his cost, even a prince's powers are limited.

Opposite A street in Florence, Borgo Santi Apostoli. Galileo returned to live in Florence in 1610, after an absence of more than twenty years.

Left Galileo's house on the Costa San Giorgio, Florence. From a nineteenth-century engraving. *Below* Galileo's sketch of what he called the 'triple nature' of Saturn. From a letter written to his friend Marcus Welser in December 1612.

Galileo left for Florence in September 1610 and by the next month he had set up his telescope and begun observing again. Almost at once he made two discoveries. The first was that the planet Saturn appeared to have two companion stars, one on each side; the other was that the planet Venus was seen to have phases like the Moon and to suffer periodical changes in size. As for Saturn's rings which, in October 1610, were tilted over at their greatest inclination to an observer on Earth, they could be mistaken for two satellites in a telescope magnifying only thirty times. It was not an epoch-making observation although its misinterpretation was to plague him later but, on the other hand, the observations of Venus were vitally important to his cause. If Venus showed phases and changes of size, then this must be because Venus orbited round the Sun, not the Earth: it was a conclusion that not even the most bigoted Aristotelian could deny, and Galileo was not slow to use it as yet another proof of the validity of the Copernican theory, even though it could fit equally well into Tycho Brahe's system of the

universe. Since others were beginning to use the telescope astronomically and might make these discoveries themselves, Galileo decided he must announce them without delay. On the other hand, the false claims of Mayr and the Capras had made him wary of giving too much away, and in the end he decided the best way to make them public was in the form of Latin anagrams. The triple nature of Saturn he announced in the form of a jumble of letters that, when properly, transposed, read quite straightforwardly 'I have observed the most distant planet is triple'. For the vital observations of Venus, Galileo was more cautious, and he incorporated the details in what was more a cryptogram than an anagram which he sent direct to Giuliano de' Medici for transmission to Kepler. Decoded, the message read 'The mother of love emulates the shapes of Cynthia'. Kepler needed no more clues and three months later, after confirming Galileo's observations, he replied enthusiastically.

The Aristotelians were in a quandary. If Galileo's observations were true, then quite clearly they would have to revise not just Aristotelian astronomy, not only their view of the universe, but the whole edifice of Aristotelian physics and with it, the entire Aristotelian philosophy. *If* the observations were true; but were they? Was what the telescope showed really what the universe was like? Even with the eye alone, optical illusions like mock suns and mirages could be seen. What then when a telescope intervened between the eye and a distant scene? Could its images not be illusions to mislead the unwary, to bedevil those stupid Copernicans who, after all, must be men of inferior intellect if they believed that the Earth really did move in space? Were these men really saying that one should jettison an entire philosophical scheme for a few observations made while using some new-fangled and imperfect instrument? Surely they could not be so presumptuous?

We can now look back and see the Aristotelians as obscurantists, as men whose minds were closed to any new interpretation, and in a sense we should be right. Yet it is important to remember that they were not used to assessing experimental evidence from any but their own viewpoint: to them observations, tests even, could never be more than demonstrations to underline the validity of Aristotelian doctrine, not a means of probing that validity. It was in Aristotle's writings, in the books of his learned commentators that the basic truth was to be found; these were the touchstone, an attitude typified by Magini, by then professor of astronomy at Bologna, who openly declared that he would see Galileo's Jovian satellites 'extirpated from the sky'.[2] Bookish argument was more to be trusted than the evidence of the senses. Galileo, of course, severely criticized this refusal to let observations speak for themselves, and when some of the Pisan academics declined even to put an eye to the telescope, he wrote to Kepler: 'What would you say of the learned here, who, replete with the pertinacity of the asp, have steadfastly refused to cast a glance through the telescope? Shall we laugh or shall we cry?'[3] And he was right, at least as far as the astronomers among them were con-

Cosimo II by Josse Sustermans. The Grand Duke was greatly attracted by astronomy and added an observatory to his villa at Poggio Imperiale in which he set up one of Galileo's telescopes.

cerned: they should have been sensitive to observational evidence for, after all, the whole Ptolemaic doctrine they accepted was based on 'saving the phenomena', on making theory fit the observed behaviour in the heavens. Even if the bibliomanic philosopher might be excused, not so the astronomer; Magini was culpable of putting prejudice and hatred above honest enquiry.

Galileo decided he needed independent confirmation of his observations. He had Kepler's pamphlets to support his case, but Kepler was far away in Prague. What he wanted was some authoritative support nearer at hand. His one answer, he felt, was to go to Rome and there see the Jesuit Christopher Clavius; here was someone whose scientific honesty he respected, an astronomer of whose integrity he had no doubt, even though he was no Copernican. Galileo wrote to him, and to his old pupil Castelli, and then put his case to the Grand Duke who immediately agreed and, to show his esteem, not only granted his philosopher leave of absence, but also a litter to carry him, expenses for his journey and, as if this were not enough, instructed the Tuscan ambassador in Rome to entertain Galileo as his guest at the embassy. The original intention was that Galileo should travel south during January 1611, but he was ill at that time, possibly with one of his periodical attacks of arthritis, and he was forced to postpone the trip until late March. When at last he set off, he was armed with letters of introduction to Cardinal Barberini, an influential prelate who was later to succeed to the Papacy.

The Roman College of Jesuits. From a contemporary engraving.

Galileo arrived safely in Rome and lost no time in getting in touch with Father Clavius and the other Jesuit astronomers at the Roman College. He took one of his telescopes along and demonstrated it, and then left it at the College so that they could observe at their leisure, for his discoveries could not all be checked in a single night and some, such as Jupiter's satellites, would require at least days of careful observing. Yet it was not long before the Jesuit astronomers saw the phenomena for themselves, were convinced, and turned to honouring and feasting Galileo: after all, was he not Jesuit trained, a true son of the Church, whose fame brought distinction to the Order. But to praise Galileo for his 'invention' and for the observations was one thing; to agree that what was seen unequivocally supported the Copernican theory was another. Indeed Clavius who had to report to a special Church commission said just this: the observations were confirmed but were not in themselves incontrovertible evidence for a heliocentric doctrine. The Commission, a high-powered one under the chairmanship of Cardinal Roberto Bellarmine, shows just how significant the Church thought the implications of Galileo's discoveries might be; for Bellarmine was a champion, one might almost say *the* champion, of Roman Catholicism, and the bane of the Protestants who had irreverently immortalized him in the 'Bellarmine', a glazed earthenware jug with capacious belly and narrow neck.

Once Clavius had reported to Bellarmine, Galileo went on to present his credentials to Cardinal Maffeo Barberini, basically a mathematician but also a

127

Opposite, top Cardinal Maffeo Barberini, later Pope Urban VIII, whom Galileo first met in the spring of 1611. *Bottom* The Palazzo Barberini, in Rome.

Above The Lincean Academy, the first true scientific society in the world, to which Galileo was elected in 1611. *Below* Preparation for a banquet, from a contemporary engraving. Galileo's visit to Rome in the spring of 1611 was an unqualified success. He was given a triumphal reception and several banquets were arranged in his honour by Prince Cesi and Cardinal Borghese among other people.

member of a rich Florentine family, who was able to indulge himself in the patronage of science and art. With him Galileo seems to have felt at ease, and thought he detected a sympathy for heliocentrism; indeed, as a mathematician Cardinal Barberini was probably an incipient Copernican who could be persuaded to accept the new theory openly, or at least this is what Galileo came to hope in the years that followed.

During this visit to Rome Galileo went to see Pope Paul V in the Vatican. The Popes had long been patrons of science as well as art, and some of the decoration in the Vatican bears witness to this: an allegory of Astronomy by Raphael on the ceiling of the Stanza della Segnatura, in the apartments of Julius II.

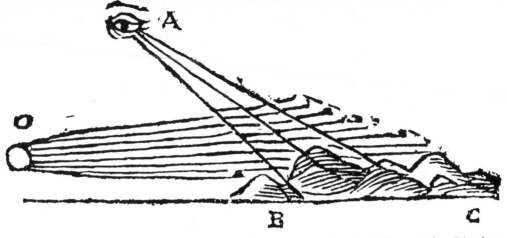

Method of measuring the height of lunar mountains from a letter written by Galileo to Father Cristoforo Grienberger of the Roman College in 1611.

While in Rome, Galileo made another powerful friend, Prince Federico Cesi, an extraordinarily keen botanist who had founded the Lincean Academy – the Academy of the Lynx-eyed – the first true scientific society the world had seen. To have Cesi as an ally was indeed something for Galileo to be pleased with and, for his part, Cesi obviously had an unbounded admiration for his new friend: he saw that he was elected as a member of the Academy and gave a banquet in Galileo's honour, a banquet which had more than a passing significance. Held during April, with Galileo's telescope standing by so that the guests could see the wonders of the heavens for themselves, it was more than a great social occasion for, during the evening, Cesi announced that the wonderful spy-glass of his guest of honour had a new name. Previously everyone had taken their choice of a variety of descriptive words like 'eye-glass', 'spy-glass', 'perspective' and 'perspective trunk', and even Galileo himself had used various names as the mood moved him. It was, Cesi said, too noble an invention not to have its own special name, its own unique place in the language, and it was to be called the 'telescope', a word not coined, however, by Cesi himself but by his friend, the poet Johannes Demisiani.

On this visit to Rome Galileo also had an audience with the Pope, Paul v, during which he seems to have made such a favourable impression that afterwards church dignitaries vied with one another to do him honour. In brief, the trip was an unqualified success, a triumph for Galileo and his telescope. Indeed the Florentine Cardinal del Monte wrote to the Grand Duke to say that, during his stay in Rome, Galileo 'had given the greatest satisfaction'.[4] As far as Galileo was concerned, he was overjoyed with the reception he had received; his telescopic observations had been confirmed by the highest astronomical authority in the land; he had the support and friendship of Prince Cesi and, it seemed, the sympathy at least of a prelate as senior as Cardinal Barberini. Church and society were on his side; what more could he ask?

Galileo returned to Florence in June 1611, flushed with success, quite unaware that storm clouds were already gathering, generated by a body of dissident professors at Pisa who, for further support, had allied themselves with a set of courtiers at Florence. They were all jealous of the special treatment Galileo was given, of his large salary and of the continual favours bestowed on him personally by the Grand Duke. In addition, the academics were furious that this braggart of an anti-Aristotelian should be in a position to promote his iconoclastic views. He must be attacked, but since his astronomy was receiving such adulation, it seemed better tactics to leave this alone and do battle on problems of physics. Led by Ludovico delle Colombe, an arrogant academic, they decided to begin in the restricted intellectual atmosphere of Florence where Galileo had the fewest allies, rather than in Pisa where he would receive more support, and they met to argue in Filippo Salviati's villa. Salviati was well known; his Villa delle Selve on a hillside above Signa, close to Florence, was a beauty spot, with terraces overlooking the river Arno, and a regular meeting place for courtiers and academics on leave from Pisa. Salviati himself was a friend of Galileo's, he had one of Galileo's telescopes in a small observatory attached to the villa, and the two met frequently, not only to discuss science but also to indulge in their taste for burlesque poetry and low comedy. That the attack on Galileo's physics should occur at the villa of a close friend and supporter was of no moment to the delle Colombe set; their purpose was only to get Galileo involved in arguments and see him bettered, for they knew he could not refuse to take part. After all, had he not assured Vinta that whilst he would not lecture or reside at the university, he would always be ready to discuss scientific matters 'with the most distinguished members of his profession'?[5]

The first sally began with someone stating the Aristotelian doctrine that the action of cold was to condense, citing ice as an example; ice, they said, was simply condensed water. No, replied Galileo, it was not; it was solidified water, certainly, but not condensed. Ice was lighter than water since one could watch it float, and therefore the action of cold was to rarify, not to condense. The Aristotelians were ready for this; ice floated on water, they said, because of its shape, not because it was light. Sheets of ice on a frozen pond were flat and that is why they floated. This Galileo recognized as the common mistake nearly everyone made; it was the error that had dogged Giovanni de' Medici's plan for dredging Leghorn Harbour. No, sheets of ice floated because they were lighter, he said, and ice would float on water whatever its shape. The question remained unresolved, but a few days later Ludovico delle Colombe himself came on the scene, determined to draw Galileo out. He brought with him pieces of ebony cut to various shapes, and with great aplomb performed a series of 'experiments' to show that while the flat pieces of ebony floated, those shaped like cylinders and spheres sank. Aristotle, he claimed, was vindicated and it was shape not substance that mattered. Ebony was denser and heavier than water yet it floated when the shape was right; that, too, was the reason why ice floated: Galileo was demonstrably wrong. And to make matters worse, Ludovico delle Colombe began to perform his demonstration in public, making his point and commenting unfavourably on the ill-founded beliefs of the Grand Duke's philosopher.

A corner of the garden of Filippo Salviati's palazzo in Florence. It was in Salviati's villa, outside Florence, that the first organized opposition to Galileo, led by Ludovico delle Colombe, took shape, though Salviati himself was a friend of Galileo's.

The situation was now beginning to get out of hand and Galileo wrote to Ludovico delle Colombe pointing out his errors, but delle Colombe remained unrepentant, and only after much further correspondence did he agree to a contest at the house of a mutual acquaintance, Francesco Nori. For some reason now quite unknown delle Colombe never turned up, but on the other hand as Galileo had once failed to appear for a discussion at the Villa delle Selve, it would be wise not to read too much into delle Colombe's lapse. Nevertheless the controversy had now become notorious; what had started quietly was now the talk of the cognoscenti, and other Aristotelians took up the matter; so that when Flaminio Papazzone visited the Court in the autumn of 1611, he felt in duty bound to raise the subject with Galileo. The ensuing discussion was so lively that the Grand Duke arranged for the arguments to be repeated for the enjoyment of Cardinals Barberini and Fernando Gonzaga who were also visiting the Court at the time.

On this second occasion Barberini sided with Galileo, and Gonzaga upheld the traditional view. Galileo was so successful that he decided to publish his ideas, and in May 1612 the pamphlet *Discourse concerning Things which Stay on the Top of the Water* appeared. Like *The Starry Messenger* it was a best-seller, and a second printing was called for before the year was out.

The pamphlet was more than just a refutation of Ludovico delle Colombe, because Galileo used it to set out his thinking on questions of hydrostatics, questions that he had been turning over in his mind ever since he had first come across the works of Archimedes nearly thirty years before. This gave him the opportunity to emphasize that the basic reason why a body sinks is due to the fact that it weighs more than the water it displaces – if it is lighter then it floats, as ice does. Typically he used geometry to analyse delle Colombe's arguments and his own, as well as the results of a whole series of experiments, and it is here that the pamphlet shows Galileo at his full stature, clearing up a question that is immensely involved and had once got him so muddled that he had drawn what later proved to be the right answer by making a wrong interpretation of experimental evidence. By the time the pamphlet was written he had, however, sorted out his difficulties, got everything clear in his own mind, and was able to extend Archimedes' principles beyond the confines of problems in hydrostatics alone. The experiments he quoted were more elaborate than delle Colombe's, and penetrated far deeper into the basic issues involved; they were also incomparably more ingenious. What he did was to take pieces of wax, which he could readily mould into any shape and mix the wax with lead shot, so that he had a flexible material which allowed him to do two things: make pieces of a given shape weigh either less or more than the water they displaced, and alter the shape of any piece whose weight he wanted to keep constant. His subsequent mathematical analysis made it evident that shape was not the governing factor.

Yet the Aristotelians, not so much because of an innate pig-headedness as of an inherent mental inflexibility, remained unconvinced. Galileo's arguments were not based on Aristotelian philosophical principles which held that shape and matter were inseparable; instead he had discussed each factor alone and analysed them piecemeal. This gave him the opportunity of removing a whole lot of confusion and presenting the issues clearly; today it seems the ideal way of tackling a problem of this kind, but to the Aristotelians it was no such thing, it was anathema. Galileo had committed the sin of dealing with disembodied 'forms' and then allying them to abstract mathematical reasoning. Moreover he had used wax, a material that would not sink whatever shape one gave it, and thus in the Aristotelian mind, had avoided the issue: that he had mixed lead shot with the wax to weigh it down only confused the experiment further as far as they were concerned.

What the Aristotelians were saying in essence was that one must accept basic Aristotelian theory and then do experiments in the light of it: what was totally inadmissible was to disregard the theory and perform tests to see where they might lead: that was to court error. Certainly it was nothing more than a mental block-age, but it was so deep-seated, so ingrained, that only a few very independent spirits could or would make the break. It was this mental attitude that Galileo set himself the task of changing; this is what he constantly campaigned against, often with such enthusiasm that he was led on to scientifically shaky ground, as hap-pened for instance soon after the pamphlet had come out. Frustrated by the obtuseness of his opponents, Galileo decided he must attack the whole Aristotelian doctrine of qualities and so initiated a whole new series of arguments and counter-arguments that gradually moved from the flotation of ice to questions of cold, and then on to the subject of heat. What happened when water boiled, where did the bubbles come from? To avoid the Aristotelian arguments about qualities and keep away from what he judged to be mere word spinning, Galileo adopted an atomic view of matter, egged on, perhaps, because he knew this was a theory that Aristotle had condemned. Unfortunately he had no sound evidence to rely on, and soon he began to go wildly astray, talking of fire atoms that could pass through solid mass in order to explain how bubbles arrived in a boiling liquid; and as his ground became more uncertain so he became more arrogant until the whole controversy developed into abuse, with Galileo writing: 'This, Colombe, is but a sample of Galileo's method of philosophizing. I think it is much safer than introducing mere names of generations, transmutations, alterations and other operations, brought in and often used when someone does not know how to cope with problems that he does not understand.'[6] No man, particularly a philosopher, likes to be told he is word-spinning and does not understand what he is talking about, and delle Colombe's rancour increased until, a few years later, he was able to get his own back and in a more serious way than by purely scientific controversy.

Overleaf, left The Viottolone Avenue in the Boboli Gardens, laid out from 1550 onwards behind the Palazzo Pitti for Grand Duke Cosimo I by Tribolo, Buontalenti and Giovanni Bologna.

Right Votive image of Cosimo II in prayer made in the grand-ducal workshops by Orazio Mochi and Giovanni Bilivert, 1619–24. Mosaic relief in gold and semi-precious stones, studded with sapphires, rubies and diamonds.

Page 138 The Dowager Grand Duchess Christina of Lorraine to whom Galileo wrote a famous open letter in 1615 which, however, was not published until 1636. French school.

Page 139 The Annunciation, by Lodovico Cardi, more commonly known as Cigoli. A close friend and lifelong supporter of Galileo, Cigoli claimed that he had learnt perspective from the mathematician.

II
Arguments and Accusations

The first half of 1611 had begun on a triumphant note with Galileo's visit to Rome, but the second half struck a more sombre chord, for besides the argument with Ludovico delle Colombe, Galileo started another controversy that was to have more serious consequences. On the face of it this was a purely astronomical disagreement, but its implications ran deeper, for Galileo impugned not only the scientific ability, but also the honesty of a powerful opponent, the Jesuit astronomer Father Christoph Scheiner.

Scheiner was a lecturer in mathematics at the university of Ingolstadt, in upper Bavaria, who had constructed small but successful telescopes based on Kepler's design, and had then used them for observing the Sun. To obviate the glare and protect the eyes of the observer, Scheiner let the brilliant image fall on a sheet of card, and so instituted a method of solar observing that became universal until the advent of photography more than two centuries later. Yet this was not what led to the argument with Galileo, but the observations themselves for, after he had been studying the Sun for some time, Scheiner suddenly found that the solar surface was blemished by spots. As soon as he was certain of his results, Scheiner began sending them together with comments to Mark Welser, chief magistrate of Augsburg and a man noted for the breadth of his scientific interests. Welser at once grasped the significance of Scheiner's work and determined to publish the correspondence, although, in deference to Scheiner's superiors in the Society of Jesus who still feared the observations might be proved mistaken, he allowed the astronomer to use the pseudonym Apelles. Once they were printed, Welser distributed copies to anyone and everyone he thought might conceivably be interested, and naturally enough one ended up on Galileo's desk.

The correspondence showed clearly that, although Scheiner had made his first solar observations in April 1611, no spots were noticed until seven months later, but that there was no doubt about their existence: the question was, what was their cause. He suggested that there were a number of possible explanations, which he then explained and discussed. First, could the spots be some kind of optical illusion? If they were, did the source of the illusion lie in the observer's eye, or was it caused by a defect in the telescope? If neither, might it be due to some atmospheric effect? Scheiner claimed that since they had been seen by several observers, the suggestion that they were due to some peculiarity in the observer's eye was ruled out: he also rejected the possibility that the telescope was at fault because he had tried eight different telescopes, and the spots had been observed through every one. What of the idea that they might be due to some atmospheric

Opposite Portrait of Galileo by Ottavio Leoni.

The projection of the Sun's image through a telescope onto a screen in order to study sunspots. From Christoph Scheiner, *Rosa Ursina*, 1630.

effect? This, Scheiner said, would not do because the spots displayed no shift across the Sun's disk when observed from different places, yet if they were caused by the upper air, then such a shift would be expected. No, the only possible conclusion that fitted all the facts was to accept the spots as real. What, then, could they be?

Scheiner decided that the observations allowed only two answers: either the spots lay on the Sun's surface, or they were caused by small planets orbiting close to the Sun; and he plumped for the second possibility because there were grave philosophical objections to the first. If the spots really did lie on the Sun's surface, then the Sun was not unblemished and no longer could it be claimed that it was a perfect celestial body, as Aristotle had taught. The doctrine was quite clear; celestial bodies were not subject to change and decay, they were made of a fifth essence which had divine overtones and the Sun could not, then, be pock-marked. And in all fairness it must be confessed that Scheiner made out his case pretty well. It was not plausible to have dark spots on so bright a surface, and, further, by observing the rate at which the spots moved, he found that they should reappear after a fifteen-day period, which they did not. No, the only logical explanation was that they were caused by a collection of bodies orbiting close to the Sun, just as a host of bodies of which Galileo had seen just a few doubtless orbited round Jupiter. It was this last remark that Galileo did not like; as far as he was concerned it implied that his observations were inadequate. Yet he knew what he had seen: there were four not forty satellites, a few not a handful, and if Scheiner's solar spots were transposed to Jupiter they certainly would have been visible in his telescope. Galileo therefore took Scheiner's comment as an implied criticism although Scheiner probably meant nothing of the kind.

142

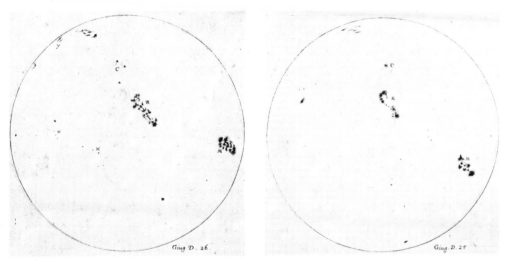

Galileo's observations of sunspots. From his *History*, 1613.

Furthermore Galileo, did not favour Scheiner's interpretation of the spots at all; he wanted them to be on the Sun because he wanted to claim that the Sun, like the Moon, was merely an ordinary imperfect body similar to the Earth, yet he had to be cautious. Rumours, due perhaps to Magini, were circulating in Bologna that Galileo's work was the subject of ridicule, and he had to take great care in this new controversy to say nothing hastily. He must not propose views that could readily be disproved, or were obviously ill-considered. Galileo therefore did two things that he thought would squash the Bologna rumours and, at the same time, open up the question of whether Scheiner's interpretation was correct: he claimed priority of observation and offered an alternative but, nevertheless, tentative explanation that put the spots down unequivocally on the Sun. He began to do this in June in a series of three letters to Welser, a series that the Lincean Academy later published. Galileo said that he had observed sunspots 'for about eighteen months having shown them to various friends of mine, and at this time last year I had many prelates and other gentlemen at Rome observe them there'.[1] Yet why had he not announced his results if he had been the first to see the spots? Because, as he explains earlier in the letter, 'certain recent discoveries that depart from common and popular opinions have been noisily denied and impugned, obliging me to hide in silence every new idea of mine until I have more than proved it'.

Galileo next goes on to consider the question of what the spots really are, and here he describes observations that show clearly that he had made his own examination of the Sun. 'Sunspots are generated and decay in longer and shorter periods; some condense and others greatly expand from day to day; they change their shapes, and some of these are irregular; here their obscurity is greater, there less.'[2] They show also a quite surprising additional fact: Scheiner had not examined his own observations carefully and had jumped to his hypothesis of orbiting planets without enough care. For Galileo was quite right – sunspots do change their shape, they are irregular and this is just what Scheiner's, as well as Galileo's, drawings actually showed. Yet Scheiner seems to have missed this vital point which put the explanation that they were orbiting bodies into jeopardy, as Galileo was quick to point out. What could they be? What could change shape and behave in so irregular a manner? Clouds, said Galileo: 'of all the things found with us, only clouds are vast and immense, are produced and dissolved in brief times, endure for long or short periods, expand and contract, easily change shape, and are more dense and opaque in some places and less so in others.'[3] Next he goes on to develop the theme that they must be on the Sun, not orbiting round it, by discussing their motion across the Sun's disk and their continual change of shape.

> The spots at their first appearance and final reappearance near the edges of the Sun generally seem to have very little breadth, but to have the same length that they show in the central parts of the Sun's disk. Those who understand what is meant by foreshortening on a spherical surface will see this to be a manifest argument that the Sun is a globe, that the spots are close to its surface, and that as they are carried on that surface toward the centre they will always grow in breadth while preserving the same length.[4]

This appeal to apparent foreshortening was a powerful argument that would convince any of his readers who were familiar with perspective, since drawings from still life or from living models would have already brought them experience of this very kind.

When Galileo's letters appeared in Rome in 1613 as *History and Demonstrations Concerning Sunspots and their Phenomena* two things were clear: Galileo was not only anti-Aristotelian, but he was also a thorough-going Copernican. Out of consideration for Welser who was also a member of the lynx-eyed fraternity, Galileo was gentle in his criticism of 'Apelles', although ten years later, when he published his most scathing and most brilliant polemic, he referred to Scheiner's work in less delicate terms, openly claiming that Scheiner had been wilfully dishonest: 'and some ... attempted to rob me of that glory which was mine by pretending not to have seen my writings and subsequently trying to make themselves the original discoverers of such impressive marvels.'[5] Although he did not mention Scheiner by name there was no doubt about whom he meant, and Scheiner was furious. In an attempt to counteract the criticism, Scheiner prepared and published under his own name a book of his entire sunspot observations, a book that made clear the considerable amount of good work he had done. Yet this did not appear until 1630, and long before then he was busy behind the scenes in Rome working out the grudge hatched by Galileo's intemperate criticism.

If the full implications of the sunspot controversy were to take time to manifest themselves, there was another more immediate danger that Galileo had to face in 1613. Ludovico delle Colombe's anti-Galileo faction, disappointed with the way

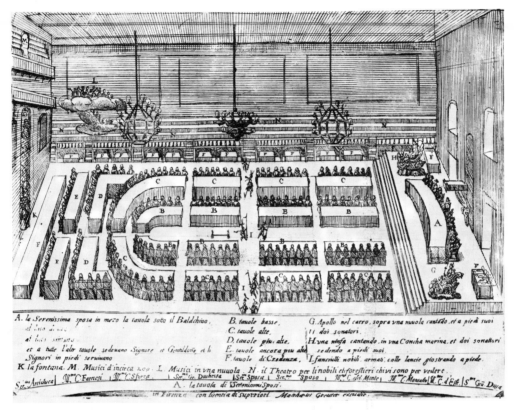

A formal Medici banquet. Note the allegorical figures of Apollo and a nymph on either side of the high table, and the jousting children in the central aisle.

the argument on floating bodies had gone, decided that it was time to carry the attack on Galileo into court circles, and to shift the emphasis from problems in physics to the far more dangerous ground of religious fidelity. Formal court banquets provided suitable occasions, and one day, when Galileo was not present, the opening salvo was fired by the pious Dowager Grand Duchess Cristina who raised the question of the religious orthodoxy of the Copernican view. Unwittingly primed by Boscaglia, the university's strongly pro-Aristotelian professor of philosophy, the Grand Duchess questioned the Benedictine monk Benedetto Castelli, who was a well-known pupil of Galileo's, asking him whether a moving Earth was not contrary to the Scriptures. Castelli made no bones about his reply, and since he was a theologian, his answer seems to have appeased the old lady. Castelli, naturally enough, told Galileo, who now became deeply worried that Colombe's anti-Galileo faction, whom he had punningly nicknamed the 'doves' (*colombe*), should let their spite carry scientific questions into the deep and perilous waters of religious orthodoxy. He therefore felt he must write a long and carefully worded letter on the subject to Castelli.

The letter, ready a little before Christmas 1613, set out Galileo's views, and while displaying his orthodoxy clearly enough, tackled the basic question of whether the Scriptures should be taken as claiming categorically that the Earth stood still. For instance, when the Psalmist writes 'Who laid the foundations of the Earth, that it should not be removed for ever',[6] should his word be taken literally or not? If not, on what authority should it be doubted? Galileo pointed out that these were totally mistaken questions; there was no challenge to Scriptural authority involved, no implication that the Church's teaching about Holy Writ was wrong; it was purely and simply a matter of recognizing the tenor of scriptural language. The Bible, he agreed, was inviolate truth, yet it was obvious that at times, it spoke in figurative language, expressions were frequently used that were symbolic and not meant to be taken literally. For instance, no one imagined that 'the hand of God' was anything but a metaphor, that the 'tent of heaven' was other than a figure of speech. And he also dealt with a question that was frequently raised whenever the Copernican theory and the Bible collided: the account in the book of Joshua of God making the Sun stand still so that there was no sunset and the Israelites could pursue their enemies. As Galileo was quick to point out, if the universe were Aristotelian, then this story implied not only that the Sun stood still, but that the whole universe stopped moving since the Sun's motion was derived from the movement of the outermost sphere of space. On the other hand, if one accepted the Copernican theory and took the account literally then only the Sun and the planets need be stopped, and there was no need to postulate that the stars stood still as well. If you were going to take the story literally, then it was preferable to be a Copernican.

In essence Galileo believed, and stated quite specifically, that he thought the world of nature and the world of the spirit should be dealt with separately. God had given Man his senses to understand the one, Holy Writ to guide him in the other, and the Bible was not written to be used by one philosophical school to beat another over the head; such an idea led to intellectual arrogance.

For who would set a limit to the mind of man? Who would dare assert that we know all there is to be known? Therefore, it would be well not to burden the articles concerning salvation and the establishment of the Faith – against which there is no danger that valid contradiction ever may arise – with official interpretations beyond need; all the more so, when the request comes from people of whom it is permitted to doubt that they speak under heavenly inspiration, whereas we see most clearly that they are wholly devoid of that understanding which would be necessary, I will not say to refute, but first of all to grasp the demonstrations offered by science.[7]

This letter delighted Castelli, and no wonder: it showed Galileo at his best, arguing persuasively yet exercising restraint, and it was a fine example of dialec-

Opposite Benedetto Castelli, Galileo's most devoted friend and probably the greatest of his scientific pupils. A Benedictine monk, Castelli wrote several treatises on the measurement and control of running waters and may be considered the father of hydrostatics.
Overleaf The Dominican cloisters of Santa Maria Novella, Florence, where one of Galileo's bitterest enemies, Fra Tommaso Caccini, resided and preached.

D: BENEDI: CASTELLI

tical skill, setting out an attitude to the basic question of science and religion epitomized in the phrase Galileo loved to quote: 'The Bible shows the way to go to heaven, not the way the heavens go.' Yet Galileo's opponents who could not answer the letter by rational argument, decided to resort to rumour and innuendo: Galileo had impugned the scriptures, he had shown himself to be a disbeliever they said. And among some churchmen who were already suspicious of Galileo uneasy feelings began to arise, for even though the letter had some circulation, there were plenty who had not seen it. Prejudice and ignorance began to make fools of some but dangerous enemies of others.

Galileo seems either to have been quite unaware of the forces that were gathering to try to destroy him, or else he had too much faith in the dictates of reason. Perhaps, too, he thought his position unassailable or, at least, far stronger than happened to be the case; yet he had warnings. As early as 1610 Francesco Sizi, a young religious fanatic had been egged on by Magini to publish his incredible numerical aberration *Diana's Astronomy*, in which he advanced semi-religious arguments why there should be seven planets, and claiming that Galileo's 'Medicean stars' orbiting round Jupiter must, therefore, be an illusion. It was a silly book, but it was a straw in the wind. More direct, though, was a *caveat* from his trusted friend Paolo Gualdo. 'As to this matter of the Earth turning round, I have found hitherto no philosopher or astrologer who is willing to subscribe to the opinion of Your Honour, and much less a theologian; be pleased, therefore, to consider carefully before you publish this opinion assertively, for many things can be uttered by way of disputation which it is not wise to affirm.'[8]

Throughout 1614 the undercurrents of anti-Galilean slander went on. Not only was he accused of undermining the Scriptures but of meddling in theology as well. Copernican ideas became increasingly unpopular, and the Bishop of Fiesole went so far as to demand that Copernicus be jailed, totally unaware that the astronomer had been dead for the past seventy years. Yet if ill-informed presumptions were to be expected in the turbulent underworld of half-truths that the 'pigeons' stirred up, what happened on 20 December 1614 was quite unforeseen, even by the most pessimistic of Galileo's friends. On that day Tommaso Caccini, a Dominican, preached a sermon at the church of Santa Maria Novella in Florence openly attacking mathematicians, and so condemning both Copernicus and Galileo. Basing his address on the allusive text 'Ye men of Galilee, why stand ye gazing up into heaven?'[9] and the account in Joshua that Galileo had dealt with, he developed his thesis that mathematics was the work of the devil and that mathematicians should be banned from all Christian countries. Ideas of a moving Earth were, Caccini proclaimed, tantamount to heresy.

The effect of Caccini's sermon was electrifying. Here, openly and from the pulpit, Galileo's views had been condemned. No longer might one suppose the Earth went in orbit round the Sun; it had become a heresy. Galileo was dumbfounded but could not stand silently by, so he elaborated his letter to Castelli and saw to it that a copy was put into the hands of the Dowager Grand Duchess. Castelli, for his part, circulated the new letter and made a point of showing it to a senior Dominican whom he knew, a man who, however, secretly made a copy which he forwarded to the Inquisition in Rome 'for investigation'.

It is important at this stage to attempt to get the whole matter into perspective and to see why the Dominicans especially, were so anti-Galilean. After all Caccini was no fool – he had some reputation as a theologian and a preacher – and it was no light thing to launch an ecclesiastical attack on anyone, let alone so well-known a figure as Galileo, a man of international reputation with a high position at court. Caccini was, admittedly, a crony of the 'pigeons', yet however persuasive Ludovico delle Colombe may have been, there must surely have been some deeper-seated reasons for Caccini to attack so virulently. One simple and obvious cause may have been the fact that St Thomas Aquinas, who had laid the foundations of Christian Aristotelianism, was a Dominican, and an attack on Aristotelianism was seen as an attack on him; another could, conceivably, have been that since the Dominicans and the Jesuits did not then have the most cordial of relationships, Galileo was attacked because he was Jesuit-trained. Yet neither reason would seem sufficient, and the cause probably lies at the door of that Renaissance magus and firebrand Giordano Bruno.

Giordano Bruno was an astonishing, and in some ways pathetic, figure. A Neapolitan, sixteen years older than Galileo, he had entered the Dominican order at the age of fifteen and while showing himself to be a great Thomist he was also influenced by Giambattista della Porta who, in the 1560s, ran an academy in Naples much taken up with investigating the secrets of nature. Yet Bruno's main interest was not science but ecclesiasticism; he was more concerned with the laws of the Church than the laws of the natural world, and like many clerics of his time he grew to be dissatisfied with the way the Roman Church was governed and the abuses he found in it. Being at heart something of a mystic he turned to Hermetism and although he was not alone in this, he went further than his contemporaries: an emotional and passionate man, he decided that nothing would do but to wipe the slate clean and go right back to the pure religion of the past. Yet to Bruno this did not mean, as it did to so many reformers, a return to the Church of the early Christians, but to the Hermetic mixture of pseudo-Egyptian Christianity. Only by these means he thought, would the Roman Church find itself purged of its errors and yet still retain its divine identity.

It needs little imagination to see that Bruno's views were hardly likely to commend themselves to his superiors, and while still at Naples he fell under suspicion of heresy. Proceedings were instituted against him, so he quickly left and travelled to Rome, but again he ran into trouble there and, as a last resort, he shed the Dominican habit and fled from Italy. For a time he travelled in western Europe, then moved to France and arrived finally in England under the protection of the French ambassador. It was here that he came across Copernicanism, untrammelled

Giordano Bruno, burnt as a heretic in 1600, not for his support of the Copernican system of the universe, but for his religious heresies.

by any ecclesiastical disapproval or secular restrictions, but a Copernicanism that was wedded to the idea of an infinite universe. The theory appealed to him for it both defied authority and put the Sun, that arch-symbol of Hermetism, in the centre of the universe. Moreover an orbiting Earth and a central Sun also fitted in well with Bruno's current ideas of astral magic and mystical numerology, and so he not only adopted it enthusiastically but, typical of him, elaborated it. With the impassioned excitement of the convert, he coupled the Copernican theory with his other beliefs, including his hopes of Church reform, and when he returned to Europe he lectured and promoted his new-found conception with astonishing vigour and even more astonishing lack of propriety. In fact, he seems in the end to have suffered from illusions of grandeur for in 1591 he returned to Italy in the mistaken belief that, with the help of a new book he had written, he could convert the Pope. Instead the cold light of reality shone down not on a messianic conquest but on the walls of a prison cell, for he was denounced to the Inquisition and, in

1600, after a protracted imprisonment, was burned as a heretic.

It must be emphasized that it was for his religious heresies that Bruno was burned, not for his support of Copernicanism. In the nineteenth century a myth grew up that Bruno was condemned because of his scientific views, but this was totally mistaken. He was not burned at the stake as 'the first martyr of science', and any but the most casual glance at his published work will show that his science was not science as we understand it, or even as the Renaissance understood it; Copernicanism and the infinite universe were no more than useful props to support his mystical cosmos peopled by angels and archangels. And it is relevant, too, that until his time the Roman Church had raised no objections to the helio-centric theory and Pope Paul III had been pleased to accept the dedication of Copernicus' book. Only after Bruno's imprisonment did that attitude change, because many clerics first met Copernicanism by way of Bruno's hermetic polemics, and so linked it in their minds with heresy. And of course the Domini-cans had little love for it as it refuted the divine Aristotle and the equally divine Aquinas, as well as being a lever used by an apostate of their order. So it seems clear that Bruno's heresies lay behind Caccini's blast from the pulpit of Santa Maria Novella. He damned all mathematicians, a seemingly intemperate and even ludicrous thing to do until it is remembered that Bruno laid claim to a special occult mathematics, a 'mathesis' that was greater even than that used by Coper-nicus, and doubtless it was this to which Caccini was taking exception: Galileo was a Copernican, like Bruno, and so in Caccini's eyes was probably tarred with the same brush. So the burden of Caccini's sermon is obvious: Copernicanism and mathematics were heretical and its advocates should be banned. It was a natural reaction to the Bruno affair, even if Ludovico delle Colombe and his 'doves' had egged him on to say it in public.

Galileo was deeply worried by this ecclesiastical attack, and when Father Maraffi, Preacher-General of the Dominicans, wrote a letter of apology saying that Caccini had got carried away in his holy zeal, he was still not mollified. The Dominicans in Rome were obviously strongly anti-Copernican, and the Domini-cans were close to the Inquisition. What should he do? Should he make a reply? Could he proclaim his religious orthodoxy? Prince Cesi advised him to keep quiet and lie low, and Piero Dini, the Archbishop of Fermo, gave him the same counsel, and for once Galileo was rattled enough to comply. Yet if he kept quiet, his opponents did not. The Caccini sermon acted as a stimulant, and Niccolò Lorini, another of delle Colombe's cronies, got hold of a copy of Galileo's second letter to Castelli and made a duplicate, changing a few key words with the aim of proving Galileo's religious infidelity; this he sent to Rome. Lorini's attempt mis-fired and little if any notice was taken of the letter, but Caccini was more success-ful; he went to Rome and he busied himself sowing seeds of distrust among the Dominicans in the Holy Office of the Inquisition, an errand that was later to prove its worth to the anti-Copernican cause.

12
A Visit to Rome

After the Caccini affair Galileo lay low and worried; he fell ill and was confined to bed, yet still he could not let things rest and turned the matter over and over in his mind. Was Cesi right that he must keep quiet? Could Archbishop Dini's advice that he must do nothing be wrong? If he remained in Florence would he not be tacitly admitting his error, surely the authorities who knew him and respected him would anticipate some reply? He was known to be a vehement critic, a powerful and forthright opponent; total silence would be uncharacteristic. And had he not been fêted when he was last in Rome, entertained by cardinals, lauded by the Jesuits, granted a long audience by the Pope? Was it sensible for him to sit back and say nothing? Should he not, like David, go into the lion's den, and proclaim his innocence; was it not imperative that he make another journey to Rome? And as he lay and pondered, a new fear arose in his mind: what of the Copernican theory? Was it not possible that the Caccinis of this world would do their best to silence it, to have it proclaimed a heresy? Possibly news of Caccini's visit reached his ears, but even if he was ignorant of it, the fear was real enough, for Dini himself had hinted as much. And once an official pronouncement condemning the helio-centric theory had been made, once there was a papal bull or a formal proclama-tion, it would not be easy to have it changed; better, by far, that he should go to Rome and talk to those who mattered, the men of influence who could take a broad and enlightened view, and persuade them that the Copernican position could be a stance of the orthodox as well as the heretic. Yes, as soon as he was well again, he would make the journey to clear his name and set the mind of authorities at rest over the heliocentric doctrine.

With these thoughts in his head, in March 1615 Galileo sent Dini some copies of his letter to Castelli, asking him to let Clavius and the other Jesuit mathe-maticians read it and see if, by any chance, he could pass on a copy personally to Cardinal Bellarmine and even, perhaps, get a copy to the Pope. Dini did what he could and managed to get the letter into the hands of Bellarmine, who read it and immediately put out a theological challenge; psalm 19, he remarked, said the Sun moved, not the Earth and it was quite explicit; the Sun's 'going forth' it said 'is from the end of heaven, and his circuit unto the ends of it; and there is nothing hid from the heat of it'. What, Bellarmine queried, says Galileo? Once again Galileo was propelled into the realms of doctrinal enquiry, once more he found himself on the unfamiliar theological ground where mathematical arguments held no sway and experiment was impossible. What should he do? He could not decline to answer since this would be taken as a rebuff and a tacit admission that the Scrip-

Opposite The Vatican City. Detail of a vew of Rome, 1630, by Goffredo van Schayck.

Cardinal Roberto Bellarmine, *Consultor* of the Holy Office, took a prominent part in the first examination of Galileo's writing.

tures were an authority on physical science, just the thing he wanted to avoid. So Galileo carefully prepared a reply, splitting textual hairs just as Copernicus had been forced to do half a century before, but it was dangerous ground. He knew Bellarmine's reputation as a theologian and realized only too well that his excursions into biblical exegesis must be made with great care. But he did not know, as the Cardinal did, the firm ruling of the Council of Trent against a multiplicity of interpretations of Scripture: however sound his arguments might appear, they were signs of heresy if he went against the official ecclesiastical line.

Yet, paradoxically, Bellarmine's response encouraged Galileo; it seemed to confirm that rational argument would win in the end, but he felt he must go to Rome to argue his case personally. So much could be done by word of mouth that was impossible in writing, however skilful the phrases used, and at last, with letters of recommendation from the Grand Duke, Galileo set out on 3 December 1615. Piero Guicciardini, the Tuscan ambassador, at whose embassy Galileo was to stay, was much put out; writing to the Tuscan secretary of state, Guicciardini

Opposite Ferdinand II de' Medici succeeded his father, Cosimo, in 1621. Interested, like his ancestors, in intellectual and scientific pursuits, he helped found the famous Accademia del Cimento in 1657. Portrait by Josse Sustermans. *Overleaf* A view of Rome by an anonymous painter of the early seventeenth century, showing a papal cortege leaving the Castel Sant' Angelo.

GIUSTO SUSTERMANS
(1597–1681)

S. ROBERTVS CARD. BELLARMINVS
E SOC. IESV
MARCELLI. II. P. M. NEPOS

The Villa Medici, the Florentine embassy built by Michelangelo and A. Lippi, and where Galileo stayed whenever he was in Rome.

said: 'I do not know whether he has changed his theories or his disposition, but this I know, that certain brothers of St Dominic, who are in the Holy Office, and others, are ill disposed toward him, and this is no fit place to argue about the Moon or, especially in these times, to try to bring in new ideas.'[1] Guicciardini's protestations fell on deaf ears, and he was firmly instructed to make ready quarters for his visitor, a valet, and a secretary.

Galileo arrived in good spirits, and formally his reception was all he could wish. He was widely entertained, and although he was not fêted to the degree he had been when he had last come to Rome flushed with the triumphs of his telescope, he met no open antagonism; everyone was charming and his social life was an endless round of pleasure. Yet it was all a gay façade, for none of his detractors would come out into the open; those who had spread rumours that he had fallen into disgrace in Florence may have been discomfited, but they took care not to show it. For his part Galileo wanted to display himself in a good light, to be seen among those who mattered as an orthodox man of science unbesmirched by whispers of heresy. Yet on a less superficial level things were not so good; try as he would he could not directly reach those he wanted. He allowed himself to be drawn into scientific arguments and he made his point but, as often as not, they were beyond the comprehension of his listeners, and all he left behind him was a

Opposite Cardinal Roberto Bellarmine. Though he did not entirely proscribe the Copernican system, he insisted that it should be presented mainly as a hypothesis and warned Galileo of the dangers of stubbornly affirming his belief in a heliocentric universe. He died in 1621, twelve years before Galileo's trial.

string of people uncomfortable at their dialectical demolition yet totally unaware of the true reasoning behind it. He wrote home:

> My business is far more difficult, and takes much longer owing to outward circumstances, than the nature of it would require; because I cannot communicate directly with those persons with whom I have to negotiate, partly to avoid doing injury to any of my friends, partly because they cannot communicate anything to me without running the risk of grave censure. And so I am compelled, with much pains and caution, to seek out third persons, who, without even knowing my object, may serve as mediators. . . .[2]

Worse still, Galileo found that while he could put things down in writing, no one of any standing was willing to discuss controversial points face to face, and although he finally managed to clear himself of any breath of heresy, the Copernican theory he had also come to save did not fare so well.

At this time Rome was no place for new ideas. Pope Paul v was not an intellectual, not a man to find stimulation in controversy, whether theological or scientific. He was an administrator, a born executive who, as he said himself, preferred new jobs for workmen to new ideas from scholars. And as always, so many of the clergy there were making visits with an eye to preferment for themselves or for their families, men who were not in the slightest interested in some abstruse scientific theory but who would pay lip service to Galileo if it suited their book, or condemn him out of hand if that seemed likely to bring them favours. Of course not all clerics were so cynical; some were saintly men working to comfort and help the vast number of poor within the city, and the even greater crowds of impoverished pilgrims who flocked there from all over the Roman Catholic world, but they too had no time to argue about a moving Earth, to discuss the fine points of planetary movement or delicate questions of scriptural meaning. Galileo was in the wrong place at the wrong time and he was quietly told by Guicciardini and friends like Cardinal del Monte, to go back to Florence and stop raising the Copernican issue publicly; he could hold the heliocentric doctrine if he liked but for his own sake and for the good of the theory, he must keep his ideas to himself. Do not, they urged him, go shouting the Copernican doctrine from the housetops, and above all stop trying to convert everyone to it; leave things alone and they will calm down, otherwise irreparable damage may be done.

There were times when Galileo would take nobody's advice, times when he would obstinately go his own way in spite of the dangers and this was one of those occasions. However much his friends might plead, whatever Guicciardini or del Monte might say, Galileo could not, or would not, leave the authorities alone; he was determined to pester them to admit that a moving Earth was not heretical. He might have to do this by way of third parties who had no idea of the significance of the matter, but do it he must. Yet, of course, Galileo's friends were right, those prelates who had his interests at heart, knew the ways of the Church of Rome better than he did. They saw that the time was inopportune to promote any

Pope Paul v, 'so circumspect and reserved', wrote a contemporary, 'that he is held for sombre', did little to encourage intellectual controversy during his papacy.

important new scientific theory: determination to do so would very likely lead to suppression or worse. If only the authorities were left alone, if only they were given time to simmer down, to forget the allegations of unorthodoxy and the accusations of bitter men, then the situation would change and it might be possible to take some action. If Galileo were only back in Florence and quietly at work, avoiding controversy, then the Copernican theory could be gently brought up, subtle innuendos made that extolled its virtues and denigrated the mental ossification of those who condemned it out of hand. This was a technique they knew well, and this was the way to persuade the authorities; but Galileo would have none of it. He must make a direct approach, for these were intelligent men and intelligent argument must of necessity appeal to them; his enemies would prevail if he did not take some direct action himself. So, in the end, all the care his friends had taken to try and defuse a potentially dangerous situation came to nothing; Galileo charged in headlong and the authorities were forced to take notice.

Late in February 1616 Bellarmine discussed the Copernican theory with the Pope, and they decided that a commission be set up to enquire into its relationship with Christian doctrine. Naturally enough it was not primarily to be concerned with the scientific and mathematical merits of the hypothesis, whilst the observational evidence was not, to them, a relevant issue; the papal astronomer Father Clavius had reported that what was seen through the new-fangled telescope did not necessarily lead to Copernicus, so this aspect need not trouble them further. Their considerations were theological and pastoral: did the hypothesis of a moving Earth contradict the Scriptures or, to be more precise, did it go against the Church's interpretation of the Scriptures, and would it be likely to mislead the faithful from the true and narrow paths of righteousness? They concluded that it failed on both counts – it was certainly contrary to traditional biblical interpretation, and might well mislead both laity and clergy. It could, if desired, be used as a purely convenient mathematical description of planetary motion, there was no harm in that, but it must not be believed as a true, factual description of the physical universe. There was nothing for it, then, but to rule that the faithful must accept the concept of a stationary Earth, fixed at the centre of the universe, yet this should prove no stumbling block for was not the suggestion that the Earth actually moved an absurd idea? Finally, therefore, they pronounced the Earth to be at the centre of the universe and the belief that it moved, heretical. Copernicus' book was suspended 'for correction'.

All Galileo feared had come to pass, and worse was to follow. As the avowed protagonist of a moving Earth, it was obvious that he must be disciplined: the voice that was promoting a heretical doctrine must be silenced. On the other hand, those very authorities who declared a physical interpretation of Copernicanism to be heretical, had received good reports of Galileo the Catholic, of the live faith of this erring mathematician, so there was at this stage no need to arraign him before the Inquisition. Instead the Pope directed Bellarmine to summon Galileo to appear before him, and to admonish him to abandon the Copernican theory. Of course it was just conceivable that Galileo might be difficult; he might, after all, refuse. Bellarmine was therefore told that if such an eventuality occurred, he was then, but only then, to summon a Commissary from the Inquisition and, before a notary and witnesses, command Galileo to 'abstain altogether from teaching or defending this opinion and doctrine and even from discussing it'.[3] In view of what followed, it is imperative that there is no doubt about Bellarmine's instructions, that there is question about the action he was supposed to do. There were two quite separate stages of procedure: the first was an 'admonition' made without witnesses, the second a full dressing down in front of witnesses and a senior representative of the Holy Office, but it was clear that the second stage was only a last line of defence to be used on a recalcitrant Galileo. If Galileo submitted to Bellarmine's admonition, all would be well, and that would be an end of the matter; there would be no need for Galileo to say anything, to make any formal declaration of his agreement since silence would be taken as an act of submission. After all he was a famous man, a personage of high standing in the court of the Grand Duke of Tuscany, and he had to be treated with care, unless he showed himself to be arrogant and without due respect for the Church: only then would the delicate balance of relationships be upset and sterner action needed. The two stages were, therefore, kept apart quite specifically in Bellarmine's instructions.

When Galileo presented himself at Bellarmine's palace it seems probable that his reception was quite friendly. Bellarmine, a man of considerable formality, was nevertheless the soul of courtesy: no one, it is said, ever came to see him without his making them sit down comfortably before the interview began, and no one left without his removing his cap and accompanying them to the stairs 'as if they were distinguished guests'.[4] It cannot be doubted that Galileo, Copernican though he might be, would be treated in just the same way. And as for Galileo himself, it is evident that he accepted his admonition; he knew now that he must keep even his fiery temperament quiet, and heed the instruction of a prince of the Church. He had tried to avoid such an impasse but now it had come there was nothing he could do; his friends had been right, and all that was left to him was to submit, and hope against hope that some day, somehow, he could get things changed. Bellarmine did not have to move on to the second stage of his instructions.

Galileo's admonition was, of course, common knowledge amongst the Curia, but the fact that he had accepted Bellarmine's injunction did not please his enemies: he had avoided the formal condemnation which they had set their hearts on. This, however, did not prevent them from spreading rumours that Galileo had not submitted, and that he had been arraigned in front of a Commissary of the Inquisition and given salutary penance. Galileo was furious; such rumours would permeate to Florence, indeed they were probably already being whispered in Court circles, and he must clear himself. He therefore sought, and obtained, another interview with Bellarmine, and persuaded the Cardinal to write a formal note in his own hand to the effect that such allegations were false, that all that had happened was that Galileo had been duly notified by the Cardinal of the papal declaration on the Copernican theory. Armed with this, Galileo at last returned to Florence, much to the relief of ambassador Guicciardini and all his friends in Rome. The whole unhappy business seemed to be at an end: Copernicus was to be corrected and no physical belief in his theory allowed, but Galileo was free to fight again, to take up the cudgels on behalf of heliocentrism if he could possibly find a way of doing so without breaking the regulations. It might not appear likely, but in time some way could conceivably be discovered, some door, at present locked, might be opened to him.

Galileo's enemies quite clearly believed that he had only been silenced temporarily: to them his submission was too sudden and too glib to be taken at its face value, and they prepared themselves for another confrontation at a later date; some time in the future there would surely be a recrudescence of the heresy, and at Galileo's instigation. They therefore decided on a course of action that totalitarian authorities inevitably turn to when no other way seems open to them: they faked the records. They inserted into the Vatican archives a false report of Galileo's arraignment before Bellarmine, a report of which the crucial part ran:

Galileo ... was in the presence of the Most Reverend Michelangelo Segizi of Lodi, of the Order of Preachers, Commissary-General of the Holy Office, by the said Cardinal [Bellarmine] warned of the error of the aforesaid opinion and admonished to abandon it; and immediately thereafter, before me and before witnesses, the Lord Cardinal being still present, the said Galileo was by the said Commissary commanded and enjoined, in the name of His Holiness the Pope and the whole Congregation of the Holy Office, to relinquish altogether the said opinion that the Sun is the centre of the world and immovable and that the Earth moves; nor further to hold, teach or defend it in any way whatsoever, verbally or in writing. . . .[5]

That this document is an untrue account will be obvious from the events it purports to describe: Galileo is admonished by Bellarmine and 'immediately thereafter' he is commanded by the Commissary-General. Yet we are not told whether Galileo agreed to the Cardinal's admonition, if he did not then the reporter would hardly have omitted to say so; and if he did (which we know from Bellarmine's personal note was what actually happened), there was no need for the formalities of stage two. But above all it is the phrase 'immediately thereafter' that gives the lie to the veracity of the document: this was contrary to the instructed procedure, an irregularity that Bellarmine would never have countenanced for a moment.

Right Cardinal Alessandro Orsini, a supporter of Galileo's in 1615.
Below The Gallery of Geographical Maps in the Vatican.

Yet false though this report might be, it was later to play a significant part when Galileo was finally brought before the Inquisition.

It would be wrong to give the impression that Galileo's visit of 1615 to Rome was a total disaster, although it very nearly became so. There was one ray of light to brighten the overcast skies and that was the effect his dialectical skill left in its wake. There was no one who was not impressed by the cogency of his arguments, and in particular there were a number of people who had almost been converted to the concept of a moving Earth by Galileo's claim that a study of the tides proved unequivocally that the Earth really does move in space. We now know that Galileo's argument was wrong and that the regular period of the tides does not, in fact, prove that the Earth is in motion, but at the time it seemed most impressive. Based on an analogy with the motion of water in a boat, Galileo argued that just as water piles up and then levels out when in a to-and-fro motion in the bottom of a boat, so the orbital and rotational movements of the Earth give a similar reciprocating motion to the seas, causing the phenomena we call the tides. Typical of him he did not just state his argument but furnished it with a geometrical proof, in which he showed how a point on the Earth's surface moves faster at one time of day than it does twelve hours later when this movement is measured with respect to the Sun. We can now see that this proof, quite valid from a geometrical point of view, is actually fallacious because the motion of the seas and oceans must be considered with respect to the Earth itself, not the Sun, but that is to be wise after the event, and when Galileo put forward his ideas in his own impressive way the reasoning appeared incontrovertible. Indeed the young Cardinal Alessandro Orsini was so impressed that he persuaded Galileo to put it all down in writing and send copies to a few carefully selected friends. Naturally Galileo needed no second prompting; here was an instruction he was delighted to obey since, with men like Orsini around, his hope of changing the Church's decree might after all prove to be more substantial than the pious dream it sometimes appeared.

GALILEO GALILEI LINCEO FILOSOFO E MATEMATICO DEL SER.mo GRAN DUCA DI TOSCA.

F. Villamœna Feat.

13
More Controversy

On the surface Galileo played the part of a penitent after he returned to Florence: the circulation of the note on his theory of the tides was done discreetly and, outwardly, he no longer concerned himself with Copernican doctrines. His friends had been right after all and, even if it were a little late in the day, he did not intend to give his enemies an excuse for further action; he had no wish to suffer a full-scale investigation by the Inquisition. On the other hand there was no need for him to pretend to embrace the Aristotelian fixed-Earth doctrine; no one, not even his most ardent detractors, would expect him to do that.

Bellarmine's admonition did not mean forsaking science, only heliocentrism, so once again he moved to the ecclesiastically safe ground of physics and, as a start, concentrated on optics and busied himself with the microscope, an instrument for which he probably deserves the credit. Although no biologist, although uninterested in entomology, his invention of the microscope was a logical enough step from the telescope: both used two lenses, an object-glass in front and an eye-piece at the rear, and the salient difference was only one of the focal length. Anyone experimenting with pairs of lenses, as a telescope maker would be bound to do, was likely to hit upon the right combination if his trials went on long enough. Indeed there is a definite possibility that Galileo may have come across the combination as early as 1610, for a former pupil of his, John Wedderborn, in a work published in Padua that very year, referred not only to the telescope, but also to an instrument for seeing small things close to: 'He [Galileo] perfectly distinguishes with his spy-glass the organs of motion and of the senses in the smaller animals; and especially in a certain insect. . . .'[1] Galileo himself made no reference to the microscope at this time, but that is not surprising since he was more than usually occupied with hammering nails in the coffin of Aristotelianism by using the lens combination as a telescope. However, four years later, when he was in bed with a bout of illness, he was visited by Giovanni du Pont who, in a detailed account of his travels, shows Galileo to have been more explicit: 'the tube of the telescope for looking at the stars is no more than two feet in length, but to see objects which are very near, but which we cannot see on account of their small size, the tube must have two or three lengths. He tells me that with this long tube he has seen flies which look as big as a lamb, and has learned that they are all covered with hair. . . .'[2] Galileo himself did not refer to the microscope in correspondence until 1619, but it is quite clear that he was familiar with a lens arrangement for magnifying small objects, and he often seems to have used an instrument he had made to delight his visitors. How much time he spent on it after his return

Opposite Portrait of Galileo from the frontispiece of his *History* (1613) and *The Assayer* (1623). The cherub at the top left holds Galileo's military compass, and the one on the right holds what may have been his first design for a telescope.

from Rome we do not know, but there seems no doubt that he developed it to a stage where he was able to have his workshop make microscopes for friends who wanted them. However, his own interest in it was rather superficial; he looked on the device as a curiosity, as an interesting exercise and perhaps an amusing device for looking at insects, but he never seems to have seriously considered it as a scientific tool. That privilege he reserved for the telescope, and in 1614 he turned his attention to it once more, although this time for rather more practical reasons than pure astronomical research: he hoped it could be used for determining longitude at sea.

At this time, and indeed for many decades to follow, the maritime nations of western Europe were all engaged in trying to discover an accurate and reliable method for finding longitude so that their ships could make trans-oceanic journeys in safety. The problem was a difficult one: any ship could determine its latitude north or south of the equator with comparative ease by observing the altitude of the Sun, the Moon or a bright star; but longitude was quite another matter. Here the mariner needed to know his distance east or west of his port of departure, and this entailed determining the moment when the Sun was exactly on the meridian. Observations could readily be made to show when the Sun was due south but these provided only half the answer, because one also had to find the instant this occurred. With an accurate clock on board there would be no difficulty, but accurate clocks were not available, and did not become so until well over a century later. The only way out of the impasse was to use the sky itself as a clock, and make other astronomical observations with sufficient precision to determine the time this way. Over the years various suggestions were made about how best to achieve this and, in the end, the general consensus of opinion was that the most convenient way would be to use the Moon as a clock hand and note the instant when its rim appeared to touch one of the bright stars in the sky. Unfortunately observations like this required accurate tables of the Moon's position, and no such tables were available in 1614; indeed, there were none of sufficient precision until at least a century and a half later. Galileo, however, believed he had another method of solving the problem.

In his investigations of Jupiter's satellites, he had observed that as they orbited the planet, they regularly went into eclipse when moving behind the disc, and into transit when crossing in front of it. Tables giving timings of all these motions could be computed and, Galileo argued, if one could use a telescope on board ship, then the Jovian satellites would act in a way analogous to a clock. But could telescopic observations be made on board ship? Certainly Jupiter and his satellites could not be observed by a hand-held telescope; a tripod was needed to hold the instrument steady, yet on the high seas, with the ship tossing first one way and then another, a tripod would be of little use and some other method was needed to keep the telescope still. Galileo therefore decided, first, that the telescope should be attached to the observer, and second, that the observer should himself be seated in a floating chair, a kind of 'vessel within a vessel' as he put it. The idea of using a floating seat was not new; in 1567 the French engineer Jacques Besson had suggested suspending an observer in a similar way, although he had proposed an arrangement of pivots to hold his navigator rather than an actual flotation system; but what was novel was Galileo's idea of anchoring a telescope to the observer's head. It should, he decided, be built as part of a helmet that had to be an individual fit for the observer who was to wear it: only in this way would it be supported firmly enough to obviate having the telescope on a separate stand. As for the instrument itself, Galileo decided it must be a binocular telescope, with the two components separated by the exact inter-ocular distance of the observer's eyes.

Galileo designed his 'large helmet' first and tests were made in Leghorn harbour in March 1617 on board the *Molo*, but the vessel pitched about so much that there was no use in pursuing matters until the floating seat was available, and as soon as plans were ready, one was built at the Arsenal in Pisa. Further experiments were then carried out in September with the help of Castelli using galleys in Leghorn harbour, but the arrangement does not appear to have worked very well or, at least, not satisfactorily enough for observing Jupiter and his satellites, and in spite of the practical importance of longitude determination, Galileo did not follow the matter up, although Castelli kept on talking about it and trying to gain government interest.

These excursions into practical optics were innocuous enough; they did not worry the authorities or sting Galileo's enemies into action. Nor did his return to the more overt anti-Aristotelian subject, the motion of bodies, because on the face of it, it had nothing to do with the Copernican theory and therefore seemed safe enough from the ecclesiastical point of view. As usual, his studies were mathematical; they dealt with accelerated motion and were concerned, in particular, with the changing rate at which a falling body drops to the ground: a vitally important question for any analysis of planetary motion, and the centre pivot for Newton's studies later in the century, but not understood in this context by the Aristotelian faction. So, when he was ready, Galileo could publish his results unmolested, and this he did in a small Latin treatise which, although undated, appears to have come out at this time, about 1617 or 1618. The results were not exactly new, for recent research on Galileo's notebooks has shown that he had discovered the exact law of accelerated motion in 1604 but had never made his work public. Now he did so, and showed that a falling body gathers speed at a specific rate that bears no relation whatsoever to its massiveness, thus completely contradicting Aristotle. Yet there was no storm of protest, even from Ludovico delle Colombe and his doves. Perhaps they did not read it or, more likely, did not understand its implications, and intellectual peace continued in Florence, at least for a time. But Galileo could not remain free from controversy for ever and soon he was to be drawn into a bitter feud, even though at first it was none of his making.

In August 1618 a comet appeared, to be followed three months later by two

Obverse of a medal commemorating the comet of November 1618 which prompted, amongst other pamphlets, Galileo's polemical masterpiece, *The Assayer*.

others; all were readily visible to the naked eye and one of them, that lasted from November until well into the following January, was particularly notable. With their bright, diffuse heads and long, glowing tails, naked-eye comets are even today awe-inspiring sights in the night sky. In 1618, when they were widely believed to be harbingers of evil, presaging death and disaster, they were quite literally a terrifying sight. We now know that they are no more than swarms of dust and rocky particles, probably bound together by frozen gas, and travelling in very elongated orbits, becoming visible only when in the Sun's immediate neighbourhood. Their power to foreshadow calamities is, of course, completely fallacious, although three centuries and more ago the belief did seem to have some rational foundation. After all the Aristotelian concept of an eternal and un-changing universe, made it necessary to assume that a comet, which appeared for only a few months at the most, must be some kind of meteorological pheno-menon, and the most widespread belief was that they were vapours of some kind that had become ignited in the upper air. As hot vapours they would have a drying effect on the lower reaches of the air and bring about just those conditions which always accompanied plagues and pestilences: to assume they were heralds of disaster was not so far-fetched. And even the more imaginative belief that a comet presaged the death of a ruler – a serious event that could alter the balance of power and even the fortunes of an entire nation – did not seem in any way illogical to minds steeped in the tradition of microcosm and macrocosm, to those who

172

took it for granted that the universe was anthropocentric and believed the heavens had no purpose but to glorify God and serve the needs of Man.

In 1577 the astronomical view of comets had begun to change due to observations of a very bright one that had appeared during November. Tycho Brahe had made careful measurements of its position and, coupling these with measures taken by a few selected acquaintances, he had reached the conclusion that whatever the comet might be, it certainly was not a meteorological phenomenon. His reason was simple: the comet lay beyond the sphere of the Moon. He could not, it is true, say precisely how far away it was, but he was able to quote figures that proved it was far off in space so that there was no doubt that it was an astronomical object. Not everyone accepted Tycho's results, and when other comets appeared, there were the inevitable astrological speculations about what they meant and, among astronomers, controversies about whether they were beyond the Moon or not. The 1618 trio of comets started all the arguments and conjectures off again, the very bright one coming in for special consideration, and a host of pamphlets rolled off the presses. Unfortunately Galileo was ill in bed when the brightest comet appeared and was not able to observe it for himself, so although he received a string of requests for his opinion, he could do nothing in the way of giving an answer. Always loath to pronounce about something he had not seen for himself, he was provided by his illness with an ideal excuse to remain quiet and stay out of the controversy. Yet this diplomatic and cautious attitude was not to remain with him for long and in 1619 he was soon drawn into what was to turn into a bitter polemical battle.

It all began with the publication, early in 1619, of a pamphlet entitled *On The Three Comets of the Year 1618*, a pamphlet that claimed to be about 'An Astronomical Disputation Presented Publicly in the Collegio Romano of the Society of Jesus by one of the Fathers of that same Society'. It was unsigned but its source, the Roman College, was the centre, the heart, of Jesuit learning: this much Galileo knew. What he did not know was that the author was Orazio Grassi, architect of the magnificent Church of St Ignatius attached to the College, as well as philosopher, physicist and mathematician, and who also, at the time the pamphlet appeared, held the chair of mathematics. The pamphlet itself was eminently reasonable but, unfortunately, it contained a glaring misunderstanding about telescope magnification. Grassi, like so many others, had been puzzled that the Sun, Moon and planets seemed larger in a telescope whereas the stars did not, but was disinclined to accept Galileo's explanation that the effect is simply due to the immense distances of the stars: the comet displayed a disk in the telescope and Grassi thought that Galileo's reasoning gave too strong a lever to those who believed all comets lay just above the Earth. He therefore tried to find an alternative explanation for the differential magnification and, to do so, involved himself in serious optical misconceptions. But on the credit side, he did come down in favour of the view that the very bright comet of 1618, like that of 1577, had been

further away than the Moon, and as Tycho had done, that it had travelled in an orbit round the Sun. This is not to say, of course, that Grassi held Copernican opinions – at the centre of the Jesuit Order he could hardly do that – but on the other hand he was too well informed to accept the Ptolemaic geocentric universe. With the new cometary evidence there was little he could do, but adopt Tycho's hybrid system which kept the Earth fixed and put the planets into orbit round a moving Sun: at least the Scriptures were satisfied and, who knew, it might, after all, prove to be true.

Grassi's discourse was only one of the many pamphlets that found their way into Galileo's hands, yet it was the one he chose to attack; out of them all it was Grassi's well argued disputation that was the solitary object of his invective. Why? Why did Galileo not bring his polemics to bear on some of the others? Why did he not choose to vent his wrath on the astrological pamphlets, on those who supported Aristotelian cometary beliefs, instead of picking on a pamphlet that, if it did nothing else, at least destroyed the Aristotelian case by proving comets to be truly celestial bodies with orbits that broke through the crystal spheres? There seems to be two reasons for his attitude. The first was that rumours reached him that everyone was saying the Jesuits had proved Copernicus wrong, even though Grassi's pamphlet had specifically avoided either mentioning the Copernican theory or launching an attack on it; indeed if the discourse was anti-anything it was really anti-Aristotelian. Yet there were plenty who would take a perverse delight in seeing Jesuit support for Tycho as Jesuit condemnation of the heliocentric theory, and Galileo's reaction was understandable; he wanted to denigrate a pamphlet, whatever its intrinsic merits, if it could foster an attack on Copernicanism. The second reason for Galileo's decision to blast Grassi was that, once again, he thought his position at Rome was stronger than it in fact was. This was due to a letter he received from Virginio Cesarini, a young Roman nobleman, who had written to say that Galileo's discussions and arguments during his Rome visit had acted 'like an insect's sting',[3] only having their due effect after Galileo had left, and he had time to think them over. What was true for Cesarini must, Galileo thought, be true for others – on reflection the intelligentsia would be coming to realize how right the Copernican view was, and in those circumstances Grassi's pamphlet provided an ideal excuse for driving his points home.

Galileo was, of course, well aware that he had to be very careful; on the one hand he had to avoid publicly advocating Copernicanism, on the other he must not openly attack the Jesuits, and so he decided to enlist the aid of a young pupil and disciple, Mario Guiducci. Guiducci was an ideal choice; academically sound – he had trained at the Roman College and taken a law degree at Pisa – he was a recent convert to science who had thrown up prospects of a diplomatic career to do scientific work. And, equally important at the time, he had just been elected as Consul to the Florentine Academy which meant that he had to give an inaugural address, a ready-made opportunity for him to act as a public mouthpiece for

Opposite Interior of the Jesuit Church of St Ignatius, built by Galileo's opponent, Orazio Grassi, and attached to the Roman College.

Galileo's criticisms of the Jesuit pamphlet. For his part, Guiducci seems to have entered into the spirit of the whole idea, and let Galileo not only prepare his brief but even decide precisely what should be said; so the lecture was delivered, and then printed and published in Florence under the simple title *Discourse on the Comets*, with Guiducci's name as author. Ostensibly moderate in tone, at least by the standards of the day, it began innocuously enough by giving a review of cometary theories and only Scheiner, under his pseudonym of Apelles, came in for any innuendos. Of course, the error over telescope magnification was corrected, but Galileo's main blast was reserved for Tycho and his concept of the universe, for only if he could discredit this would he silence those critics who claimed that Tycho's theory had disproved Copernicus. Unfortunately this criticism could not but involve the mathematicians at the Roman College who, in their enthusiasm for Tycho's theory, had tripped up by taking what were in fact unwarranted assumptions about cometary paths as facts.

> If the comet's orb is as these authors depict it, [Guiducci and Galileo had written] it is a great source of wonder to me that the Fathers at the Collegio have later been persuaded to call the comet the offspring of heaven; being in effect a triple goddess, it would have to be made an inhabitant of the heavens, of the elemental regions, and also of hell. Since the elongation of our comet from the Sun exceeded ninety degrees, a smattering of geometry suffices to show that if its orb encircles the Sun [but not the Earth], it must, after running through the sky a long way, traverse the elements and then plunge into the infernal bowels of the Earth. . . . I cannot believe that the author . . . would wish to maintain such a monstrosity.[4]

Grassi had been guessing and Galileo had caught him out, but his own ideas about comets and cometary paths were no better. The fact of the matter was that at this time no one knew enough to be certain what sort of path a comet pursued, and the observations Grassi had available could equally well fit a host of possible orbits, or even no orbit at all, and not until Halley's comet was observed on its return in 1758, was the question cleared up once and for all. Yet if both Galileo and Grassi had been guessing, the language of the Guiducci *Discourse* was hardly conducive to an amicable solution of the scientific question, and as soon as the Jesuits had read it they were up in arms. And, of course, Guiducci's name did not fool them for a moment: the style of the prose, the arguments used, the optical knowledge displayed, as well as the place of publication all pointed to only one man, Galileo. So they prepared a reply, attacking him openly and with vehemence.

The Jesuit polemic was called *The Astronomical and Philosophical Balance* with Lotario Sarsi [of] Sigensani credited as its author. Sarsi was supposed to be Grassi's pupil but this was a fiction; his name was purely and simply an imperfect anagram of Grassi's own name and birthplace and the book itself a compilation by a number of Jesuits, Grassi and Scheiner among them. According to its full title its pur-

---

The painter Cigoli, a man who dearly loved a good fight, set himself up as his friend Galileo's partisan and unofficial representative in Rome.

pose was to weigh Galileo's views on comets, but in fact it did more than this: it defended Grassi's original contentions and did so with dangerous theological overtones. For instance, in excusing the bias towards Tycho, Sarsi said: 'But consider, let it be granted that my master adhered to Tycho. How much of a crime is that? Whom instead might he follow? Ptolemy?...Or Copernicus? but he who is dutiful will rather call everyone away from him and will equally reject and spurn his recently condemned hypothesis.'⁵ And this extract is no isolated case; all the way through the mêlée of physics and mathematics which constitutes the *Balance*, the authors adopted the same tone. Galileo had dared to criticize the Roman College which had welcomed him as an honoured guest not so long before, he had poured scorn publicly on the work of their very able mathematicians, and they would see to it that he paid the price.

If the Jesuits hoped that the *Balance* would reduce Galileo to silence, they had seriously miscalculated. In the first place Galileo was not a man to let taunts and criticisms cower him into submission; he was made of sterner stuff, and nothing short of a formal directive from the Church could curb his scientific and intellectual independence. He was also a man with a mission – to convert the Aristotelian and Tychonic heretics to the pure faith of Copernicanism – and nothing was going to deflect him from this. Indeed although Grassi and his co-authors could never have realized it, the *Balance* played right into Galileo's hands, for scholarly though they were, all their learning was confined within the intellectual strait-jacket of authority; they discussed their results with all the formality of Aristotelian syllogistic reasoning and continually found it necessary to bolster their case by quoting the opinion of this or that accepted authority. Attacking this method of argument and satirizing ancient authorities was something Galileo could do better than anyone else, and since his friends told him he must not keep silent because of the accusations of heresy implied in the *Balance*, he set about the task of completely demolishing the Jesuit case. This was to take time, and as an interim measure Guiducci published an open letter to Tarquinio Galluzzi, his old professor of logic at the Roman College, making some temperate criticisms of the *Balance* and defending the opinions in 'his' *Discourse*.

Galileo worked on his destruction of the *Balance* during 1621 and 1622 and, as soon as it was finished, sent a draft to Prince Cesi in Rome, where it was read to the Lincean Academy. For their part they suggested some slight changes and Galileo reworked the text here and there, so that it was not until 1623 that it finally appeared. Called *The Assayer*, it was a substantial book of over two hundred pages 'in which with a delicate and precise scale' the arguments contained in the *Balance* were 'weighed'. Written in the form of a letter to Cesi and dedicated to the Pope, it was published in Rome by the Lincean Academy, and turned out to be a monumental polemic in the best Italian prose that heaped ridicule on the head of the unfortunate Grassi. For Galileo had not restrained himself at all, he had made use of every literary device that would serve his purpose, and, although *The Assayer* is not a

Opposite Drawing by Cigoli of a triumphal arch for the Medici.

great scientific treatise, it is a masterpiece of satiric prose.

Grassi under the guise of 'Sarsi', for Galileo found it convenient to continue the fiction, is severely taken to task for his scientific methodology or, rather, his lack of it.

> It seems to me [Galileo wrote] that I discern in Sarsi a firm belief that in philosophizing it is essential to support oneself upon the opinion of some celebrated author, as if when our minds are not wedded to the reasoning of some other person they ought to remain completely barren and sterile. Possibly he thinks philosophy is a book of fiction created by some man, like the *Iliad* or *Orlando Furioso* – books in which the least important thing is whether what is written in them is true. Well, Sig. Sarsi, that is not the way matters stand. Philosophy is written in this grand book – I mean the universe – which stands continually open to our gaze, but it cannot be understood unless one first learns to comprehend the language and interpret the characters in which it is written. It is written in the language of mathematics. . . .[6]

And as if this blast were not enough, Galileo then went on to pick holes in Grassi's arguments, and although he could not prove his own theory that comets were ignited vapours, at least he was able to rip the ground from under Grassi's feet.

For his part, Grassi had tried in the *Balance* to demolish Galileo's theory of vapours by attempting to prove that they would display effects that comets never could. Unfortunately, however, he had not been content to rely on the evidence of simple experiments, but had decided to bolster up his results by quoting authorities and giving examples of their reasoning, and one of these turned out to be a singularly unhappy choice. 'Therefore' wrote Grassi 'Suidas in his Histories . . . narrates this: "The Babylonians whirling about eggs placed in slings were not unacquainted with the rude hunter's diet, and by this method which the solitude of the army required, by that force they also cooked raw eggs". Thus he. Now if one seeks the causes of such things, let him hear Seneca the philosopher, since he among others is approved by Galileo, when he discusses these things philosophically.'[7] This attempt to drag in Seneca whose view of comets Grassi approved, gave Galileo a golden opportunity for ridicule, and he excelled himself:

> I cannot help wondering that Sarsi still wishes to persist in proving to me by means of witnesses that which I can see at any time by means of experiment. . . . If Sarsi wants me to believe from Suidas, that the Babylonians cooked eggs by whirling them rapidly in slings, I shall do so; but I must say that the cause of this effect is very far from that which he attributes to it. To discover the truth I shall reason thus: 'If we do not achieve an effect which others formerly achieved, it must be that in our operations we lack something which was the cause of this effect succeeding, and if we lack but one single thing, then this alone can be the cause. Now we do not lack eggs, or slings, or sturdy fellows to whirl them; and still they do not cook, but rather they cool down faster if hot. And since nothing is lacking to us except being Babylonians, then being Babylonians is the cause of the eggs hardening.'[8]

Galileo's polemic masterpiece did not please the Jesuits. He had impugned the Roman College and told them in so many words that their philosophers did not know how to philosophize, their logicians how to practice logic; their science was at fault and their authorities were fallible. But at last Galileo had made his comeback as a fighting force; with *The Assayer* he showed himself to be a literary giant as well as a master of philosophy, and once again he had triumphed over the opposition. Furthermore he had also provided something good to read, and *The Assayer* was a great success; even the Pope had it read to him at meals and obviously enjoyed it. But this was a mathematically minded Pope: Paul v with whom he had his audience twelve years earlier had died, as had his successor Gregory xv, and now the triple crown rested on the head of Galileo's friend Maffeo Barberini. Suddenly the future looked bright: the Jesuits had been silenced, and if the Copernican theory could not at the moment be openly proclaimed, at least the alternatives had been disposed of. Who could tell what the years ahead would bring, but equally who could doubt that Galileo's star was once again in the ascendant?

14
Barberini and the Dialogue

In August 1623, two months before *The Assayer* appeared, Maffeo Barberini became Pope Urban VIII. Giovanni Ciampoli, one of Galileo's staunchest clerical supporters was appointed Secretary of the Briefs (one of the coveted private secretary posts), and another pro-Galilean, Virginio Cesarini, was made Master of the Chamber. The clouds of intellectual lethargy were dispersing fast; a papacy of the virtuosi was heralded everywhere; and when Prince Cesi went to congratulate Barberini, the Pope asked him how Galileo was and when he was coming to give his congratulations: the auguries were indeed favourable. So once more preparations were begun for yet another visit to the Holy City, but this time Galileo was in high spirits and, since there seemed no urgency, he took his time, travelling at a leisurely pace and spending a fortnight with Cesi at his villa at Aquasparta. It was not until the end of April 1624 that he finally arrived in Rome, to be received by the Pope 'with infinite demonstrations of love'.[1]

All portended well, Galileo's gift of a microscope had delighted the Pope and surely, he thought, there seemed now to be every hope that the edict on Copernicus could be rescinded. Yet although Galileo stayed in Rome for six weeks and had many audiences of the Pope, he gradually came to realize that his hopes were going to founder. He was no longer dealing with Maffeo Barberini but Urban VIII, with a man who must now set his ecclesiastical authority above his scientific preferences; he was Pope first, mathematician second. As head of the Church on Earth, his first responsibility was to the faith, to his religious leadership, not to the promotion of a scientific theory or the acceptance of a particular mathematical interpretation of planetary motion. Moreover Urban was an ambitious man who was elected at a time that seemed to him to provide every opportunity to show that he was a Pope in the great Renaissance tradition. The Thirty Years War was five years old, and Urban hoped to help end it victoriously by engineering a great political campaign that would alter the balance of power in Europe and demolish the Reformation: if he could achieve this then his name would indeed go down in history, he would be hailed as no ordinary Pope – and nothing less would do. Beside so grand a plan, the fate of a scientific hypothesis seemed of little moment.

Galileo was not a man to give up easily. His ecclesiastical friends assured him that he could, in fact, now support the Copernican theory, provided only that he caused no scandal and, of course, remained a faithful churchman. If they were right, and he had no reason to doubt that they were, surely he could at least raise the matter with the Pope; Urban might have become more overtly ecclesiastic but surely he would discuss the matter rationally? And so Galileo broached the

Opposite The so-called Barberini armillary sphere, which may have belonged to Urban VIII.

question, delicately and tactfully, but making his point quite clearly: had he not proved the case of a moving Earth with his explanation of the tides? Would the Church not admit as much, and permit the Copernican doctrine to be advocated once again? After all, the Church had never set its face against disputation, never turned its back on rational discussion; surely then one could legitimately consider arguments based on natural phenomena for and against new scientific views? Was he not right in assuming that the Church did not wish to curtail that? Indeed would it not be desirable for the whole case to be considered dispassionately, for all the facts to be laid out and looked at without bias; might not such a course lead one to see that Man alone could reach no final decision, that he must turn to God, the ultimate authority, for the complete answer? A subtle argument, showing Galileo at his most persuasive; and Urban agreed. Good, he said, go and put forward your ideas with that exquisite balance of scruples with which you always test the truth, but be sure you do not come down in favour of any one hypothesis. Remember, he emphasized, that God was ever free to design the universe just as He wished and cause it to display just those very phenomena that you will persist in calling your 'proof'. To claim otherwise is tantamount to proscribing God's omnipotence, limiting divine power to what can be conceived within the narrow compass of the human mind. No man should have the temerity to do that.

It was an incontrovertible argument, at least to the faithful, and Galileo knew it. He knew, too, that it implied the underlying belief that it was pointless to try to determine the real nature of the world: to the Church science was no more than an interesting intellectual exercise that could never enable Man to probe the essential truths of material creation. Needless to say, this was not an opinion that Galileo could share, but he realized it was no good arguing about so fundamental an issue. And as a faithful member of the Church, he was well aware of the sin of intellectual arrogance; indeed for a time he seemed torn between the two opposing outlooks, the dichotomy between the Church's authoritarianism and science's empiricism, between the dogmatism of the Scriptures and the enquiring mind of the scientist. Yet one thing above all was now clear in his mind: he could at last discuss the Copernican theory. Of course, he must take care to present other views, and must avoid coming down heavily in favour of the heliocentric hypothesis: Urban's argument about divine omnipotence must also be quoted. But these were small matters compared with the essential thing – he could bring Copernican doctrines out into the light once more, and for this he was truly thankful.

Galileo began work on his discussion about the universe soon after his return to Florence, but he took his time; there was no sense in rushing what was to prove a very delicate balancing feat, for in spite of the Pope's requirements, he wanted to present the Copernican hypothesis in the best possible light. At the start he decided to use the familiar form of a dialogue, and use three characters – Salviati, Simplicius and Sagredo. Salviati, modelled directly on his friend Filippo Salviati, who had died in 1614, is the advocate of the Copernican theory and, of course, really speaks for Galileo himself. Simplicius is an Aristotelian and so Salviati's antagonist; based on a sixth-century commentator on Aristotle's physics and astronomy, Galileo casts him as the archetype of the obstinate, unimaginative university professor, a veritable epitome of delle Colombe and his Pisan colleagues, a man so steeped in Aristotelianism that he cannot free himself from its shackles. Salviati and Simplicius were to be set the task of vieing with one another to convince the third disputant, Sagredo, of the truth of their cause. The model for Sagredo was another deceased friend, the Venetian nobleman Giovanfrancesco Sagredo, the paradigm of the best type of leisured Italian intellectual, a man-of-the-world, outspoken, practical and broad-minded, prepared to judge any case on its merits. With these three Galileo knew he could do everything he wanted.

Although Simplicius was in some ways Salviati's butt, Galileo took great care in the way he handled the character. He avoided all bitterness, all cantankerousness; Simplicius was always to be good natured, and even when driven into a corner by argument, never allowed to display anger or become spiteful – at the worst he was allowed to become a little pompous. For instance when Salviati demonstrates that Aristotle really does no more than equivocate when it comes to the question of the difference between celestial and terrestrial bodies and their motions, Simplicius does not argue, he pontificates. 'This manner of thinking tends to the subversion of all natural philosophy and to the disorder and upsetting of Heaven and Earth and the whole Universe. But I believe the fundamentals of the Peripatetics [Aristotelians] are such that we need not fear that new sciences can be erected on their ruins.'[2] And this extract is typical of Simplicius' outlook: it is set. He knows all the answers, not from experiment and observation, not even from logical discussion, but because the authorities have said so. When Sagredo asks Simplicius 'How do you know that celestial rarity and density do not depend on heat and cold?', he receives the simple reply, 'I know it because those qualities do not belong to celestial bodies which are neither hot nor cold';[3] to which he might well have added 'because Aristotle said so'. Yet in spite of his mental rigidity, in spite of Salviati's enthusiasm for a totally opposed viewpoint, the discussion is always a very gentlemanly affair, at least on the surface. But then Galileo was drawing on real characters who would have behaved in this very way; as Fulgenzio Micanzio later wrote to Galileo, 'How beautifully you have given life to our dear Sagredo. God help me, it is as if I heard him speak again.'[4]

How hard Galileo tried to exercise those virtues of impartiality that seemed foreign to his nature, how much he really wanted to balance the arguments for and against Copernicanism, we shall never know, because he was completely and utterly unsuccessful. Admittedly none of the disputants come to any firm conclusion, ostensibly the Copernican view does not win the day, Salviati does not emerge triumphant with Simplicius hanging his head in shame. Nevertheless the uncommitted reader is bound to come to the conclusion that the Ptolemaic theory is dead, with nothing to offer; Salviati pumps it so full of holes that it is no longer a viable proposition. Aristotelian physics and the peripatetic style of argument fares equally badly: Simplicius retreats into dogmatism, relies not on argument but on statements of position, and visibly weakens the Aristotelian-Ptolemaic case in the glare of Salviati's penetrating arguments. One can see, too, the way Sagredo is thinking; one senses how his mind is going, even though he does not commit himself in so many words. In brief, by a masterly use of language, and a subtle delineation of character, Galileo wrote a book that could not be faulted, that would stand up to any amount of textual analysis, and yet made the case for Copernicus as strongly as if he had just settled down and repeated all the arguments he had used so effectively over the previous thirty years. He had kept to the letter of the law – Copernicanism was still treated as a hypothesis – but the spirit was very different. Certainly it is true that Galileo wrote a preface to the book that seems to support the anti-Copernican view, but his enemies remained unconvinced when they later saw it, and referring to it bitterly as a 'wretched hypocrisy',[5] and they were, to a great extent, right. The preface was hardly Galileo's, since the major part of it was dictated to him by his friend Niccolò Riccardi, Master of the Holy Apostolic Palace, who saw below the surface of the text the minute he had read it and was thereafter a very worried man. However it did contain one piece of pure Galileo, and this was the short section that expressed some measure of his own feelings:

I have personated the Copernican in this discourse, proceeding upon an hypothesis purely mathematical; striving by every artifice to represent it superior not to that of the immobility of the Earth absolutely, but as it is defended by some who, claiming to profess the Peripatetic doctrine, retain of it no more than the name, and are content, foregoing the old ways, to adore shadows, not philosophizing with their own intelligence but with the sole remembrance of a few principles badly understood.[6]

As far as the text itself was concerned, Galileo divided it into four 'days' of discussion. The first of these was devoted to explaining the Aristotelian case and running over all the stock arguments, but with a liveliness and a literary skill that prevents the reader from being bored: indeed by a kind of dialectic magic he manages to make the whole philosophical discourse generate emotion as well as acting as a mental stimulant. Yet the subtle anti-Copernican feeling is there: Simplicius is for ever dogmatic and authoritarian, Salviati continually stresses the need to test what the authorities say by mathematical analysis. And when we come to matters like the solid crystal spheres of the heavens so beloved of the Aristotelians in Galileo's day, and a subject of philosophical faith over which no argument could ever prevail, he resorts to ridicule: Simplicius says how hard and yet how utterly transparent the heavenly spheres are, and Sagredo immediately comments 'What excellent matter would the heavens afford us to make palaces, if only we could procure a substance so hard and so transparent!',[7] while Salviati goes one better: 'Rather how improper, for it being, by its transparence, wholly invisible, a man would not be able, without stumbling at the thresholds and breaking his head against the walls, to pass from room to room.' No, says Sagredo continuing the mockery, 'This danger would not befall him, if it be true, as some Peripatetics say, that this matter is intangible; and if one cannot touch it, much less can it hurt him.' 'This would not serve the turn,' Salviati says, 'for while the intangible matter of the heavens cannot be touched, yet it may easily touch the elementary bodies [i.e. the stars and planets]. But let us leave these palaces, or, to say better, these castles in the air, and not interrupt Simplicius.' So poor Simplicius is forced to proceed, admitting that 'the question which you have so casually started is one of the most difficult that is disputed in philosophy. . . .', and one can almost hear Galileo chuckling 'you bet it is!'

The second and third days are concerned with the diurnal rotation of the Earth and the possibility of its annual orbit round the Sun. All the Aristotelian arguments are trotted out: if the Earth rotated on its axis, everything would have a tendency to fly off into space, terrible winds and tempests would arise, and no birds would be able to fly. Counter arguments are given; for instance Galileo shows that to be consistent, an object chopped from the mast of a ship should fall to the deck some distance away whereas it does no such thing; instead it drops straight down to the bottom of the mast. And above all, he draws the important scientific distinction between horizontal and vertical motions, a subject on which he was utterly clear and the Aristotelians completely bemused. He also takes the opportunity of attacking that mental quirk, still present with us in the twentieth century, of giving something a name and then thinking we understand it. What, says Salviati, makes the Earth move? He will tell Simplicius, 'if he can only tell me what moves the parts of the Earth downwards'. 'The cause of this is most manifest,' retorts Simplicius, 'and everyone knows it is gravity.' No, Salviati replies, 'You are out Simplicius; you should say that everyone knows that it is *called* gravity, and I do not question you about the name but about the essence of the thing. Of this you know not a little more than you know the essence of the mover of the stars. . . .'[8]

Particularly in these sections of the text, Galileo makes brilliant use of the Socratic method of extracting the facts by a series of carefully phrased questions. This comes out very clearly in the discussion of the Aristotelian argument that if the Earth rotates on its axis, things would be thrown up into the air: *Simplicius*: 'The argument seems to me very well proved and enforced; and I believe it would be a hard matter to try and overthrow it.'[9] Ah, says Salviati, 'Its solution depends upon certain notions no less known and believed by you than by myself; but, as they do not come into your mind, you do not perceive the answer. Wherefore, without telling you (for you know it already), I shall, by only assisting your memory, make you refute this argument.' After a slight diversion by Simplicius and Sagredo, Salviati goes on, using the behaviour of a stone in a sling as his example: 'Let Simplicius tell me what motion the stone makes when it is held fast in the slit of the sling as the boy swings it about to throw it.'[10] *Simplicius:* 'The motion of the stone, so long as it is in the slit, is circular. . . .' *Salviati:* 'And when the stone leaves the sling?' *Simplicius:* 'It will continue no longer to swing round. . . .' *Salviati:* 'With what motion does it then move?' *Simplicius:* 'Give me a little time to think; for I have never considered it before.' Simplicius then comes to the conclusion that the stone would move outwards. Precisely by what path? Simplicius is forced to give a geometrical answer. Salviati then changes the questions to the behaviour of a projectile – a subject on which the Aristotelians were seriously in error – and makes Simplicius conclude that 'gravity' pulls it down. Salviati then ties the two arguments together and Simplicius is forced to declare that 'like a simpleton, I have suffered myself to be persuaded that stones could not be extruded by the revolution of the Earth!'[11] Subtle, clever: the Aristotelian is persuaded against his will, the opposing view is extracted out of his own mouth, and the Copernican case receives another sound argument which would tell with the fair-minded reader, even though Galileo allows Simplicius in the next breath to repudiate his conclusion.

By the time the text of the dialogue was complete Galileo was in his mid-sixties, but his mind was alive as ever. In the fourth 'day', in which he discusses his theory of the tides as a proof of the Earth's motion in space – the argument that he believed proved that Copernicanism was a true explanation of the universe – he suggests a number of novel astronomical ideas. He speculates about a large and extensive universe, and proposes a method for determining stellar distances that was based on the orbital motion of the Earth and which astronomers were to use successfully two centuries later. And of course, in the context of the dialogue, he uses these as yet other points with which to bolster the Copernican cause. But the theory of the tides was really the culminating point, the apex to which all the rest of the discussions and arguments had led. Indeed, Galileo felt so strongly about it, he believed it to be so crucial, so important, that it was his original intention to call the book *On The Flux and Reflux of the Sea*. However Urban would not agree: the book was about the two main philosophical systems of the universe? Then its title should make that clear, and finally it was decided that it should be called *Dialogue on the Great World Systems*.

What of the text itself, of the book as a whole; was it really acceptable to the authorities, would the Church give its *imprimatur* so that publication could become a reality? Anticipating this, Galileo had made sure that the Pope's argument about divine omnipotence was quoted, at least in general tenor even if not word for word. At the end of the fourth and final day, he makes Simplicius say:

As for the past discourses, and particularly this last, of the reason of the ebbing and flowing of the sea, I do not, to speak the truth, very well comprehend it. But by that slight

Frontispiece of the first edition of Galileo's *Dialogue*, 1632. The figures represent, from left to right, Aristotle, Ptolemy and Copernicus.

idea, whatever it be, that I have formed thereof to myself, I confess that your hypothesis seems to me far more ingenious than any of all those that I have ever heard, besides; still, I esteem it neither true nor conclusive, but, keeping always before the eyes of my mind a solid doctrine that I once received from a most learned and eminent person, and to which there can be no answer, I know that both of you, being asked whether God, by his infinite power and wisdom, might confer upon the element of water the reciprocal motion in any other way than by making the contained vessel to move, I know, I say, that you will always answer that he could, and also knew him to bring it about in many ways, and some of them above the reach of our intellect. Upon which I forthwith conclude that, this being granted, it would be an extravagant boldness for anyone to go about to limit and confine the Divine power and wisdom to some one particular conjecture of his own.[12]

To this peroration Salviati answers: 'An admirable and truly angelical doctrine . . .', with Sagredo not daring to disagree, but hoping for further dis-

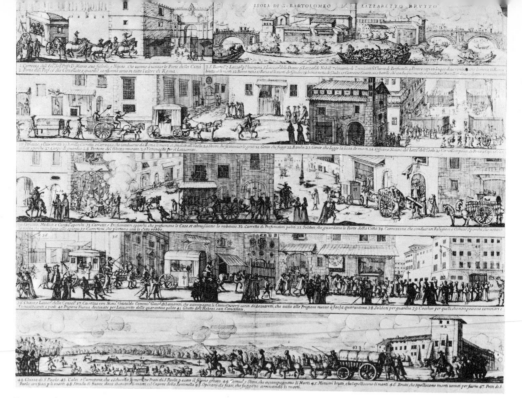

In 1630 there was a vast epidemic of plague throughout northern and central Italy. A seventeenth century engraving showing the municipally organized fumigation of houses and the disposal of the dead during an epidemic in Rome.

cussions at some other time. A somewhat tame ending to an anything but a tame discourse, yet one that at least met the Pope's expressed wish.

Galileo's original plan was that the book should be published by the Lincean Academy, Prince Cesi making all arrangements for the printing, and Niccolò Riccardi seeing that it was licensed for publication. Everyone was happy with the arrangement and on 3 May 1630 Galileo arrived in Rome with the manuscript, Urban endorsed the idea of publishing a dialogue, repeated his conditions and made his specification about the title. All seemed plain sailing and Riccardi took the manuscript and read it, but the more he read, the more worried he became. He therefore handed the manuscript over to his assistant Raffaello Visconti, who read it through, changed a few words, but saw nothing in it to give ground for concern. Riccardi, on the other hand, remained doubtful: rumours were reaching him that Galileo's enemies knew that he had prepared a new book, and although they did not know precisely what it said, they were stirring up as unfavourable an atmosphere as they could for its reception. So in the end he decided to go over the entire text in detail himself. This made for delay which neither pleased Galileo nor the dedicatee, the Grand Duke Ferdinand who had now succeeded Cosimo as Tuscan ruler, and between them they managed to persuade Riccardi to send the sheets to the printer as soon as he had read them, but as the printer could only print if he had a licence, Riccardi was also forced to arrange for one to be issued. It was at this juncture that he persuaded Galileo to write the special preface which, he fondly hoped, might cut some of the ground from under the feet of Galileo's enemies. And so, by the end of June 1630, Galileo returned to Florence, away from the 'unhealthy air' of Rome where there was a lot of malaria, with a promise that he would have the new preface ready by the autumn for, as he knew, precious little, if anything at all, would be done during the rest of the summer.

A few weeks after Galileo's return, he received a serious blow: Prince Cesi died. This was an irreparable loss, for Cesi was the ideal mediator and executive to see that the whole operation ran smoothly, and without him there was hardly a soul in Rome on whom Galileo could rely. Possibly he might have asked Ciampoli, but in spite of an official position, he had nothing like Cesi's influence, and, as it soon transpired, things were not well in Rome; late in August Castelli, who was not a man ever to harbour suspicions, wrote to Galileo begging him 'for many most weighty considerations'[13] which he did not wish to commit to paper, to get the book published in Florence, and as soon as possible. Galileo hesitated but only temporarily: the plague, which had already become a serious emergency in the north of Italy, had now spread to the central areas, quarantine stations were established and communication between even local regions was difficult, so if the book was to be published at all it must now be under his own personal direction. But to have the book published in Florence meant that it must be licensed there and not in Rome; so the text was given to the Florentine Inquisitor, Giacinto Stefani to read. Stefani could find nothing wrong; he did change the odd word here and there but, in general, he said he was 'moved to tears at many passages by the humility and reverent obedience displayed by the author'.[14] Thus far, so good, but there was still Riccardi to contend with. He had the revised preface and the conclusion but refused to part with them, so pressure had to be brought to bear once again, and as a start the Tuscan ambassador in Rome was instructed to do what he could. The ambassador now was another Galileo supporter, Francesco Niccolini whose wife was Riccardi's cousin, but only after a good deal of persuasion, could Niccolini write back to say that the 'Monster' (the family name for Riccardi) agreed to the final revision being made in Florence. Yet still there was delay because Niccolini did not have the remaining sections of the manuscript. By now the trouble seems to have been that Riccardi, who was a Jesuit, had learned that Scheiner and Grassi were on the warpath and had stirred up the whole of the Roman College; naturally enough he feared for his own position and hoped to procrastinate until a more opportune time for publication should arrive, if it ever did. How frightened Riccardi was may be judged from the fact that he even tried to defy the Grand Duke himself, who besides his elevated position had the extra lever of being liege lord of the Riccardi family. But in the end, he could hold out no longer, and on 19 July 1631 'dragged by the hair',[15] wrote Niccolini, the Monster brought the outstanding documents to the Embassy; and seven months later, in February 1632, Galileo was at last able, to hand a copy of the book to the Grand Duke. *The Dialogue of the Two Great World Systems* was out in the open.

15
The Storm Breaks

The *Dialogue* was a dangerous book. Written in Italian, its influence, its subtle arguments and its advocacy of the Copernican system, could percolate through to anyone who could read, and the response of the public was enormous: it quite literally sold out as it came off the press. Due to quarantine problems publication in Rome was delayed by four months, but as soon as it was available there, the same thing happened. Indeed, there is a story that while Scheiner was in a Rome bookshop, a friar from Siena came in and began to be vociferous in his praises of the *Dialogue*; Scheiner blanched, began to tremble and then offered a high sum to anyone who could procure a copy for him.

It was soon after this that rumours began to circulate of serious disapproval of the *Dialogue* within the Church, or at least within some sectors of it, and Riccardi, who feared the worst from his brother Jesuits, sent warnings post-haste to Florence. He also tried to get all the copies held at the embassy out of Niccolini, but failed. The Grand Duke was appraised of the situation and forthwith instructed Niccolini to deliver a very stiff diplomatic letter to the Pope, a decision which on the face of it may look like premature over-reaction, but was due as much to political as ecclesiastical reasons, since by the time the *Dialogue* came out, Rome and Tuscany were at loggerheads on the question of foreign policy. What had happened is that Barberini had been pursuing his aim of shifting the balance of power in Europe, since the Thirty Years War had reached a stage when he thought he could at last act the part he had cast for himself. In France Cardinal Richelieu, in an attempt to break the Hapsburg influence, had made a deal with the Protestant Swedish king Gustavus Adolphus who, since the Hapsburgs were staunch supporters of the Counter-Reformation, was quite prepared to accede to Richelieu's request to refrain from molesting certain Catholic princes in exchange for a chance to reduce Hapsburg power by force. For his part Urban VIII feared the Hapsburg influence in Italy, so he too concluded a secret alliance with Gustavus Adolphus. On the other hand the Medicis, and especially the Grand Duke Ferdinand, had no love for Richelieu who, in 1630, had exiled Marie de' Medici from France, so they countered his moves by allying themselves with the Hapsburgs. A potentially explosive situation, fraught with undercurrents of distrust and suspicion, it had seriously deteriorated two months before the *Dialogue* had appeared in Rome, when Gustavus Adolphus had suddenly died and the Pope's secret treaty had come out into the open. Urban was furious, both at the failure of his master plan, and the fact that it had become common knowledge that for political reasons he would even ally himself to a Protestant prince.

Urban VIII by Pietro da Cortona.

Left Ferdinand II de' Medici whose support of Galileo so angered Urban VIII that he went as far as to utter veiled threats of excommunication. Marble bust with porphyry head.

Below The Sala dei Santi Pontefici, in the Vatican, with decorations by Pinturicchio.

When Niccolini went to the Vatican to deliver his note about the *Dialogue*, he knew then it was likely to be a stormy interview, but even he was surprised at the Pope's anger. Urban shouted at him, 'Your Galileo has ventured to meddle with things he ought not and with the most grave and dangerous subjects that can be stirred up these days.'[1] Niccolini replied that the *Dialogue* had received Vatican approval, but Urban retorted that Niccolini and Ciampoli had circumvented him by the action they had taken to get the book published, and deliberately misled him by saying all was well with the text. But Niccolini had his answer: surely, the Pope would not stop the sale of a book already approved without, at the least, talking to Galileo himself and hearing what he had to say? In other words he deliberately implied that Urban had found it convenient to believe hearsay evidence and accept a specific interpretation of the text just because he did not see eye to eye with the Grand Duke, and gave him a veiled warning not to precipitate an 'international incident'; those who had the Hapsburgs on their side were in the stronger position. But Urban was not to be intimidated, and countered Niccolini's remarks with veiled threats about excommunicating the Grand Duke if he opposed papal authority.

Urban's reaction was partly political, but this was not the sole reason for his outburst: Riccardi was right, the Jesuits had been busy. Thanks mainly to Grassi and Scheiner, the powerful Roman College had been inflamed to fever pitch, and was now determined on bitter retaliation against Galileo and everyone connected with the book. Scheiner had been nursing a dull fury ever since Galileo's *History and Demonstrations Concerning Sunspots* had come out some twenty years earlier, but it had only come to a peak when the *Dialogue* appeared, and after he had convinced himself that Galileo's argument that sunspots were evidence for the Earth's motion, was plagiarized from his *Rosa Ursina*. It was a totally unfounded supposition since the *Dialogue* was already in the press long before *Rosa Ursina* appeared, but coupled with the *Dialogue*'s claim that Galileo was the first to observe sunspots, it was inflammatory enough, while for his part Grassi, it is now clear, was still smarting under the whiplash of Galileo's *Assayer*. The Roman College itself, a centre of learning with a collection of scholars who could comprehend the *Dialogue*'s text and also read between the lines, was a hot-bed for the kind of antagonism that Scheiner and Grassi cultivated. But hatred within the College was not enough, they had to stir up the Pope's antagonism, for whatever political overtones there might be, Urban was still Galileo's friend. Their ploy was simple, direct and eminently successful: they simply pointed out to Urban that the crucial criticism of the powerful tidal theory had been put into the mouth of the foolish Simplicius. Yet this was His Holiness' own argument, given direct by him to Galileo, who had therefore betrayed his trust and friendship by using Simplicius, the archetype of the bad Aristotelian philosopher, the butt of Salviati and Sagredo, to quote it. There was, of course, no sure evidence that this was so: indeed if Urban himself had made a careful study of the text he would have seen that the burden of his argument – the omnipotence of God – had been given earlier as well, and by one of the other disputants. On the 'third day', when they were discussing the fixed stars and Galileo implied, through Salviati, the infinite extent of space, Sagredo indirectly supported him by saying: 'Great in my judgement is the ineptitude of those who would have had God to have made the Universe more proportional to the narrow capacities of their reason than to his immense, rather, infinite, power.'[2] But the Pope was in no mood to look at the book in detail; he was in dire trouble politically and, as far as the *Dialogue* was concerned, out of favour with the Jesuits for having it published, and he well knew their displeasure could readily turn on him. Always a sensitive man, his ego was now most vulnerable, and what the Jesuits had pointed out hurt deeply; but for good measure the Roman College had not left things there. They had warned him that the text was a subtle advocacy of the Copernican doctrine, a doctrine which they claimed was far more dangerous and insidious than anything of Luther's or

Opposite A meeting of cardinals. From a contemporary engraving.

Left The Barberini bee, part of the arms of Urban VIII. Motif on a mantelpiece in Castel Sant' Angelo. During Urban's papacy the Vatican court was dominated by members of the Barberini family and the bee is a recurrent symbol in the paintings and sculptures of that period.

Below Giovanni Ciampoli, one of Galileo's most devoted friends, was sacked as Secretary of the Briefs and never allowed to return to Rome as punishment for his staunch support of the rebel. Engraving after Ottavio Leoni.

Calvin's. And of course, for his part, Galileo had been less than frank; he had paid lip service to the Papal injunction, he had legally obeyed Urban's ruling but had denied the spirit of their agreement. To Urban it could seem that Galileo was guilty of double dealing; that he had meddled with things that he should not, and in devious underhand ways at that. Moreover, he had ridiculed the Pope, but no man could insult the Holy Father with impunity; Galileo must pay the price. And not Galileo only: others had been party to this disgraceful charade, and they too must suffer.

Urban's fury was intense and long-lived. First he summoned Riccardi who, however, was able to extricate himself by pleading that he had his doubts and offer his ineffectual attempts at procrastination as evidence that he had tried to

Another steadfast Galilean supporter was Ascanio Piccolomini, Archbishop of Siena. Engraving after Ottavio Leoni.

withhold publication. Riccardi escaped, but not so Ciampoli who was sacked as Secretary of the Briefs, and exiled first to the small town of Montalto della Marca as governor, and then kept on the move from one provincial centre to another but never allowed to return to Rome, his hopes of a cardinal's hat dashed for ever. Yet, surprisingly, Ciampoli took his demotion philosophically; he never turned against Galileo, whom he always called 'my persecuted Socrates'.[3]

And what of Galileo himself: how did he view the papal temper? Surprisingly, he seems to have been completely at a loss to understand what all the fuss was about. As far as he was concerned, he had obeyed the injunction, treating the arguments as inconclusive; he had been specifically permitted to discuss Copernicanism as a hypothesis and this is what he had done; and he had been careful to reach no firm answer. He had dutifully and deliberately quoted Urban's argument twice, and the fact that he had put it at its fullest into the mouth of Simplicius had been unintentional; indeed it did not even cross his mind that this could be construed in any way derogatory to the Pope. And this was also the view of his friends, Niccolini and Ascanio Piccolomini, the archbishop of Siena. The Pope, they told him, was very upset over other things and that if he would only stay quiet, the whole affair would blow over. Issue no denials about your intentions, they explained, give no cause for irritation and in time the matter will be forgotten. There was, it is true, idle chatter that since Galileo still supported Copernicanism, he would be arraigned for heresy, but no one really took any notice. Niccolini, the experienced career diplomat, dismissed the rumours as exaggerated, and Piccolomini could see no cause for such a charge after the clever way Galileo had handled the arguments in the *Dialogue*. And their assessment seemed to be confirmed when, in September, an obscure young scientist, Evangelista Torricelli, a pupil of Castelli, wrote to Galileo, and by way of introduction, openly declared himself to be 'Copernican by conviction, by profession and sect Galileist':[4] if charges of heresy were rumoured, no one would dare to be so frank.

For once Galileo's friends were wrong; they had miscalculated the forces that were ranged against them. And as for Galileo himself, he should perhaps have realized that his text was not everything it should have been: he had given the impression that Aristotle's universe and Aristotle's physics were totally wrong, and the heliocentric theory with a moving Earth was a true physical picture of the real nature of things. Above all, the ending of the fourth day was undeniably weak. But perhaps Galileo was too close to the book to see it as a whole, and anyway all along he had the feeling that the original papal injunction about Copernicus would soon be swept away in the new 'papacy of the virtuosi', so he doubtless felt no one would object to his giving the movement new impetus. Certainly, he seems to have felt sure the Pope would support him for, after all, Urban VIII had already shown himself to be broadminded; in 1626 he had intervened to have Tommaso Campanella, ex-Dominican, Hermetist, occultist, overt practitioner of magic, released from prison. Surely a Pope who could do this would not object to

Cardinal Francesco Barberini was appointed by his uncle, Urban VIII, as chairman of a special committee to investigate Galileo's *Dialogue*. School of Bernini.

the way the *Dialogue* was written, would even applaud the witty discussions that followed, for Galileo's early experience of Urban had convinced him that here was a man who found the obscurantist Aristotelian as much an anathema as he did himself. Unhappily Galileo never realized the resentment and bitterness his *Assayer* and his earlier *History and Demonstrations Concerning Sunspots* had caused, yet it was here, above all, that the trouble lay; indeed if any persons are to be charged with responsibility for the tragedy that was to follow, it is probably Grassi and Scheiner who should share the blame. Urban was guilty of blind fury, but he was goaded into this by others: given time things would have simmered down, just as Niccolini and Piccolomini thought they should. But time was not on their side, and Galileo's hopes that the *Dialogue* would be allowed to circulate freely, turned out to be unfounded.

In the middle of August 1632 the Florentine publisher, Battista Landini, was ordered to suspend all sale of the *Dialogue*, and at the same time the Pope appointed a special committee under the chairmanship of his nephew Cardinal Francesco Barberini to examine the book and report on its contents: did it do as the Jesuits were claiming or not? Francesco Barberini was well-disposed towards Galileo and it is a point in Urban's favour that he did not immediately ban the book and castigate Galileo; he did not allow himself to be browbeaten into irrevocable action before he had at least had a report from some 'independent' advisors. The report of the young cardinal's committee was soon made and, unhappily, it was not favourable to Galileo. He had, they said, presented the Copernican doctrine of a moving Earth as a fact of reality rather than a pure hypothesis, giving the reader the impression that it was the true explanation of the universe instead of just an ingenious proposal. Yet this was not all: the supposition that the tides proved the motion of the Earth was wrong, a totally erroneous idea and the whole book, in its approach and in the tenor of its text, went against the edict of 1616. The *Dialogue* as it stood was unacceptable to the Church and it must be suspended for correction.

The report itself is not surprising, especially since the Barberini Committee had some members serving on it who were not well disposed towards Galileo, but what is unexpected is the mild verdict. Galileo had broken the Church's very definite ruling about promoting the Copernican view – the Committee was in no doubt about this – yet they do not rave about dire penalties, they make no suggestion that the author should be taken to task: the worst they do is to recommend that the book be suspended until it is corrected. Obviously then, they considered the 1616 ruling something that should be obeyed, but not serious enough in intent to make it necessary to recommend that the Inquisition should be alerted. The book would be withdrawn and the emphasis changed, that was all. But Urban had different ideas, and in spite of Niccolini's report that the Grand Duke thought the Committee's report was rubbish, Urban called the Inquisition in and in no time the Inquisitor at Florence called at Galileo's house and served him with a formal summons to present himself at Rome within thirty days to answer charges that were to be brought against him.

Galileo immediately retired to bed in a state of shock, appalled at the sudden turn of events, stunned that his old friend Urban could permit so cruel a blow to fall completely unheralded. Now he was in no doubt about how serious matters were, how badly he had miscalculated the licence he thought Urban would permit, yet what could he do? How could he extricate himself from the terrifying situation in which he was enmeshed? Perhaps Urban would remember his age, recognize the rigours of a wintertime journey of more than two hundred miles to Rome and rescind the order. So Galileo wrote and pleaded that he was now sixty-eight and too frail to make the trip; if he tried to do so, it was more than likely he would not reach Rome alive. Nor was this just an excuse, for he suffered severely from arthritis and, by this time, had a double hernia that forced him to wear an iron truss, so a long journey was certainly no light matter. Hoping against hope, he waited for a reply, and meanwhile his plight became a talking point outside court circles. Surprisingly, the first reaction came not from Rome but from Venice: with that show of independence for which they were famous, the Venetians offered him sanctuary there. The old statesman Francesco Morosini, asked Galileo if he would not return to Padua: his precipitous departure of twenty years before would be forgotten and the Venetian State would prove to be deaf to the Pope's demands. But Galileo declined. He seems to have felt that he must obey his Church: if the Pope stood firm, if the summons to Rome was not withdrawn, then he would have to go. Of course he would try hard to extricate himself, to plead, to make excuses, and genuine ones too, but in the end it was the Pope's will he must obey: if Urban would not relent, then as a good Catholic he must do as he was told. And perhaps, after all, there were alternatives the Church would accept: possibly the Inquisition could deal with the matter in Florence, perhaps His Holiness might permit Galileo to revise the book and send his revision to Rome? But Urban was implacable, and a second summons was delivered. Galileo was still ill in bed, so he had a certificate signed by three medical men saying he was suffering from fits of giddiness, 'hypochondriacal melancholy',[5] a weak stomach, insomnia, and various sudden pains; yet it did no good. The Holy Office of the Inquisition replied with a papal mandate which bluntly stated that no more procrastination would be tolerated, either Galileo travelled to Rome or an officer and a physician from the Holy Office would come and collect him, and bring him back in chains. And if, when they arrived, they did find him too ill to travel, they would wait until he was well enough. There was no way out.

Further resistance seemed impossible. The Grand Duke, although ruler of Tuscany, had not sufficient power to withstand the Pope: he could not rely on Hapsburg support on a matter like this, and did not possess the political independence of Venice. All that was left to him was to ameliorate the situation as best he could. He ordered his own litter to be prepared for the journey and his embassy in Rome to receive Galileo and put quarters at his disposal and, ignoring the advice of his Secretary of State, Ferdinand instructed Niccolini to do everything he could for Galileo's defence. Fortunately, Galileo's health had now begun to improve and by the middle of January 1633 he was fighting fit. He seems to have come to terms with the situation, and was ready to do battle with the ecclesiastical authorities over the whole Copernican question; indeed he was, he said, ready even to argue about the theological points, about the Scriptures, if they wanted it that way. This was the Galileo of old. Not so Urban; still all fury and righteous indignation, he was also beside himself with worry about his political failure and its possible consequences, so that it was even said that he lived in daily fear of being poisoned. And this seems to have been more than idle gossip, for not only did he retreat to Castel Gandolfo, some ten miles outside Rome, but he ordered the road to be constantly patrolled and would see no one until they had been thoroughly searched.

When Galileo arrived in Rome at the Tuscan embassy on 13 February, after twenty-three days on the road, he found a warm bed awaiting him and Caterina Niccolini, the ambassador's wife, saw to it that his every need was met: she was, Galileo wrote, 'queen of all kindness'.[6] As for the Holy Office, this took its time:

Chiesa di S Tomasso Villa noua edificata da N Sig· PROSPETTO DELLA PIAZZA DI CASTELLO CANDOLFO AMPLI 3 Fontana ristaurata da N Sig·
PP·ALESSANDRO VII· ATA E RABBELLITA DA N·S·PP·ALESSANDRO VII
Palazzo Pontificio restaurato da N Sio· Gio Batta Falda def et fec Per Gio Iacomo Rossi in Roma alla Pace con Priu del S Pont·

The papal residence and church of Castel Gandolfo, on the outskirts of Rome, where Urban VIII retired in righteous indignation as Galileo made his way to Rome to face the Inquisition.

it did not try to stampede Galileo into an ill-considered confession, nor did it threaten him with an immediate trial. Instead he was allowed to stay quietly in the Embassy for a few weeks, and only after this did they begin to take any action, and that was limited to visits from a few officials, who seemed friendly and courteous enough. Indeed Niccolini could write 'We find a wonderful pleasure in the gentle conversation of this good old man',[7] and later on say that as far as he could make out, the whole business merely boiled down to the question of what the edict of 1616 was all about, and that on this Galileo had a private letter from Bellarmine and felt very confident. The Grand Duke was relieved and reckoned that he could now begin putting pressure on the Pope to send Galileo back home. After all, a situation that had once looked so serious, so terrifying in its proportions, was now being cut down to size; soon the whole silly business would be over.

M.ᵃ ſopra Minerua il di 3. ſbre 1697. alla preſenza de g...
...rali Inquiſitori in tutta la Republica Chriſtiana, e di tutto
gio. Di tutti li Conſultori, e molti altri Prelati, Prencipi,
Popolo numeroſiſſ.ᵒ di queſt' alma Città di Roma.
All' Em.ᵐᵒ e Reu.ᵐᵒ Pnp̄e. Sig.ʳᵉ e Pron̄ mio Col.ᵐᵒ Il
FLAVIO CHIGI.

16
Trial

The Grand Duke Ferdinand was too sanguine, and so was his ambassador Niccolini; the courtesy of the visitors from the Holy Office and the whole tenor of Galileo's treatment gave them both a false sense of security. But they had not reckoned on Urban's implacability, on his determination to stage a formal trial. Certainly this was due partly to personal pique, partly to his fear for his position and his hope that by humbling Galileo, he could get at the Grand Duke, but it was in part due also to a real ecclesiastical problem that faced the Roman Catholic Church at the time. A number of books of doubtful orthodoxy, expressing new and not always welcome opinions, had been appearing, and although their authors had been forced to submit to their ecclesiastical superiors, they had been un-molested provided only that they acquiesced. Now this movement towards freedom had begun to show its dangers; Galileo had joined its ranks, and Galileo was famous; what he said carried weight, and since he wrote in the vernacular his opinions were spreading far outside the limited circles of the cognoscenti. He advocated independent thought and continually attacked authority, scientific authority it is true, but authority none the less; and he recommended an individual approach to every problem, a testing of every fact, an acceptance of none just because they had the patina of age or the aura of antiquity. But this way lay danger, danger to the sacred authority of Mother Church, and none realized it more than the Jesuits, who were not slow to point out to the Pope that the health of the Church must come before the fate of a man and his theories.

The possibility of a trial had always been there, but as far as Galileo and his friends were concerned, the Inquisition's case seemed a weak one: the edict of 1616 and Bellarmine's admonition were not strong enough for a formal con-demnation. Yet what none of them knew was that the document in the Vatican files purporting to record the events of 1616 was a false one which stated that Galileo had received a solemn command from the Commissary-General of the Holy Office, and had been instructed to 'relinquish absolutely' the concept of a moving Earth and a central Sun, and told categorically that he must not 'hold, teach or defend it in any way whatsoever, verbally or in writing'.[1] This was a very different matter: a strong legal case could be made out on the basis of that docu-ment, since there was absolutely no doubt that in writing the *Dialogue*, Galileo had failed to comply with the injunction. He had put into Salviati's mouth argu-ments that specifically 'defended' the Copernican theory, whilst the very publica-tion of the book could be construed as evidence that he had ignored the instruction to do nothing 'in any way whatsoever, in verbally or in writing'.

Opposite A seventeenth-century engraving of a public recantation before the Inquisition in the church of Santa Maria Sopra Minerva.

When Galileo and Niccolini heard there was to be a trial after all, they were of course confident Galileo would clear himself quite easily; all that Niccolini warned Galileo about was that however strong his case he must not be arrogant, he must answer 'gently and submissively'. So it was with some assurance that, on 12 April 1633, Galileo presented himself before the Dominican Commissary-General of the Holy Office and his assistants. And everything seemed to begin innocently enough, questions being put to Galileo about his visit to Rome in 1616, and enquiring its purpose. Galileo answered fully, without prevarication, and with due deference just as Niccolini had advised. The questioning then moved on to the injunction itself, and only then did it become evident to Galileo that something was wrong: he began to get suspicious and become more chary in his answers. At last the Inquisitors came out into the open and began to quote from the false document. Galileo was astounded for this was not his recollection of what had happened. No, the Commissary-General had not done what the statement said, he, Galileo, had only been 'admonished' by Cardinal Bellarmine. No, he did not recollect being instructed 'not to teach', and certainly could not remember the significant words 'in any way whatsoever'. Yes, it was indeed some seventeen years before, but he would not have forgotten anything so important, so vital to his own well-being. Of course rumours had circulated, as was well known; they had spread through Rome and even reached Florence, but they were false. Yes, he had heard them and had taken action to stop them; he had even been to see Cardinal Bellarmine, and asked for his help in contradicting them. Very graciously the Cardinal had written a letter in his own hand and with permission he would read it. Yes, he would like to submit this as evidence that he had merely been told of the Church's edict and advised to abandon the theory. And it was as well that he did, for Bellarmine's document was strongly worded:

We, Roberto Cardinal Bellarmine, having heard that it is calumniously reported that Signor Galileo Galilei has in our hand abjured and has also been punished with salutary penance, and being requested to state the truth about this, declare that the said Signor Galileo has not abjured either in our hand, or the hand of any other person here in Rome ... any opinion or doctrine held by him; neither has salutary penance been imposed on him; but that only the declaration made by the Holy Father and published by the Sacred Congregation of the Index has been notified to him, wherein it is set forth that the doctrine attributed to Copernicus, that the Earth moves around the Sun and that the Sun is stationary in the centre of the world and does not move from east to west, is contrary to the Holy Scriptures and therefore cannot be defended or held.[2]

The judges accepted the document, but it obviously presented them with a puzzle. Here, clearly, was a serious piece of evidence, and one which was totally at variance with the report in the Vatican archives. Bellarmine had been dead for more than a decade and could not be asked his opinion, so the judges were forced to take the letter away to consider at their leisure. But the questioning could con-

tinue since the second matter to be dealt with was the *Dialogue* itself, and they had
a report on it by the Inquisition's counsellors, a report that said Galileo had not
only discussed the Copernican theory, but had 'maintained, taught and defended'
it, although its words of condemnation were obviously lifted from the false
document.

After the hearing was over, Galileo returned to the embassy, shocked at the
evidence that had been offered, and in no doubt but that the Inquisition was hardly
likely to send him back to Florence immediately as the Grand Duke hoped. The
judges were to deliberate in their own good time, and who knew how long this
might take; indeed after a fortnight Galileo had still heard nothing. However the
silence was not complete. Cardinal Francesco Barberini, who had headed the
Pope's commission on the *Dialogue*, felt that the trial should not be unduly
dragged out – something that frequently happened – and brought pressure to
bear on the Commissary-General so that he went privately to the embassy to talk
with Galileo. From a letter he had recently received from Castelli, Galileo knew
that the Commissary-General, Vincenzo Maculano da Firenzuola, was really in
sympathy with his outlook and thought that the Bible was not the place to look
for scientific truth: the Scriptures were the authority on spiritual matters, not on
science. But when Maculano came, he could not hold out much hope whatever he
might feel himself about the controversy; indeed he told Galileo pretty bluntly
that once the Inquisition began to probe and examine, they did not give up lightly.
They would delve into his motives, examine his every intention, seek what lay in
his mind, and when he thought they had finished, they would start all over again.
With a book on which the report was so unfavourable, they would have no
alternative: they would be sure that evil intent lurked somewhere in his thoughts,
that in some hidden recess of his personality he had decided that he must oppose
the Holy Father's edict. And they had ways of making him confess: if they felt
certain he was guilty then they would prove it, even if they had to resort to solitary confinement or, worse still, to torture. But, the Commissary-General went
on, there was a simple and easy way out, there was one course that would auto-
matically stop the Inquisitors enquiring further, and that was to plead guilty.
Confess to forgetfulness, admit pride, acknowledge vanity and conceit, and that
would clear the matter up. The Inquisition would be satisfied, and no great evil
would result; they would demand no swingeing penalties, and in no time Galileo
would find himself back in his beloved Florence, free once more to pursue his
studies. It was wise counsel in view of the way things had gone, and Galileo was
won over. After all he was up against a powerful opponent whose methods could
be harsh and even cruel, an enemy that could and would break resistance if it was
thwarted. There was no chance of arguing his case as he had once fondly imagined
he would be able to do; he had submitted Bellarmine's letter yet there were clearly
other forces at work, and other evidence that he did not know about and of which
he never would get details. There was no system for him to be defended by an

Though Galileo was neither imprisoned nor tortured by the Inquisition, he feared that he might be if he tried to resist. An engraving of the torturing of heretics by the Holy Office.

advocate, no rule that the prosecution's evidence should be made available to the accused: it was a one-sided tribunal that might be totally ignorant of science and of the scientific issues involved, but which had the whole power of the Church behind it. Men who had tried to resist had been imprisoned for years, tortured perhaps, and then burned at the stake; no, it was as Maculano said, pointless to resist in view of all the circumstances. He would confess and throw himself on the mercy of the Holy Office.

And so, on 30 April, Galileo appeared again before the Commissary-General and his assistants. They knew what he would do, and were ready. What had Galileo Galilei to say touching the matter on which he was arraigned before them? He had, he said, been thinking things over; he had gone over the terms of the injunction about the Copernican doctrine and had re-read his *Dialogue*, and after due reflection he had to confess that it did seem to him that in places he had overstated the Copernican case; he had advocated it rather too emphatically here and there, and sometimes countered it with arguments that were too weak, too ineffectual. He had wanted to make out a clever case: indeed, as he succinctly put it, 'My error, then, has been – and I confess it – one of vainglorious ambition and of

Opposite A portrait of Galileo by an anonymous painter on a panel in his friend Filippo Salviati's Villa delle Selve at Signa, outside Florence, where Galileo often stayed.
Overleaf, left Urban VIII by Gian Lorenzo Bernini. *Right* Painting by Andrea Sacchi of Urban VIII's visit to the Church of the Gesù, the mother church of the Jesuits in Rome.

pure ignorance and inadvertence.'[3] He was then dismissed, but shortly returned to make an additional statement:

And in confirmation of my assertion that I have not held and do not hold as true the opinion which has been condemned, of the motion of the Earth, and the stability of the Sun – if there shall be granted to me, as I desire, means and time to make a clearer demonstration thereof, I am ready to do so; and there is a most favourable opportunity for this, seeing that in the work already published the interlocutors agree to meet again after a certain time to discuss several distinct problems of Nature not connected with the matter discoursed of at their meetings. As this affords me an opportunity of adding one or two other 'days', I promise to resume the arguments already brought in favour of the said opinion, which is false and has been condemned, and to confute them in such most effectual manner as by the blessing of God may be supplied to me. I pray, therefore, this holy Tribunal to aid me in this good resolution and to enable me to put it into effect.[4]

This sounds like an abject confession, and it is obvious Galileo did not want to say it: he went off without making it and then came back, because he knew he must. Yet it was not really as complete a capitulation as it sounded. He was up against serious odds, and was forced to admit his error, but if only he could get the chance to modify the *Dialogue* all would not be lost. Deep down Galileo believed that the arguments he had given in the *Dialogue* were so powerful that nothing could demolish them, that no subsequent discussion would lessen their effectiveness, and he was making a last stand so that, far from being banned, the *Dialogue* would continue to circulate. If that could be arranged, the Copernican theory would gradually become accepted. It was similar in many ways to the ploy he had used with Urban when he could not persuade the Pope to rescind the edict of 1616. Then he had obtained the agreement that had led to his writing the *Dialogue*, now, with the connivance of the Commissary-General, he would try to keep his views in circulation. Better, certainly, if he had not had to confess to the Tribunal that the Copernican theory was wrong, but Maculano had assured him this would be necessary: the important thing was that the arguments for Copernicus, for the moving Earth, and above all the proof from the tides, should be read and examined by the thinking world. Of course Galileo could have remained obdurate, have challenged the Tribunal over the events of 1616 and sworn he was being falsely accused, but it would have served no useful purpose. The Inquisitors were both judge and jury, and they would have had but one course, to condemn Galileo to death. To burn at the stake might be dramatic but it would not really do any good: better that he should live to continue the fight, and to prosecute other research. The wise man knows when to withdraw and regroup his forces.

The trial now reverted to formal procedures. Galileo had to prepare a 'defence' and this he did in collaboration with Maculano. On 10 May he appeared again, explaining that try as he would he could not remember the serious phrases that had been quoted from the injunction of 1616 – the words from the false docu-

Opposite A model of Galileo's *giovilabio,* made either on his instructions or those of his disciples.

ment – and then declared his original good intentions and confessed that vain-glorious ambition had thwarted them, and once again offered to amend the text. Then follows the most moving part of the 'defence' in which he makes an appeal for mercy:

Lastly, it remains for me to beg you to take into consideration my pitiable state of bodily indisposition, to which, at the age of seventy years, I have been reduced by ten months of constant mental anxiety and the fatigue of a long and toilsome journey at the most inclement season – together with the loss of the greater part of the years to which, from my previous condition of health, I had the prospect. I am persuaded and encouraged to do so by the faith I have in the clemency and goodness of my most Eminent Lords, my judges; with the hope that they may be pleased, in answer to my prayer, to remit what may appear to their entire justice the rightful addition that is still lacking to such sufferings to make an adequate punishment from my crimes, out of consideration for my declining age which, too, humbly commends itself to them.[5]

But the defence is not just a plea for mercy, not only a claim for special considera-tion: there is a subtle twist in its tail. Galileo does defend himself and ask that the Tribunal, in deciding on a sentence, should remember that there are those who would delight in a harsh verdict, who would rejoice in his discomfort. 'And I would equally commend to their consideration my honour and reputation, against the calumnies of ill-wishers, whose persistence in detracting from my good name may be inferred from the necessity which constrained me to procure from the Lord Cardinal Bellarmine the attestation that accompanies this.'[6] A clever move, designed to ensure that the Inquisitors do not overlook Bellarmine's statement about what happened in 1616.

The defence was accepted and everything seemed set for a mild sentence – some nominal form of penance probably – and the revision of the *Dialogue*. This was certainly what Galileo hoped and Maculano had led him to believe and, as far as one can tell, had every reason to think would be the case: the Inquisitors were not, ordinarily, spiteful men. But contrary to everyone's expectation the sentence, when it came, was a harsh one and Maculano, Commissary-General though he might be, was utterly powerless to do anything about it. Precisely what happened between the time the Tribunal accepted Galileo's defence and the pronouncement of the sentence is not certain, but everything points to Urban being behind the sudden change of attitude. This is not unlikely, for he had, by this time, gathered a number of sympathisers and sycophants around him, all strongly anti-Florentine and most with their faces firmly set against Galileo. These were suspicious men, devious men, men of the wildest ideas, who had even put into the Pope's head the idea that the title *Dialogue of the Two Great World Systems*, was full of hidden hermetic symbolism, thus linking the book with the heresies of Giordano Bruno. And not content with this calumny, they also fed another rumour started by Galileo's detractors, that he practised astrology and, in 1630, had used the art to predict Urban's death.

True or false, what is now certain is that on 16 June 1633, after the Pope had returned from Castel Gandolfo, there was a private meeting of the Congregation of the Holy Office of the Inquisition, the Commissary-General was overruled and his hopes dashed. Instead of a mild sentence, the Congregation recorded:

Sanctissimus decreed that the said Galileo is to be interrogated on his intention, even with the threat of torture and, if he sustains [the examination], he is to abjure vehement suspicion of heresy in a plenary assembly of the Congregation of the Holy Office, then is to be condemned to imprisonment at the pleasure of the Holy Congregation, and ordered not to treat further, in whatever manner, either in words or in writing, of the mobility of the Earth and the stability of the Sun; otherwise he will incur the penalties of relapse. The book entitled the *Dialogue of the Lincean Galileo Galilei* is to be prohibited. Furthermore, that these things may be known by all, he ordered that copies of the sentence shall be sent to all Apostolic Nuncios, to all Inquisitors against heretical pravity, and especially the Inquisitor in Florence, who shall read the sentence in full assembly and in the presence of most of those who profess the mathematical art.[7]

It was a sentence full of bitterness, designed not only to stamp on the Copernican theory but to grind the face of its chief protagonist into the dust. What Maculano had hoped was something far more gentle; indeed he had written to Cardinal Francesco Barberini saying that for the sake of procedure, Galileo would merely have to state his intent (probably in the terms he had previously used), receive a formal enjoiner, and then he could be sent home, the formalities of imprisonment being met as the Cardinal had suggested, by nominating Galileo's own house as a prison of the Holy Office. But now the whole tenor was different: Galileo was to make a public recantation and go through the full rigours of a rigid interrogation. Yet the sentence, severe though it was, could have been worse; if Galileo's Jesuit enemies had had their way, they would have seen to it that the *Dialogue* was publicly burned, and that Galileo himself was put on trial again, this time for heresy. That this did not happen was primarily due to Maculano who, as Commissary-General, threatened that if there were to be heresy trials then not only Galileo but also the Jesuit Ciampoli would be arraigned, since Ciampoli had supported Galileo's Copernicanism and had been sacked by the Pope for his part in licencing the *Dialogue*. All the same, the new sentence was a complete volte-face, and when the formal notification arrived, Niccolini was horrified. The Inquisition had always scrupulously followed a well-established procedure, and the Italian Holy Office had never been as vehement as its Spanish counterpart: if a confession was deemed necessary and a lenient sentence proposed, then this was what happened. The formal procedures were carried out but the result was as previously arranged, or so it invariably seems to have been; in this instance, however, the high standards of conduct were not maintained. Now Niccolini faced a completely unexpected situation, and one that he could do nothing about, yet it was his unhappy task to tell Galileo, and he broke the news as gently as he could,

ALTRA VEDVTA DELLA PIAZZA DI S·MARIA DELLA MINERVA·

1 Chiefa di S·Maria della Minerua·   2 Obelifco inalzato da N·S·PP·ALESSANDRO VII·   3 Tempio della Rotonda
Gio·Batta Falda dif·et fec·   *Per Gio·Iacomo Rofi in Roma alla pace co priu·del S·Pont·*

The church of Santa Maria Sopra Minerva with, next to it, the Inquisition headquarters.

omitting to say anything about the imprisonment to follow since it was his hope that diplomatic pressure could be brought to bear so that it was remitted.

On Tuesday, 21 June, Galileo appeared once more before the Inquisition, this time for a formal interrogation. The procedure was that he should be questioned, under threat of torture, about his intentions – did he, or did he not, really believe Copernicus? No, not since well before the Church's edict, he said when the question was formally put. But what of the *Dialogue*, for this supported Copernicus? Not his intention, Galileo said; he had tried to show that neither the Ptolemaic nor the Copernican views were certain, and when challenged again, he said, 'I do not hold and have not held the opinion of Copernicus since the command was intimated to me that I must abandon it; for the rest I am here in your hands – do with me what you please'.[8] Truth or torture, said the judges, following formalities, and once more Galileo mumbled that he was there to submit and had not held the doctrines since the time he had been forbidden to do so. Fortunately for him, Maculano was still in charge and he did not raise all the difficult points in the *Dialogue* which, according to the Holy Office's assessors, did show a belief in the condemned Copernican theory, nor did he bring up questions noted by the Pope's original commission, questions that could have shown Galileo to have been guilty of heresy, at least from a rigidly scriptural point of view. As it was, the whole interrogation was over in an hour and Galileo was kept in the Inquisition building

Opposite An engraving after an apocryphal painting by Carlo Piloty of Galileo awaiting trial in the prison of the Inquisition. It depicts far severer conditions than Galileo actually experienced.
Overleaf Robert Fleming's historically inaccurate painting of Galileo recanting before the tribunal of the Inquisition.

until the next day when he was to receive sentence. His public career finished, his hopes of converting the Pope and the Church to Copernicanism gone, he must have spent the most dismal night and, seeing how unreliable had been the promises of lenient treatment he had received, have experienced that ghastly feeling of incipient terror when he thought of what might happen the next day when his sentence would be made known.

On 22 June Galileo was dressed in the white robe of a penitent and conducted to the large hall of the Dominican Convent of Santa Maria sopra Minerva, where he knelt in penitence to hear his sentence read out. He did not stand arrogantly in court dress as shown in the famous but totally incorrect painting by Robert Henry, but waited on his knees, humble and broken, shaking beneath the folds of his loose-fitting robe. The sentence was long, setting out his sins in the *Dialogue*, his behaviour at the trial and excusing the second interrogation instigated by the Pope, on the grounds that he had not stated the full truth on the previous occasion. It closed by banning the *Dialogue* and then went on: 'We condemn you to the formal prison of this Holy Office during our pleasure, and by way of salutary penance we enjoin that for three years to come you repeat once a week the seven penitential Psalms. Reserving to ourselves liberty to moderate, commute, or take off, in whole or in part, the aforesaid penalties and penance.'[9] But this was not the end: Galileo had still to make public his abjuration of the Copernican doctrine, and this he now did:

I, Galileo, son of the late Vincenzo Galilei, Florentine, aged seventy years ... have been pronounced by the Holy Office to be vehemently suspected of heresy, that is to say, of having held and believed that the Sun is the centre of the world and immovable and that the Earth is not the centre and moves: ... with sincere heart and unfeigned faith I abjure, curse, and detest the aforesaid errors and heresies. ... [10]

Contrary to popular belief he did not end with the statement '*Eppur si muove*' ('But it still moves') – he was not so foolish, and no story about it was current in his lifetime. Indeed this uncharacteristic phrase did not appear until 1640, and then only on a fanciful portrait of him in prison painted in Madrid by Murillo or one of his pupils, but later, and most unfortunately, the story has stuck.

In spite of the phrases permitting the Holy Office to exercise some leniency, the harshness of the sentence was still disagreeable to some of the judges. Three of the ten refused to sign, one perhaps for political reasons, but two probably because they considered the whole matter an excess of authority and something of an injustice: Cardinal Francesco Barberini was one of these. And no more than two days after the proceedings were over, Galileo was allowed back to the embassy. He was very downcast over his punishment which, as Niccolini remarked, had come as a shock, although it seems Galileo had for some time been resigned to the idea that the *Dialogue* would be banned. The depth of Galileo's disgust and shock at the way things had gone was greater, though, than perhaps Niccolini realized:

in the margin of his own copy of the *Dialogue* Galileo was later to write:

In the matter of introducing novelties. And who can doubt that it will lead to the worst disorders when minds created free by God are compelled to submit slavishly to an outside will? When we are told to deny our senses and subject them to the whim of others? When people of whatsoever competence are made judges over experts and are granted authority to treat them as they please? These are the novelties which are apt to bring about the ruin of commonwealths and the subversion of the state.[11]

Signature of Galileo on the statement of his recantation.

17
Phoenix Reborn

With Galileo's public abjuration of the Copernican doctrine, the new scientific movement in Italy came to a halt; Torricelli worked on and the Academy for Experiments remained in existence, but the spirit had gone out of them. The leading light of the new mathematical-physical approach to questions about the natural world had been extinguished. It was an intellectual disaster, yet, as far as Galileo was personally concerned, it must in all fairness be pointed out that he was treated very leniently. The Pope's small pension that had been voted in happier times was still kept on, and Urban kept his word to Niccolini over Galileo's physical treatment: he had promised that 'after the publication of the sentence We shall see you again, and we shall consult together so that he may suffer as little distress as possible',[1] and he did not rescind. Moreover, during the trial Galileo was put in no prison, but stayed in the apartments of the Procurator-General, was given three rooms to himself, allowed a servant, and permitted to walk in the corridors; indeed, it is probably true to say that no one had ever been treated so gently. And this leniency continued after he was sentenced, for he was allowed to go to the Grand Duke's villa at Trinita dei Monti and then, once the sentence had been published and read, it was proposed that he should go to the monastery of Santa Croce for a rest and a short period of penance. Due, however, to his friend Archbishop Piccolomini, aided and abetted by Francesco Barberini, Galileo was allowed to move instead to the archepiscopal palace at Siena for five months, although with strict instructions that he should be allowed to see no one. Fortunately, Piccolomini was no respecter of papal injunctions that did not suit him, and as he was clear in his own mind that Galileo had been the victim of an unjust trial, he ignored the command that there should be no visitors, and threw the palace open to whomsoever should come. Although there is no doubt that Piccolomini's independent behaviour reached the ears of the authorities, no action was taken, and when in November Niccolini pressed the Pope to allow Galileo to return to Florence, this was granted. So December saw him back in his own villa and small farm a few miles outside the city at Arcetri, which he had bought so that he could be near his beloved elder daughter Maria Celeste.

Maria Celeste had always been an immense comfort to him, writing to him daily, carrying on a correspondence that became a regular feature of their lives. Unfortunately much of what they wrote is lost, but from the comparatively few letters that remain it seems that they were mostly of a purely domestic kind, referring to the mending and ironing she did for him, the napkins she made, the cakes she baked, and even the food she cooked and sent up to him by special

Opposite View of Galileo's house in Arcetri, in the hills overlooking Florence.

The Palazzo Piccolomini in Siena. After his trial Galileo spent five months there as the guest of his friend Archbishop Ascanio Piccolomini.

messenger once he had moved close enough to the convent. Even throughout the trial she had continued to write, encouraging her father, telling him of the prayers she had said for him and how, with some of Galileo's friends, she had helped remove all her father's papers from his house for fear of a raid by the Inquisition's officers. Her utter joy at his return to Arcetri can better be imagined than described but, sadly, their mutual happiness was not to last long for at the beginning of April 1634 she died. Galileo was, literally, heartbroken: for a time he completely

The courtyard of Galileo's house in Arcetri.

lost interest in science and, indeed, in life itself, and those close to him feared he too might die. But fortunately Galileo had a resilient nature, and lived on to complete yet another book, this time one that turned out to be his most important contribution to science.

How quickly Galileo's resilience asserted itself, how rapidly he got over traumatic events, can be seen from the fact that as soon as he got to Siena after the trial, he and Piccolomini, who had once been his pupil, set to work on the new

225

Above The view over Florence from the hills of Arcetri.

Opposite Galileo's daughter, Maria Celeste, whose convent was also at Arcetri. Her death, in April 1634, was a great blow to Galileo.

book. The Church had done the one thing Galileo had hoped against hope he could avoid: they had banned not only the *Dialogue* but also every one of his writings. Yet now, with what seemed almost a new lease of life, he no longer let the sentence bring on fits of depression: on the contrary he let it act as a stimulus to new activity. Admittedly both he and Piccolomini must have drawn some encouragement from the fact that the ban was almost totally ignored, at least so far as the *Dialogue* was concerned. Merchants, nobles and even prelates vied with one another to buy copies on the black market before officials from the Holy Office arrived to confiscate them, and the price of a copy rose to anything between eight and twelve times its original value. So, with their hopes raised, Galileo and Piccolomini began work together in what one visitor described as a softly carpeted and richly furnished room, spreading their papers all over the floor, and did so with such excitement that 'one could not weary of admiration'[2] for them. Forbidden to write about or even discuss Copernicus, Galileo had turned back to questions of motion, of falling bodies and problems of applied mechanics

DISCORSI
E
DIMOSTRAZIONI
MATEMATICHE,
intorno à due nuoue ſcienze

Attenenti alla

MECANICA & i MOVIMENTI LOCALI,

del Signor

GALILEO GALILEI LINCEO,

Filoſofo e Matematico primario del Sereniſſimo
Grand Duca di Toſcana.

Con vna Appendice del centro di grauità d'alcuni Solidi.

IN LEIDA,
Appreſſo gli Elſevirii. M. D. C. XXXVIII.

Above An apocryphal painting by Tito Lessi of the blind Galileo dictating his *Discourses* to his son Vincenzo.

Left The title page of Galileo's *Discourses*, 1638.

Opposite Portrait of Galileo by Josse Sustermans.

Overleaf Galileo's study at Arcetri, with his telescope, astrolabe, lodestone, and a copy of *The Starry Messenger*.

like the strength of beams, subjects that would allow him to attack Aristotle, display the powers of mathematical reasoning and, incidentally, prepare the ground for a detailed discussion of planetary motion when the time came for the Copernicus edict either to be rescinded or, at least, tactfully forgotten. Even though planned some years before, it was a bold thing for a man of sixty-nine to attempt, and it says much for Galileo's scientific perseverance that, in spite of Maria Celeste's death, he had the drive to finish it and see it published.

The book, called *Discourses and Mathematical Demonstrations concerning Two New Sciences* was, like the *Dialogue*, written in Italian, and in the form of a discussion. Once more, the interlocutors were Salviati, Sagredo and Simplicius, and the 'two new sciences' were the engineering science of the strength of materials on the one hand, and the subject of bodies in motion – kinematics – on the other. Divided into four 'days', just as the *Dialogue* had been, the first two are concerned with the engineering problem, the last two with kinematical theory, and the whole text is a brilliantly clear exposition that explodes old fallacies and replaces the woolly thinking of the Aristotelians by a fine descriptive and mathematical analysis. The *Discourses* is, in fact, a brilliant piece of writing, the text is alive – as alive as anything in the *Dialogue* – yet at the same time it shows Galileo's powers of mathematical analysis and physical description at their best: a masterpiece of scientific prose, at once readable and informative. Simplicius is still cast as a true Aristotelian but seems to have learned something from his part in the *Dialogue*: he is no longer so stupid or so hidebound, and neither Salviati nor Sagredo are so militant or so derisive; it is all more gentle, although the discussion is live enough since it is shot through and through with a true spirit of enquiry. Indeed it is still stimulating to a reader today, and it is only when one pauses, looks back and realizes that it was written well over three centuries ago, that one appreciates how far in advance it was of anything else that had been produced at that time.

Since the *Discourses* is concerned with a narrower scientific field than the *Dialogue*, since it is confined to specific engineering and kinematic problems compared with the vast canvas of the entire universe which is the *Dialogue*'s purview, it may sound too specialized to be discussed further, yet to assume this would be unfortunate. For Galileo discusses problems that are not only of importance today, but even now are still topics of conversation among thinking people. And, perhaps even more important, he deals with the basic question of the role of mathematics in describing the physical world, and so is led on to discuss the relationship between theory and experiment in probing the secrets of nature. His conclusion, that experiments could be used to test previously conceived mathematical explanations, and his rejection of the idea that experiments alone can act as a source from which theoretical explanations may be derived, shows deep insight into the nature of what we now delight in calling the modern scientific approach.

Yet the *Discourses* is not all concerned with the philosophy of science, for Galileo

Opposite The Tuscan hills beyond Arcetri, seen from the window of Galileo's study.

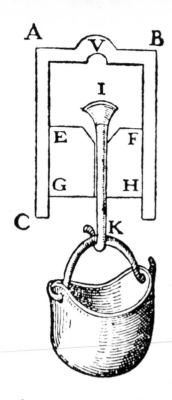

also uses it for demolishing old fallacies and outworn conceptions. For instance he gets Simplicius to quote the time-worn phrase 'Nature abhors a vacuum' and shows how this is not only a personification of nature, but embodies a basic tenet of Aristotelian physics, a belief that at once made it impossible to conceive of an atomic theory of matter or even understand as mundane a matter as the physical limitations of suction pumps. And in discounting the Aristotelian view, Galileo gives actual experimental verification for the vacuum and describes the way one can be generated, evidence which exerted a profound influence on subsequent work, not least upon his pupil Evangelista Torricelli.

In the last two days of the *Discorsi* dialogue, Galileo turned his attention once again to the fundamental questions of moving bodies, questions that he had already shown in earlier years to have been misconceived and wrongly explained by Aristotle. Now he was able to gather together the threads of his research, and join them with his mathematical analyses of movement and of falling bodies. The results were indeed impressive for, in the *Discorsi*, Galileo lays down the basic elements of the whole mathematical treatment of motion. To begin with he discusses in some detail the behaviour of falling bodies, and then goes on to examine the path of a projectile. This, of course, had important military implications, and was therefore of the utmost significance at a time when war was raging in Europe. But philosophically it was still more significant, for this was a subject on which the Aristotelians had always been mistaken. Because Aristotle had made it a fundamental rule that no body could take part in two different kinds of motion at once, those who supported Aristotelian physics had to divide a projectile's motion with two quite distinct parts; and not from a purely mathematical point

234

of view, but as a real physical fact. When shot from a bow or a gun, a projectile would first, they said, travel in a straight line and later, when the impetus causing the 'violent' forward motion had ceased, take part in 'natural motion' and plummet straight down to the ground. Galileo's analysis of motion made no such demands, asked for no such differentiation: to him there was no difference between violent and natural motion, there was just motion and, he believed, one set of laws to describe it. By a simple and elegant mathematical analysis, combining together the motion ahead with the accelerated motion of a falling body that he had established earlier, Galileo proves conclusively that a projectile must move in a parabolic path, a fact that is borne out by experience. Thus, once and for all, he cleared up a problem that had harboured confusion and misunderstanding for centuries.

Perhaps the most astonishing thing of all in the *Discourses* was how close Galileo came to the first law of motion that Newton was to enunciate half a century later. What Galileo puts into the mouth of Salviati runs as follows: 'Furthermore we may remark that any velocity once imported to a moving body will be rigidly maintained as long as the external causes of acceleration or retardation are removed. ...'[3] Newton wrote: 'Every body continues in its state of rest, or of uniform motion in a right line [i.e. a straight line], unless it is compelled to change that state by forces impressed on it.'[4] Newton's law was more widely embracing than Galileo's, for Salviati goes on to remark that the law only applies to bodies 'on a horizontal plane', in other words not to bodies falling under the force of gravity, whereas Newton generalizes for all motion. Moreover Newton takes such motion to be in a straight line whereas Galileo's motion is motion round the Earth, motion in a circle. These are important distinctions, but they do not detract from the significance of Galileo's achievement which was to break totally with Aristotle, and show that motion did not require the constant application of a motive force: the crucial phrase 'any velocity once imparted to a moving body will be rigidly maintained ...' enshrines the doctrine that is the basis of all kinematics, and remains one of the foundation blocks of modern physics.

There are indications, too, that Galileo could have gone further. Newton's second law of motion, concerned with the change of motion of a body acted on by a force, the kind of thing in practical terms that happens when, for instance, one billiard ball hits another, was a matter that Galileo fully intended to discuss – he called the subject 'percussion' – although he did not manage to get his thoughts and experiments in order in time to include them in the *Discourses*. Yet, significant though Galileo's close approach to Newton may be, the most important thing in the *Discourses* is the attitude of mind it displays. Here, for the first time, was a book that demonstrated the immense power of the mathematical analysis of physical problems, whether they be the strength of materials which are concerned with static forces, or with the basic problems of movement that concern kinematics. It placed scientific experiment in its proper context and, in short, laid

Trajectories of cannon balls in parabolic path, according to the physics of Galileo and Newton. From *Encyclopaedia Metropolitana*, 1845.

the foundations of mathematical physics. And its beautifully clear literary style was a classic example of what could be done in the way of scientific writing; no longer was there any need for involved and convoluted explanations, nor any need to write pedantic prose to appear learned. The wonderful introduction to the third day is a case in point: clear, succinct and with a stamp of modernity that is breath-taking:

Change of Position. My purpose is to set forth a very new science dealing with a very ancient subject. There is, in nature, perhaps nothing older than motion, concerning which the books written by philosophers are neither few nor small; nevertheless I have discovered by experiment some properties of it which are worth knowing and which have not hitherto been either observed or demonstrated. Some superficial observations have been made, as, for instance, that the free motion of a heavy falling body is continuously accelerated; but to just what extent this acceleration occurs has not yet been announced.[5]

And as he goes on, after mentioning the paths of projectiles: 'But this and other facts, not few in number or less worth knowing, I have succeeded in proving; and what I consider more important, there have been opened up to this vast and most excellent science, of which my work is merely the beginning, ways and means by which other minds more acute than mine will explore its remote corners.'[6] Here speaks the essential scientist who glories in opening up new fields of knowledge and rejoices in the thought that others will discover more; here too speaks a man who can use language so that his own achievements may be seen in the round, clearly and without ambiguity.

Once the book was written, there was the problem of getting it published. The Inquisitors were not stupid men, they knew Galileo was at work, and they would not have expected things to be otherwise: at the age of seventy it is not likely that a man is going to change the habits of a lifetime. And, of course, some of them at least were on Galileo's side, wishing to keep science and the Scriptures in separate compartments. And, knowing that the Pope's jurisdiction was confined to Roman Catholic lands, they may not have been averse to closing a blind eye to what might go on abroad in countries that had repudiated papal dominion. As far as Galileo's personal friends were concerned, they had no reservations; they were only too keen to see the master's work published, and through them Galileo began secret negotiations with Louis Elzevir, founder of the famous Dutch printing and publishing house in Leiden. The negotiations went well, and as soon as they were complete, Galileo received a visit from an ex-pupil, the Duke of Noailles, who was French Ambassador to the Holy See and whom Urban did not dare to forbid visiting the little villa at Arcetri. Galileo dedicated the book to Noailles for it was doubtless his assistance that made it possible for Prince Mattia de' Medici to smuggle the actual manuscript out of Italy and into Holland, so that in 1638 the book could actually appear at Leiden. In a dedicatory preface, Galileo claims that publication was arranged without his knowledge, using a manuscript copy that he had given Noailles but this was, of course, untrue and no one, least of all the Holy Office, believed it. But honour was satisfied and the Pope's hands were tied because of Noailles' diplomatic position: whatever Urban might feel, and however furious Galileo's enemies might be, there was nothing they could do without precipitating an international quarrel, and the Pope's political position was too weak to risk that. Galileo had, in the end, conquered his conquerors, and by a simple but effective subterfuge published what, as he himself knew, was his greatest work.

During 1636 and 1638 Galileo received visits from both Thomas Hobbes and John Milton. Hobbes had the most immense respect for Galileo, 'the first that opened to us the gate of natural philosophy universal, which is the knowledge of the nature of motion',[7] while Milton, who took a less scientific interest, was more concerned with the restrictions placed on Galileo and on his power to publish. Indeed, in his *Areopagitica* dealing with the very question of freedom of publication without a licence, Milton specifically referred to his Italian visit:

I have sat among their learned men, and been counted happy to be born in such a place of philosophic freedom as they supposed England was, while they themselves did nothing but bemoan the servile condition into which learning amongst them was brought; that this was it which had damped the glory of Italian wits, that nothing had been there written now these many years but flattery and fustian. There it was that I found and visited the famous Galileo, grown old, a prisoner of the Inquisition for thinking in Astronomy otherwise than the Franciscan and Dominican licencers of thought.[8]

Certainly the Church's censorship was a serious problem for the intellectual, although Galileo overcame it by a ruse and published abroad. He also kept up a

During 1636 and 1639 Galileo received visits from Thomas Hobbes *(left)* and John Milton. Milton's visit has been the subject of several romanticized nineteenth-century paintings such as this one by A. Gatti *(below)*.

prodigious correspondence with scholars all over Europe. But before the *Discourses* was complete and smuggled out of Italy, he was beset by another problem: he began to go blind. He first noticed the trouble in 1636, and asked to be allowed to go to Florence for treatment, but to begin with Urban refused: he must stay under house arrest at Arcetri. However the Grand Duke and other friends intervened, and in March 1637 he was allowed to go into Florence and stay in his son's house near the San Giorgio gate, although with strict injunctions that on no account should he leave the city. The true nature of Galileo's medical condition is uncertain, although we do know that he was not suffering from cataract. Whatever it was it was a virulent infection and by June he had lost the sight of his left eye, with vision impaired in his right one due to a permanent discharge. His one comfort was a constant flow of visitors, among them the Grand Duke who often used to come and use the opportunity to prepare Galileo's medicines himself: 'I have only one Galileo,'[9] he kept saying. Unhappily the medical treatment failed and by December 1637 Galileo was totally blind, but he stayed on with his son, Vincenzo, instead of going back to Arcetri because he was still in a poor state of health, and not until January 1639 was he well enough to return to his own villa.

Despite his blindness Galileo's last years at Arcetri were made happier by the presence of his pupils and amanuenses, Evangelista Torricelli *(below)* and Vincenzo Viviani *(opposite, bottom)*. *Opposite, top* An apocryphal painting, by Niccolò Barabino, of Galileo explaining some of his theories to Torricelli, Viviani and his son, Vincenzo Galilei.

EVANGELISTA TORRICELLI

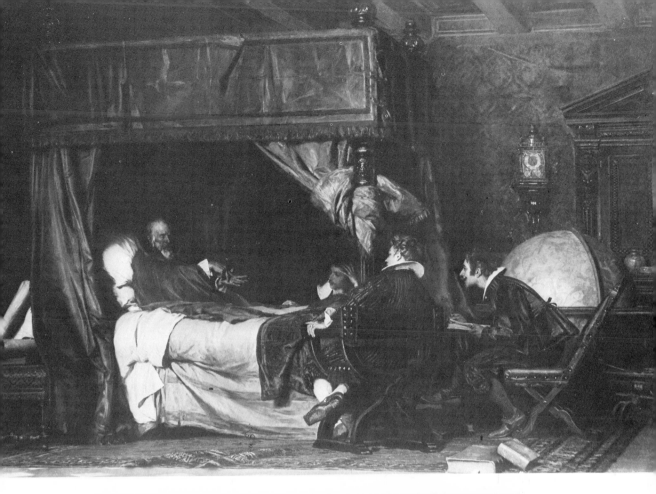

Yet now he was blind he could not be allowed to be alone with his science and both his son and his 'last pupil' Vincenzo Viviani became his amanuenses, helping to keep up his correspondence and discussing new ideas with him. In 1641 they were joined by Evangelista Torricelli, and with this small team Galileo received enough stimulus to do more scientific work, especially on 'percussion', on sound and the problem of dissonance, and on mathematics. It was during this time, too, that he dictated to his son details of a pendulum escapement based on his early ideas of isochronism which, if developed, could have led to the arrival of the pendulum clock at least a decade earlier. The fact that this did not happen was due to an out-size measure of caution on Vincenzo's part: so afraid was he that his father's idea would be pirated that it was not until 1649 that he at last had a framework built and set about cutting the appropriate gears himself. But it was then too late: his own health failed and the project was cut short by his death shortly after. Yet if the pendulum clock came to nothing, Galileo did develop the pendulum as a vibration counter which recorded the number of swings that occurred in a given time interval. This was in 1637 just before his eyesight began to fail so rapidly, and since he thought the device might be of help in determining longitude at sea he wrote to Admiral Reael in the Netherlands about it. In view of Galileo's reputation, the States–General took the suggestion most seriously, appointed four commissioners to examine the possibilities and began negotiations direct with Galileo. But by the time two of the commissioners came to visit him, bringing a gold chain

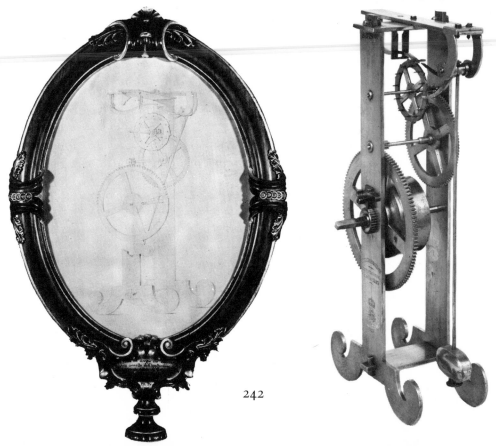

as a mark of esteem, he was blind and confined to bed, and the arrangements petered out.

One other matter in which Galileo revived his interest after his return to Arcetri was the *giovilabio*, which he had originally devised as early as 1612 for computing the positions of Jupiter's satellites. Originally this had been no more than a collection of specially prepared charts from which past and future positions of the satellites could be computed. Now, however, he suggested that the calculation could be done mechanically, and sometime during the 1640s this Jovian-satellite computer was constructed by his willing helpers probably under his personal direction. But this was Galileo's last device, for during 1641 he seems to have confined himself to theoretical discussions, and early in 1642, on 8 January, he died.

A thick-set man, lively, quick to anger and equally quick to forgive, Galileo seems to have been widely loved, at least by his pupils and his colleagues. But his caustic tongue and witty pen had made him implacable enemies, and some of their bitterness was too intense even to subside at death. Urban was still full of rancour, and positively refused to let his old friend have any memorial erected over his grave. Not until almost a century later was permission given for his remains to be interred under a large monument in the entrance to the Church of Santa Croce in Florence.

Opposite, left A drawing, by Vincenzo Galilei, of his father's concept of the pendulum clock. *Right* A model of this clock, now in the Science Museum, London.

18
Assessment

Galileo's death ushered in the end of an era. Urban VIII died in 1644, two years later, and almost at once the intellectual temperature gradually began to drop and the fury of the past decade to wither away. Slowly belief in a moving Earth came to be accepted in Roman Catholic as well as Protestant countries; and in the end no one could be found to argue against the growing evidence in favour of a fixed Sun. Yet formally the Catholic world was still geocentric. The *Dialogue* remained on the *Index of Prohibited Books* and only in 1822, after repeated protestations of the Vatican astronomer Settele, were the authorities forced to relent.

Yet because the *Dialogue* was so stimulating a book to read, and because of its dramatic associations with the persecuted Galileo, its involvement with his trial and renunciation, the book enjoyed the widest currency abroad during the seventeenth century and exerted a vast amount of influence in favour not only of Copernicanism but also of Galileo's mathematical approach and appeal to experiment. Heartbroken he may have been over the way in which his fellow countrymen were officially prevented from reading it, but he cannot fail to have been encouraged by the way it was read and used abroad, especially as this was partly due to his own foresight. Within a month of his trial and his return to Rome, Galileo had sent a copy to Matthias Bernegger in Strasbourg so that a Latin translation could be made. Latin was still the common language of scholarship and when the Bernegger edition appeared in 1637, the entire case that he built up over the four days of discussion could now be read by astronomers, physicists, philosophers and countless other scholars all over Europe. And since the trial and sentence had become common knowledge, the pious arguments of Sagredo and Simplicius which Galileo had been obliged to insert could be seen for what they were, overtures of peace to the authorities so the book could be published, and as such did nothing to undermine the real conclusions in favour of Copernicanism. Admittedly Bernegger's was a rather dull and stolid translation, lacking the fire of the original and failing to communicate the subtleties of Galileo's magnificent prose, but it was sound enough, and effectively helped to spread the Galilean gospel. But there was one of Galileo's aims that no Latin edition could meet, and this was his desire for universality, his wish to bring his ideas and methods to all classes of people: Galileo never wanted to confine his thinking to scholars alone, his aim was always to spread the habits of independent and logical thought over as wide a social spectrum as possible. This was why he wrote in Italian, and this was the aim that motivated Thomas Salusbury to prepare an 'inglished' version of the *Dialogue* almost two decades after Galileo's death.

Opposite Bust of Galileo from the monument containing his ashes in the Church of Santa Croce, Florence.

Salusbury is a somewhat shadowy figure: a Royalist who seems to have spent almost a decade on the Continent during the Civil War in England, he found favour at Court after the Restoration, probably because he had contributed financially to the Royalist cause. He was not, however, a rich man, and was employed as advisor to the young Earl of Huntingdon, and Librarian to the Marquis of Dorchester, but at some point he seems to have become involved in book publishing. He brought out a novel, then a tract and, in 1661, the first of two volumes called *Mathematical collections and translations*. The reason for doing so, was, his preface claimed, that he was disturbed that 'Mathematical learning (to speak nothing touching the necessity and delight thereof) has been so sparingly imparted to our countrymen in their native English, especially the nobler and sublimer part ...',[1] so he decided to set about 'collecting and translating from among the excellent pieces that are so abounding in the Italian and French tongues, some of those that are ... most useful and desired and, withal, most wanting in their own'.[2] The venture was, he felt certain, assured of success because there were plenty who 'either want time or patience to look into the vulgar and unstudied languages'.[3] And so in volume one, which came out in two parts, he included Galileo's *Dialogue*, the letter to the Dowager Duchess Christina and a work on hydraulics by Galileo's pupil Castelli. The second volume was also printed in two parts but was more heterogeneous, the first containing Galileo's *Discourses*, his tract on floating bodies and his early booklet on mechanics, as well as works by Descartes and Tartaglia; the second a tract by Torricelli on projectiles, one by Salusbury himself and, most significant, the first ever biography of Galileo. The second volume seems to have come out in 1665 but, unfortunately, the warehouse containing the entire stock of both volumes was destroyed in the Great Fire of London the very next year, and the Salusbury translations are now very rare; indeed only eight copies of the first part of volume two are known, and none whatsoever of the second part, so we are almost completely in the dark about the biography. In his prospectus Salusbury claimed it would be extensive, and certainly it was used in the early eighteenth century by the anonymous author of the article on Galileo in a biographical dictionary, but that is all we know, and today it is impossible even to say whether Salusbury's intentions that it should be a very full biography were met.

Salusbury's translation of the *Dialogue* into English was not the first; according to Hobbes, there was a translation made by a Dr Webbe, about which he told Galileo when he visited him, but tantalizingly little is known either of the author, who was a medical man, or of the work he is supposed to have written. But fortunately the spread of Galileo's discoveries and ideas was not confined to his own writings, much was done by his pupils and the many scientific men with whom he corresponded. In France, the chief Galilean protagonist was Marin Mersenne, an able mathematician and physicist, Jesuit-educated and a friar of the order of Minims. At their monastery in Paris, he seems to have run an unofficial

Marin Mersenne, from a sketch published in Paris about 1870 by Louis Figuier in his *Marvels of Science*.

clearing house for scientific information, acting as intermediary between scientific men who would not, for one reason or another, communicate directly, as well as carrying on an immense correspondence on his own account. A man who made little contribution in the way of new knowledge himself, he was nevertheless a stimulating force in the early days of the new science, constantly being quoted, ever encouraging others to do experiments, publish their work and answer pertinent questions. Pro-Copernican as early as 1629, Mersenne had written to Galileo to say that he understood that a new book on the movement of the Earth was ready but could not be published in Italy because of the Inquisition's prohibition, and offered, if only Galileo would send him the manuscript, to publish it in Paris. In this, of course, Mersenne was ahead of events, but in 1634 he did publish a French translation of Galileo's booklet on mechanics and in 1639 performed a great service by translating the *Discourses* into French with the title *The New Thoughts of Galileo*. Yet it was not solely because of his translations or even because of his multifarious correspondence that Mersenne was such a key figure in promoting the Galilean attitude to science: he had another string to his bow. At the Minime monastery he gathered around him an intellectual circle, composed mainly of Parisians, but vivified by travellers passing through the city either on their way to other continental countries or who were travelling to England, and it was through these men that the new scientific approach to nature was given a new and lasting impetus.

In England Galileo's outlook and methods became well-known, partly through continental visitors, partly by way of correspondence, and in part due to Salus-

Isaac Newton, from a mezzotint by James Macardel based on a portrait by Enoch Seeman.

bury's and Bernegger's translations and a translation by a Robert Payne of the mechanics booklet. The result was that when, in 1660, the Royal Society was founded to improve scientific knowledge and perform experiments, some of the founder members already had a grounding in the new physical-mathematical approach that Galileo took for granted; they had been reading the literature and attending meetings devoted to the new 'Experimental Philosophy' at Gresham College in London or in Bishop Wilkin's rooms at Oxford, so they were ready to carry on where Galileo had left off. Indeed they were so Galilean in mind that at the early meetings, the members of the Royal Society concerned themselves particularly with motion, continually referring to Galileo as a basis from which to work; in fact on one occasion a founder member, William Croone, was specific-ally asked to consult Galileo's *Discourses* 'when the translation of that treatise ... shall be printed'.4 And, of course, Isaac Newton read Galileo, for his Cambridge tutor Isaac Barrow was a staunch supporter of Galilean methods. However, there seems to have been some confusion in Newton's mind about precisely what Galileo had achieved: in his famous *Mathematical Principles of Natural Philosophy* or *Principia* he actually credits Galileo with the law of inertia that he believed he had derived from his work on falling bodies, whereas Galileo had never managed to do this even though he had come close to two of Newton's 'laws of motion'. Perhaps Newton had the idea put in his head by reading Salusbury, whose translation of the *Dialogue* was unclear on certain points, or from the mathematician John Wallis who praised Galileo for having applied mathematics to the solution of scientific problems; but no matter, the significant thing is that Newton, who was not a man to bestow praise lightly even when he could bring himself to bestow it at all, went to the trouble of referring to Galileo and his work. This indeed shows how strong Galileo's influence still was among advanced thinkers, even forty-five years after his death.

If Galileo's effect on the basic physical problem of motion was immense, so was his use of the telescope. It forced astronomers to look at the heavens in a new way, to do something more than merely measure the position of one star relative to another. Perhaps it is hard today to realize what a profound effect this had: for the first time it became possible to look at celestial objects for their own intrinsic interest instead of using them only to mark position or regulate time. And this fired the imagination: the Moon, for example, came in for intense study, and between 1610 when the *Starry Messenger* came out in Venice and Galileo's death, five different maps of the Moon or charts of parts of its surface were published, and by the end of the seventeenth century at least nineteen more. Moreover, the telescope became used for observing comets, planets and stars in a way that had never been attempted before, and then later also adopted as a vastly more precise device for measuring stellar positions compared with the old open (lensless) sights. Certainly Galileo's telescopes were far from perfect, but their potentialities led to new designs and the very optical imperfections stimulated optical theory and optical practice, so that a successful reflecting telescope, the prototype of today's large modern instruments, was designed by Newton twenty-five years after Galileo's death. All along Galileo was the driving force, for while there is some evidence that he may not have been the first to use the telescope for astronomy, it was the *Starry Messenger* that caused all the excitement and awoke an immense interest, among the laity as well as the scientific community.

How great popular interest was in the new discoveries, may be gauged from the fact that in England in 1638 a popular book incorporating Galileo's lunar discoveries was a best-seller. Called *The discovery of a new world in the moone*, it was published anonymously in London by Bishop Wilkins, and it sold so well that a second edition had to be brought out in the same year. By 1640 a third edition was called for, an edition which carried a supplement, a *Discourse concerning a new planet, tending to prove that 'tis probable that our earth is one of the planets.* In the pre-

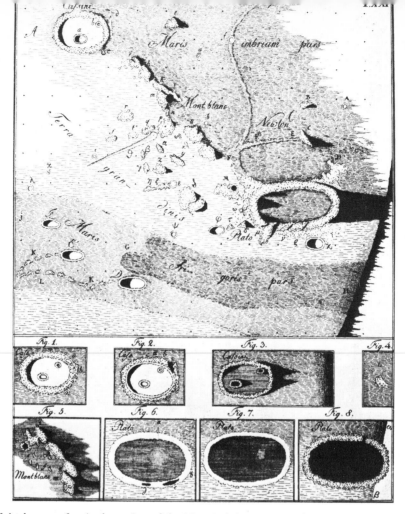

Details of the lunar surface in the region of the Mare Imbrium. From Johann Schröter, *Selenographische Fragmente*, 1791.

vious editions, Wilkins had incorporated parts of the *Starry Messenger* and the *Dialogue*, now he turned to face squarely the question of reconciling the Scriptures and the Copernican theory, and it is significant that he went to Galileo's letter prepared for the Dowager Duchess Christina for guidance and help. So not only was there wide popular interest in the observations but also in their philosophical implications which, fortunately for Wilkins' readers, could be faced without equivocation in the freer and far less doctrinaire atmosphere of England.

Galileo's telescopic work had another important effect, that of underlining the necessity of observation as a check to theories. This became widely accepted by the middle of the seventeenth century, it was part and parcel of the motivation behind the Royal Society yet, at the beginning of the century when the *Starry Messenger* appeared, it had been a hotly debated point. How far Galileo's influence had changed this can be seen, for instance, over his observations of the planet Saturn. When he had first observed it, he had thought it was a triple planet, but later it appeared only a single disc. What had happened he wondered, had Saturn consumed his attendants? Those who disliked the telescope jeered that he had

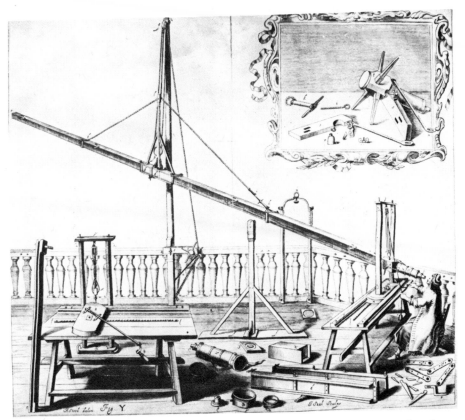

Above To overcome the optical faults which beset Galileo, astronomers began to adopt front lenses with very long focal lengths and their telescopes became extremely cumbersome. This engraving by Johannes Hevelius shows him observing through one of his long-focus instruments. From his *Selenographica*, 1647. *Below* The title page and frontispiece of the first (anonymous) edition of Bishop Wilkins' *The Discovery of a World in the Moone*.

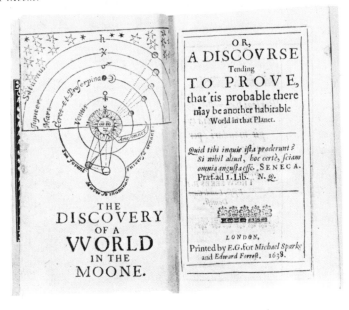

either been hallucinated or that his telescope had been displaying unreal sights, something they had, of course, known all along. Yet by the 1650s the attitude of mind was totally different: the famous Johannes Hevelius of Danzig had no doubts about the validity of Galileo's observations, no qualms over what the telescope displayed; his only problem was to determine the cause, and he discovered that the planet underwent cyclical changes, at times appearing as Galileo first saw it, at others looking as it had done later: certainly there was no question about the reality of the effect. And Hevelius was not alone in trying to solve the puzzle. The Dutch scientist Christiaan Huygens, using a telescope optically superior to Galileo's and to the one Hevelius had used, managed to solve the mystery when he observed that Saturn was surrounded by a series of flat rings whose aspect changed as the relative positions of the planet and the Earth altered. To Hevelius and Huygens, observing for themselves seemed the logical way to try to solve the problem, indeed they probably never stopped for a moment to consider the matter; the appeal to observational evidence was built into their mental outlook, but that this was so is a measure of the profound effect Galileo and his science had exerted. As Isaac Barrow said at his inaugural lecture at Cambridge in 1664, Galileo was to be numbered as one of 'those Moderns resembling and nearly equalling the Ancients in sagacity' and who had 'extended the Circuits of Natural Science beyond its ancient Bounds'.[5]

Galileo the scientist is one of those giants whose achievements are even now surprising in their scope and penetration, yet science was not his only forte. As a literary force he is not to be ignored, and his *Assayer* is still a remarkable effort, still worth reading, still a masterpiece of sound argument and witty polemic. But Galileo was more than a polemicist, more than a man who had the gift of turning a beautiful phrase; he was a master of clear unpretentious prose. He wrote succinctly, explained what he meant as straightforwardly as he could, without pedantry; his books and pamphlets made a strong contrast to the verbose and convoluted arguments of the Aristotelian philosophers, and indeed with academic writing in general. And this clarity of expression was something that caught on among the growing scientific fraternity: when the Royal Society was founded in 1660 it expressly stated that it would encourage publication in clear and straightforward language, and laid down in its statutes that reports of scientific experiments made elsewhere should be 'barely stated' and free from 'rhetorical flourishes'. Galileo's directness became a recommended virtue that the scientific world has followed ever since, even, in some cases perhaps, to the point of too impersonal an approach and too terse a style. But whatever the demerits of this, it is still to be preferred to the old pre-Galilean approach that was full of turgid ambiguity.

Galileo's scientific achievements were very real and exerted an almost incalculable effect on seventeenth-century science; his literary successes were a tonic to read and a stimulus to Italian letters, but in the public mind his image is primarily that of a martyr. Galileo is the pristine example of the oppressed scientist, the symbol of religious persecution; and of course this is true. He was a victim of the Inquisition, the thought-police of the Roman Catholic Church, he did suffer because he challenged an authoritarian system that dared not allow true freedom of belief. Yet part of the romance behind this view lies in his supposed overt defiance of his persecutors, in the myth that makes him exclaim 'But it does move' under his breath. But Galileo was too old a hand to defy the Inquisition, instead he fought on and won with a subtle and civilized defiance, and was the more effective for that. Scientifically speaking Galileo's tactics were right: open mutiny would have been ruthlessly squashed whereas apparent acquiescence allowed him to conquer his conquerors. It may not have been so dramatic but it was far more successful and allowed him to write and publish his most significant scientific treatise. This indeed was victory.

Yet even if popular legend is wrong, Galileo does stand as a classic example of the evils of a totalitarian régime. He was persecuted and prosecuted by men who were not so much scared of the new science that was coming to life before their eyes – they were too dogmatically orientated, too nurtured in the ways of Aristotle to see that – but who were afraid of the power of independent thought. Galileo queried the Scriptures, he made his own interpretation, and so cut right across the religious authority of the Church; he wrote in the vernacular and appealed to those who had never before dared to question authority, and this was too dangerous a challenge to be allowed to pass. Of course, there were political implications, the seventeenth-century Church was too involved in power politics for things to be otherwise, and there were personal scores to be paid off, but that is human nature. Yet it was essentially Galileo's danger to an authoritarian outlook that caused his downfall. We glance back with the advantages of hindsight and see Galileo as the progenitor of the new scientific man, yet this was beyond the comprehension of the administrators of his day. All they could see was a man who could disrupt their system, and they took the one course they could: they stifled the dissention at its source. It was the normal reaction of any régime that controls the mind as well as the body. It is here that the moral lies, here that the lesson of Galileo's indictment and trial is to be found. And it is a lesson that must not be forgotten even today; after all it is not fifty years since a schoolmaster was put on trial in the United States for daring to teach Darwinian evolution, and for the very reason that it conflicted with the Scriptures. And hardly more than twenty-five years have elapsed since the Lysenko affair in the USSR when scientists were actually executed for daring to hold Medelian ideas of heredity because these did violence to the state's interpretation of Marxist ideology. These are sobering thoughts. Man has not changed, dogmatism has not been exorcized, but there is hope – the spirit of Galileo is still with us, beckoning us to follow, to seek new worlds, to open new doors of the mind and glimpse something of his vision of a universe whose shores we are still trying to chart.

Notes

There are no quotations in chapters 1–5 inclusive.

Chapter 6

1   Galileo, *The Little Balance*, in an English translation from Bernardini, G., and Fermi, L., *Galileo and the Scientific Revolution*, Fawcet Premier, New York, 1965, p. 114.

Chapter 7

1   Galileo, *On Motion*, quoted in English translation from Shea, W.R., *Galileo's Intellectual Revolution*, Macmillan, London, 1972, p. 4.
2   *Ibid.*, p. 6.
3   *Ibid., loc. cit.*
4   Fahie, J.J., *Galileo, his life and work*, London, 1903; reprint, Dubuque, Iowa, 1962, p. 30.

Chapter 8

1   Fahie, J.J., *Galileo, his life and work*, London, 1903; reprint, Dubuque, Iowa, 1963, p. 36.
2   Bedini, S.A., in *Galileo, Man of Science*, ed. McMullin, E., Basic Books, New York, 1967, p. 269.

Chapter 9

1   Bedini, S.A., in *Galileo, Man of Science*, ed. McMullin, E., Basic Books, New York, 1967, p. 275.
2   Galileo, *The Sidereal Messenger*, trans. Carlos, E., reprint, Dawson's, London, 1959, p. 11.
3   *Ibid.*, title page.
4   *Ibid.*, p. 8.
5   *Ibid., loc. cit.*
6   *Ibid.*, p. 15.
7   *Ibid.*, p. 40.
8   *Ibid.*, p. 41.
9   *Ibid.*, p. 42.
10   *Ibid., loc. cit.*
11   *Ibid.*, p. 69.

Chapter 10

1 de Santillana, G., *The Crime of Galileo*, Chicago University Press, Chicago, Ill., 1955; and reprint, Heinemann (Mercury Books), London, 1961, p. 8.
2 *Ibid.*, p. 9.
3 *Ibid.*, p. 9.
4 Fahie, J.J., *Galileo, his life and work*, London, 1903; reprint, Dubuque, Iowa, 1962, p. 128.
5 Shea, W.R., *Galileo's Intellectual Revolution*, Macmillan, London, 1972, p. 14.

Chapter 11

1 Seeger, R.J., *Galileo Galilei, his life and his works*, Pergamon Press, London and New York, 1966, p. 240.
2 *Ibid.*, p. 241.
3 *Ibid.*, p. 242.
4 *Ibid.*, p. 244.
5 Drake, S., and O'Malley, C.D., *The Controversy of the Comets of 1618*, University of Pennsylvania Press, Philadelphia, Pa., 1960, p. 164.
6 *Holy Bible*, A.V., Psalm 104, v. 5.
7 de Santillana, G., *The Crime of Galileo*, Chicago University Press, Chicago, Ill., 1955; and reprint, Heinemann (Mercury Books), London, 1961, p. 41.
8 *Ibid.*, p. 45.
9 *Holy Bible*, A.V., Acts, ch. 1, v. 11.

Chapter 12

1 de Santillana, G., *The Crime of Galileo*, Chicago University Press, Chicago, Ill., 1955; and reprint, Heinemann (Mercury Books), London, 1961, p. 110.
2 *Ibid.*, p. 111.
3 Vatican MS, fol. 378^v, quoted in translation by de Santillana, G., *op. cit.*, p. 126.
4 de Santillana, G., *op. cit.*, p. 127.
5 *Ibid.*, p. 126.

Chapter 13

1 Bedini, S.A., in *Galileo, Man of Science*, ed. McMullin, E., Basic Books, New York, 1967, p. 283.
2 *Ibid.*, p. 283.
3 Cesarini, V., Letter to Galileo dated 11 July 1618 (*Le opere di Galileo Galilei*, vol. xii, p. 413).
4 Drake, S., and O'Malley, C.D., *The Controversy on the Comets of 1618*, University of Pennsylvania Press, Philadelphia, Pa., 1960, pp. 52–3.
5 *Ibid.*, p. 71.

6   *Ibid.*, pp. 183–4.
7   *Ibid.*, p. 119.
8   *Ibid.*, pp. 300–1.

Chapter 14

1   de Santillana, G., *The Crime of Galileo*, Chicago University Press, Chicago, Ill., 1955; and reprint, Heinemann (Mercury Books), London, 1961, p. 160.
2   de Santillana, G., *Dialogue on the Great World Systems*, University of Chicago Press, Chicago, Ill., 1953, p. 45.
3   *Ibid.*, p. 53.
4   *Ibid.*, p. xxxiv footnote.
5   *Ibid.*, p. 6 footnote 2.
6   *Ibid.*, p. 6.
7   For this and the rest of this paragraph, *ibid.*, p. 80.
8   *Ibid.*, p. 250.
9   For this and the next quotation, *ibid.*, p. 202.
10 *Ibid.*, p. 203.
11 *Ibid.*, p. 209.
12 *Ibid.*, p. 471.
13 de Santillana, G., *The Crime of Galileo*, p. 184.
14 *Ibid.*, p. 185.
15 *Ibid.*, p. 186.

Chapter 15

1   de Santillana, G., *The Crime of Galileo*, Chicago University Press, Chicago, Ill., 1955; and reprint, Heinemann (Mercury Books), London, 1961, p. 191.
2   de Santillana, G., *Dialogue on the Great World Systems*, University of Chicago Press, Chicago, Ill., 1953, p. 381.
3   de Santillana, G., *The Crime of Galileo*, p. 198.
4   *Ibid.*, p. 201.
5   *Ibid.*, p. 213.
6   *Ibid.*, p. 219.
7   *Ibid.*, p. 220.

Chapter 16

1   de Santillana, G., *The Crime of Galileo*, Chicago University Press, Chicago, Ill., 1955; and reprint, Heinemann (Mercury Books), London, 1961, p. 262.
2   *Ibid.*, pp. 261–2.
3   *Ibid.*, p. 256.
4   *Ibid., loc. cit.*

5   *Ibid.*, pp. 259–60.
6   *Ibid.*, p. 260.
7   *Ibid.*, pp. 292–3.
8   *Ibid.*, p. 303.
9   *Ibid.*, p. 310.
10 *Ibid.*, p. 312.
11 de Santillana, G., *Dialogue on the Great World Systems*, University of Chicago Press, Chicago, Ill., 1953, p. ix.

Chapter 17

1   de Santillana, G., *The Crime of Galileo*, Chicago University Press, Chicago, Ill., 1955; and reprint, Heinemann (Mercury Books), London, 1961, p. 302.
2   *Ibid.*, p. 325 footnote.
3   Crew, H., and de Salvio, A., *Dialogues concerning Two New Sciences*, Macmillan, New York, 1914; and reprint, Dover Publications, New York, n.d., p. 215.
4   Newton, I., *Principia* (Mathematical Principles of Natural Philosophy), trans. Motte, A., in edition prepared by Cajori, F., University of California Press, Berkeley, Calif., 1947, p. 13.
5   Crew, H., and de Salvio, A., *op. cit.*, p. 153.
6   *Ibid.*, pp. 153–4.
7   Hall, Mary B., in *Galileo, Man of Science*, ed. McMullin, E., Basic Books, New York, 1967, p. 408.
8   Drake, S., in *Galileo, Man of Science*, p. 423.
9   Fahie, J.J., *Galileo, his life and work*, London, 1903; reprint, Dubuque, Iowa, 1962, p. 384.

Chapter 18

1   de Santillana, G., *Dialogue on the Great World Systems*, University of Chicago, Chicago, Ill., 1953, p. liii.
2   *Ibid., loc. cit.*
3   *Ibid., loc. cit.*
4   Quoted by Hall, Mary B., in *Galileo, Man of Science*, ed. McMullin, E., Basic Books, New York, 1967, p. 410, from Birch, T., *History of the Royal Society*, London, 1756, vol. I, p. 109.
5   *Ibid.*, pp. 413, 414 and quoted from Barrow, I., *Mathematical Lectures*, trans. Kirkby, J., London, 1734, p. xxvii.

Further Reading

1 *Ancient and Medieval Science*

Aristotle, *Physica*, translated Hardie, R.P., and Gaye, R.K., *De Caelo*, translated Stocks, J.L., and *De Generatione et Corruptione*, translated Joachim, H.H., *The Works of Aristotle Translated Into English*, vol. II, Clarendon Press, Oxford, 1970.

Butterfield, H., *The Origins of Modern Science*, Bell, London, 1949.

Copernicus, N., *The Revolutions of the Heavenly Spheres*, given in *Great Books of the Western World*, vol. 16, Encyclopaedia Britannica, Chicago, 1952.

Dreyer, J.L.E., *A History of Astronomy from Thales to Kepler*, Dover Publications, New York, 1953 (reprint).

Grant, E., *Physical Science in the Middle Ages*, Wiley, New York and London, 1971.

Koyré, A., *From the Closed World to the Infinite Universe*, Johns Hopkins Press, Baltimore, Md., 1957 (and John Hopkins Paperback, 1968).

Sarton, G., *A History of Science*, Harvard University Press, Cambridge, Mass., and Oxford University Press, London, vol. I, 1953; vol. II, 1959.

2 *Galileo's Works*

For those who read Italian and Latin, all Galileo's works, almost all his correspondence, and most of his manuscripts are to be found in *Le opere di Galileo Galilei*, edited by Favaro, A., 20 volumes, Florence, 1929–36, and 1965.

Selected translations in English are:

Carlos, E., *The Sidereal Messenger*, Dawson's, London, 1959 (reprint).

Crew, H., and de Salvio, A., *Dialogues concerning Two New Sciences*, Macmillan, New York, 1914; (reprint) Dover Publications, New York, no date.

Drake, S., and O'Malley, C.D., *The Controversy on the Comets of 1618* (containing besides Grassi's and 'Sarsi's' works, Guiducci's *Discourse* and Galileo's *The Assayer*), University of Pennsylvania Press, Philadelphia, Pa., 1960.

de Santillana, G., *Dialogue on the Great World Systems*, University of Chicago Press, Chicago, Ill., 1953.

Some translations of extracts from the *Discourses* and Galileo's other works on physics and sunspots are to be found in Seeger, R.J., *Galileo Galilei, his life and his works*, Pergamon Press, London and New York, 1966.

3 *Modern References*

Bernardini, G., and Fermi, L., *Galileo and the Scientific Revolution*, Fawcet Premier, New York, 1965.

Drake, S., *Galileo Studies*, University of Michigan Press, Ann Arbor, Mich., 1970.

Kaplon, M., editor, *Hommage to Galileo*, M.I.T. Press, Cambridge, Mass., 1965.

McMullin, E., editor, *Galileo, Man of Science*, Basic Books, New York, 1967.

de Santillana, G., *The Crime of Galileo*, Chicago University Press, Chicago, Ill., 1955, and reprint, Heinemann (Mercury Books), London, 1961.

Shea, W.R., *Galileo's Intellectual Revolution*, Macmillan, London, 1972.

Chronology

1564   Galileo born.

1574   Family moves to Florence.

1575–8 Galileo at Jesuit school of Vallombrosa.

1581   Galileo to Pisa university as a student.

1582   Supposed discovery in Pisa Cathedral of isochronism of the pendulum.

1585   Return to Florence from Pisa.

1586   Writes *The Little Balance* about hydrostatics but makes no attempt to publish.

1587   First visit to Rome.

1588   Lectures on Dante to Florentine Academy.

1589   Professor of Mathematics at Pisa.

1590–1   Supposed experiments from Leaning Tower of Pisa, and tract *On Motion*.

1591   Father dies and Galileo returns from Pisa.

1592   Professor of Mathematics at Padua.

1593   First 'edition' of his student notes on mechanics.

1597   Designs popular 'geometric and military' computing compass.

1600–1   Daughters Virginia and Livia born.

1604   Galileo shows mathematically that argument that the Earth is at the centre of the universe is wrong, and lectures on the new star (supernova) of 1604.

1607   Court case against the Capras.

1609   Constructs his first telescopes and presents one to the Doge. Also makes first surveys of the heavens with the telescope.

1610   Publication of *The Starry Messenger*, and return to Florence as the Grand Duke's chief mathematician and philosopher.

1611   Triumphant visit to Rome with the telescope. Arguments about floating bodies and the nature of heat.

1612   Publication of tract on floating bodies; argument with Father Scheiner over sunspots.

1613   Publication of tract on sunspots; letter about science and religion to Castelli.

1614   Galileo denounced in sermon by Caccini.

1615   Revision of letter to Castelli as *Letter to Madam Christina of Lorraine, Grand Duchess of Tuscany*; third visit to Rome and admonishment by Cardinal Bellarmine.

1617   Binocular telescope for determining longitude at sea.

1618   Three bright comets appear.

1619   Controversy over the comets and publication of famous polemic *The Assayer*.

1621   Death of Grand Duke Cosimo II, and succession of Grand Duke Ferdinand II.

1623   Cardinal Barberini becomes Pope Urban VIII, and Galileo visits Rome for the fourth time.

1623–31   Galileo at work on the *Dialogue*.

1632   The *Dialogue* published, then banned. Summons from the Inquisition.

1633   Trial and recantation in Rome. Move to Siena and then to Arcetri.

1634   Virginia dies.

1636   Visit from Thomas Hobbes.

1637   Total blindness.

1638   Publication of the *Discourses* at Leiden. Visit from Milton.

1639   Arrival of pupil, Vincenzo Viviani.

1640   Construction of *giovilabio*.

1641   Torricelli comes to work with Galileo; pendulum escapement devised.

1642   Death of Galileo.

Index

FLO

ARNUS FLU.